GASLIGHT

A NOVEL BY

RACHAEL ROSE

GASLIGHT

wattpad books

wattpad books

An imprint of Wattpad WEBTOON Book Group

Content Warning: abuse, intimate partner violence, gaslighting, child abuse

Published in Canada by Wattpad Books, a division of Wattpad Corp.
36 Wellington Street E., Toronto, ON M5E 1C7

www.wattpad.com

First Wattpad Books edition: March 2022

ISBN 978-1-98936-561-8 (Trade Paper original)
ISBN 978-1-98936-562-5 (eBook edition)

Library and Archives Canada Cataloguing in Publication information is available upon request.

Printed and bound in Canada
1 3 5 7 9 10 8 6 4 2

Cover design by Jill Caldwell
Images © Mosuno via Stocksy

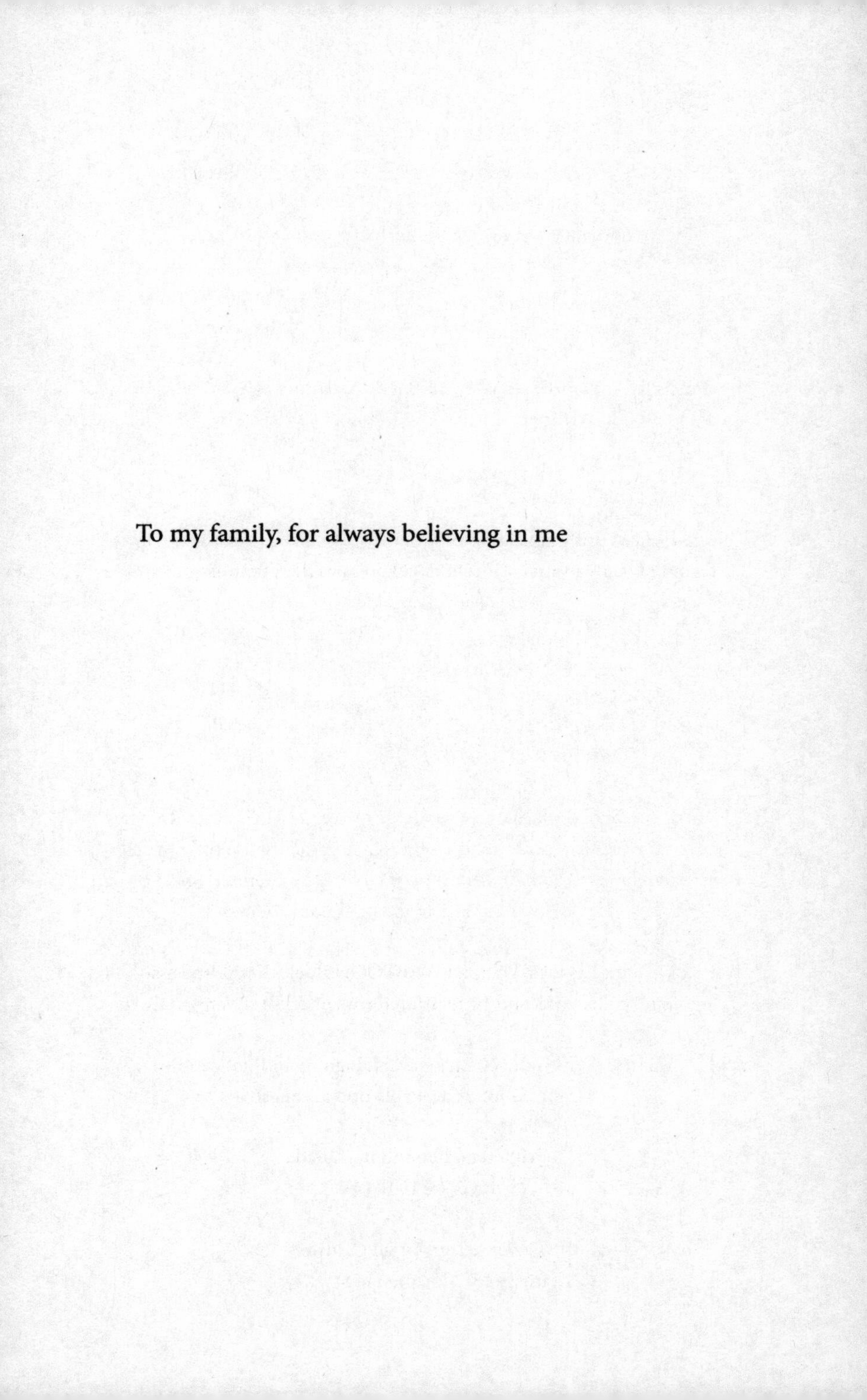

To my family, for always believing in me

CHAPTER ONE

This place is my version of hell. It isn't just that it's crowded, or that the air smells distinctly of sweat. It's that someone like me, someone who operates on structure and order, does not handle chaos well.

"Stay close, Maddie!" Dylan shouts. "Your mom will kill me if I lose you."

"Forget her mom," his twin, Oliver, yells. "*Lilly* would kill us." He reaches behind him and grabs my hand, pulling me through a throng of sweaty bodies.

Everything about this screams chaos, from the black heavy bags suspended by chains to the loud, rowdy patrons. In the corner is the boxing ring, its once-black canvas stained with blood and sweat. In less than ten minutes, I'll get to see why.

This is the last place I ever thought I'd be. I am not the kind of girl who agrees to go to a boxing match, especially the day before starting a new school, but then that has always been my problem. I'm a yes girl: *yes, I'll move to California, yes, Aunt Lilly, your stepsons can kidnap me, and yes, I'll pretend to enjoy it.* Because that's what I do, I say yes when I want to say no.

We fight our way to the ticket booth, manned by a stocky guy named Ray. For reasons unknown, Ray is shirtless and sporting a thick serpent tattoo across his broad chest. He snatches our tickets, raising an eyebrow at my outfit. I can only imagine what I look like right now. Sweat prickles my neck, soaking into the cotton of my favorite pink hoodie, and my bun is on the verge of unraveling—we have that in common. As discreetly as I can, I run my palms down the side of my head, smoothing down any potential flyaways. My hair, like my skin, is an equal mix of my half-Black mother and white father, which means it's neither straight nor curly, thin nor thick, but something in the middle.

Ray lifts his gaze to give us the go-ahead. We squeeze past more bodies, trying to push to the front. *Close enough*, Olly had said, *to see all the action, but far enough away that we won't be sprayed with blood.*

Reason number two this is hell. I'm pretty sure when Lilly asked her stepsons to show me around, she'd meant a trip to the mall or a walk along the beach. Maybe I'm wrong, but a boxing match in Burbank isn't exactly what she'd meant—it's not like I'd know. Before last week, when she picked us up from LAX, I'd mostly only ever seen Lilly through FaceTime. I'd known she'd moved to California to be an editor; that her husband of three years, Tim, is a goofy, divorced writer with sons. But other than that, Lilly's life in the suburb of Granada Hills remains a complete mystery.

What happened to us is a mystery too. As far as everyone's concerned, this move was a much-needed break after Mom's split from Dad. It's a half truth, which according to my mother is better than a lie; sometimes, I'm not so sure.

"You made it!" Something latches on to me, spinning me around into a hug. My new best friend, June, all five foot two inches of glossy black curls and sun-bronzed skin. I say new best friend, because ever since Olly introduced us last week at Lilly's Welcome barbecue, she's stuck to me like a barnacle. Beside her is Kavithra, Kavi for short, who traps me into another hug.

It's the one thing I can't get used to about California. Say what you want about New Yorkers, but at least we have rules: keep to yourself, don't stare at strangers, and don't take up space. It's been less than five minutes, and already I've had to dodge two elbows and several unsolicited hugs.

But I make the effort to hug June back properly. Part of making sure these next few months run as smoothly as possible means trying my best to make friends. Back home I never needed them, I always had my boyfriend, Jamie, but now he's not here to be my buffer.

"For the record," Kavi says, pulling away, "I wanted to take you surfing today. Obviously, I was out voted." She shakes her head, sending her pin-straight black hair back and forth. Kavi's Sri Lankan, which means she's got this thick, shiny hair that I can't help but envy.

"It's fine," I say.

She squeezes my hand as we're rocked by the crowd. Something about her calmness reassures me in all of this chaos. She's the epitome of a laid-back Californian, the kind of girl I could never—will never—be.

"Quick question," I say. "Are you sure this is legal?"

"Quick question," Olly says as his dark eyes flit to mine, "are you always this uptight?"

The word cuts through me, settling in the back of my mind with all of the others. *Crazy, irrational, paranoid.* They form together, shifting and pulsing like an entity of their own.

June's eyes narrow. "God, do you even have a filter?" To me, she says, "Don't worry, it's legal. They're doing an open-night thing to promote some boot camp they're pushing. Our tickets were free."

Relieved, I turn to the ring. Through a gap in the crowd, Kavi spots her boyfriend, Zion, and starts toward him. June goes to grab my hand, but I tell them I'll wait back here with the twins, and they push through the crowd without me.

Six weeks ago, when Mom and I made the decision to move, a part of me had been hopeful. California was my do-over. I'd reinvent myself as the cool girl, the laid-back West Coast girl who drinks vegetable smoothies and surfs on the weekend, but so far, my life has been nothing of the sort—it's hard not to feel disappointed.

The crowd suddenly parts as an older man wearing a GymCon T-shirt pushes through. He's in his midforties, much older than the rest of this crowd, with salt-and-pepper hair, a squashed nose like he's taken too many hits, and hooded, no-bullshit eyes.

"Here," he says, and he pulls a flyer from his bag, handing it to me, "take one of these so it looks like I'm doing my job."

For about a millisecond, I wonder what it would be like to take it. To be the kind of girl who could step into a ring, face her opponent, and be brave. But then *his* voice is back, a low familiar hum in my ear. *That's not you, Maddie.*

"No, it's oka—" but he's already shoving it in my hand.

Olly laughs as the man carries on behind us. "Keep it as a souvenir," he says. "You can hang it in your new bedroom and think about how nice we were to bring you along tonight."

Dylan thumps him in the ribs and says, "Leave her alone, dick."

You'd think being twins, they'd have something in common, but they don't. Other than sharing the same brown skin—their dad, Tim, is Black and their mom is white—they look nothing alike. Dylan is tall and lean, with short, dark hair and a narrow, angelic face. Olly, it seems, is still catching up. He's three inches shorter, with rounded cheeks, a curly taper fade, and an immature grin. Out of the two of them, I know which one I get along with, and which I'd like to kill.

In a desperate attempt to speed up time, I get out my phone and reread old messages between me and Jamie. Despite the chaos of the past few days, his name immediately calms me.

Jamie and I have been joined at the hip since the day he sat next to me in the library, a year ago. I'd been working on a poem for English, struggling to think of a word that rhymed with *broken*, when he leaned across the table, flashed that boyish grin, and said, "Token."

It's not like it was love at first sight or anything, but whenever he'd see me around after that, he'd make sure to say hey. Eventually, those heys turned into sentences and those sentences into full-blown conversations. Before I knew it, Jamie and I had become inseparable, two halves of the same person.

Still, it's hard not to feel the strain. There's a three-hour time difference between New York and California, which means the structure we've built, the routine we'd safely established back home, is gone.

It's this thought that unravels the last of my resolve. My stomach knots, a sudden panic settling over me, and I stand up, telling the twins I'm heading to the bathroom. There's a short line outside, but once I'm in the cubicle, I sit on the toilet and take a deep breath.

I thought I could do this. Thought I could come here—not just *here*, but all the way across the country—and be this carefree version of myself. Instead, I feel like a fraud.

Leaning my head back, I pull out my phone. Jamie's name is the first one on my call list, and even though he'll be asleep, I need to hear his voice. It rings a few times before going to voicemail. My phone is almost in my pocket when I pause. Even though I know I shouldn't, I press the photo album icon and scroll through pictures of Dad.

My favorite is one of us at Coney Island, during a rare trip to visit my grandparents. Cheesy grins peek out from behind our cotton candy, the lights of the Coney Island Cyclone blurred like stars as Mom struggled to focus the camera. There's nothing special about it, no significant moment that marked the occasion, I just like how happy we looked. Whenever I think of him, it's *this* version I remember. Kind, loving, with a smile that could warm you right up—it's what made leaving so hard.

Throat tight, I clutch my necklace, focusing on the feel of the pendant between my fingers. It was a birthday present from Jamie, a thin-cut gold necklace with a bean pendant in the center. He'd said when he learned the bean represents the origin of all things, he immediately thought of us. Now when I hold it, it's like I don't just think about a memory, I'm recalling a feeling: slightly blurred and out of focus, but soft, warm—safe.

A wild pounding vibrates the door, making me jump. "Are you going to be in there all night? Some of us need to pee!"

Exhaling, I get to my feet and unlock the door. The girl who'd been waiting pushes past me into the cubicle, locking the door behind her. I move to the sink to wash my hands and risk a look in the mirror.

I was right about the bun. I pull out the bobby pins, twisting my hair at the base of my neck, the way my mom used to do every night before ballet. That was the deal: Mom would do my hair, Dad would take me to the studio and afterward, the park, where he'd spin me on the merry-go-round.

"When I'm a ballerina," I'd shout through bubbles of laughter, "I'm going to spin as fast as this!"

My mom would have told me not to be silly, that no person could spin as fast as a merry-go-round, but not him. Dad just looked at me, eyes warm, and said, "You'll be the fastest-spinning ballerina the world has ever seen." I ended up quitting once I got to nine or ten, but the sentiment carried with me through everything I did, because that was my dad. He'd build you up until anything was possible, until you were up in the clouds. But the higher you went, the farther you fell when he pushed you.

After drying my hands, I step into the hallway to join the others. At the end of the hallway is a steep set of stairs. My body acts before I can think, propelling me down the steps and through the fire exit, out onto the back street.

The blast of warm air is startling. The streets are still frostbitten back in New York, the air the kind of cold that makes you involuntarily gasp. I'd known it wouldn't be like that in Southern California, but considering it's early March, I'd expected the evenings to be a lot cooler.

"You're not supposed to be out here."

My gaze shifts to the tall, tanned boy leaning against the wall. He's about five feet away, but there's enough light from a nearby streetlamp to irradiate his face in a warm, yellow haze.

He's strikingly handsome, but not in the clean-cut, LA type of way, more in a rugged, *I don't give a shit* way. His hair is jet black and short, curling slightly at the ends. He's wearing an old black T-shirt and faded gray sweatpants, but even fully clothed he looks strong, muscled, like he spends all his time lifting weights. His eyes skate over me in the same fashion, from my bun to my lips and back up again. An odd feeling flutters through me, halfway between nervousness and alarm.

"I needed to get out of there," I say, leaning against the wall. If my mother could see me now, tucked away in the dark with a boy, she'd have a coronary. "I'll head back inside in a minute. Unfortunately."

"Why did you come tonight if you don't want to be here?" He's looking right at me, head tilted slightly, a glimmer of intrigue in his eyes.

"Believe me, it wasn't my idea." I'm not usually this straightforward, this *honest*, but here in the shadows, I don't feel like pretending. "Watching some idiots fight is not my idea of fun."

His smile immediately fades and he pushes himself off the wall. He walks right past me, stopping when he gets to the door. His eyes flit to mine, bright, green, and no longer filled with amusement. "You should probably get going, then," he says in a low voice near my ear. "I doubt you'll be missed." With that, he slips back through the door and heads up the steps as I'm left, openmouthed, staring after him.

Back in the gym, Kavi and June are beside the twins, taking selfies by the ring. Kavi turns midselfie, takes one look at my face, and says, "Hey, are you okay?"

"I'm fine."

At last, the first competitor has arrived. The sooner this night is over, the better.

The crowd goes wild as the boxer in question is introduced as Moby. He raises his gloves, turning in a circle until every inch of him is seen. There's a collective roar, and I'm surprised by the sudden jolt in my stomach. It's like the feeling I get when Jamie drags me to a football game. I might not like the sport or care much about the players, but for one brief moment, I'm a part of something collective; something bigger, a swell of excitement over a shared moment. For a brief moment, I don't feel so alone.

Moments later, his competitor, Red Gloves, makes his grand entrance, and it's like that moment in movies where time stops, and everything clicks into place. The exchange outside, the hostility of the boy I'd met—the guy from outside is Red Gloves.

Slowly, they face one another. Leaning forward slightly, I try to see past the head of the person in front. Despite being similar in size and stature, they couldn't carry themselves more differently. While Moby looks fierce, intimidating even, Red Gloves is calm, like he's mastered the art of restraint.

The bell rings. Moby gets into a defensive stance, but Red Gloves darts forward. He's quick and controlled, dodging Moby's blow before returning the effort with a jab to the nose. June and Kavi tense beside me as the thwack of Red Gloves's fist connecting with Moby's face echoes around the gym. My fists clench, too, willing it on.

Blood sprays the air and splatters across the mat. Red Gloves moves forward, his body a blur, and lands another blow. I grip my necklace, waiting for that feeling of horror to hit, but it doesn't come. It's *enthralling*. The soft glow of the overhead lights, the sheen that clings to each of their faces, the organized chaos. I'm standing here, pushed back and forth by a sea of bodies, and it feels like I'm finally awake.

"We probably should have checked if you're squeamish around blood," Dylan shouts. "Are you all right?"

I nod, suddenly aware of the commotion around me: people are cheering, calling out to the boxers, stomping on the floor. I turn back to Moby, watching as blood trails his lips and his chin, curving down the length of his neck. Gone is the posturing and bravado from before, the two men stripped bare for the crowd.

"I can't believe I let you talk me into this," June says to the twins through her fingers.

Desperate, Moby takes a blow to the chest in order to land a face punch. Red Gloves jerks back, stunned, and falls to his knees. For a split second, it's like I'm reliving that night.

Flashes of his snarl come roaring back, of his words like lashes of a whip. *Stupid, crazy, bitch*. I lean forward, fists clenched, and will him to get up. *Get up, get up, get up*!

The countdown begins. Moby steps back into the overhead lights, and his bloody snarl lights up like something from a horror movie. My fists are packed tight, and I wish I could go up there and punch it right off. I know that snarl, that look of superiority; I've seen it more times than I can count.

The countdown reaches six. I hold my breath, but at the last second, Red Gloves straightens up, circles back around, and crashes his fist into Moby's nose. The crowd goes wild as Red Gloves reverts to his typical stance. Despite the noise, the chaos, the pain, he's the only one still in control.

I feel the lump in my throat—sharp, solid—before the tears press my eyes. I fought back like this once. Not when it counted, but every night after, in my dreams. I stood up for myself the way Red Gloves is now, and I was brave.

Moby falls to the mat, and for a brief moment, as the countdown begins, the room is completely silent. Then, all at once, the room explodes with noise. Red Gloves lifts his glove to the air and searches the crowd, looking for someone in particular. His eyes find mine, bright and severe and alive.

CHAPTER TWO

Anxiety keeps me awake half the night. I give up on sleeping and sit up in bed, glancing at the clock on the nightstand. My eyes strain against the brightness of the neon blue light. It's not even five, but my heart is still pounding like a drum in my chest, convinced that I've woken up late.

Dad hated lateness. If you were late, it meant you thought your time was more valuable than his, and he'd give you the silent treatment. Out of all of the weapons he had in his arsenal, this was the one I hated most. You never knew how long it would last, so you'd tiptoe around, breath held, waiting for the moment he acknowledged you again—the moment you could finally exhale.

It's strange, most would see silence as a good thing—a prerequisite to peace—but Dad saw it as a weapon. Silence became a punishment, and he was our judge, jury, and executioner.

The photos on the nightstand slowly come into focus. I

hadn't brought much in the way of possessions—there was only so much I could fit in two cases—but as I fretted over what to pack, I found myself tearing them from the Goodwright family album.

The first is my favorite, a polaroid of Mom in her senior year. She's leaning against an old red truck, her high school boyfriend on one side and her best friend on the other as they prepare for their precollege road trip.

She's always hated the picture—she claims she wasn't ready—but it's my favorite *because* it's so candid. She's clutching the camera she'd spent months saving up for—a graduation present to herself—and for once she isn't posing, she's looking up, mouth open, on the brink of an almighty laugh.

My mother had to sacrifice a lot of her teenhood when Grandma got sick with cancer. She says it's like they went from living comfortably to drowning in medical bills overnight. Grandpa had to sell his café to help pay for it all, and Mom and Lilly got part-time jobs while trying to survive high school. Thankfully, Grandma made a full recovery, but their savings didn't until many years later. It's why, when my mother got accepted to Cornell with full financial aid, she said it had felt like a miracle.

Gently, I brush my thumb over her face. There's always this strange sense of sorrow when I hold it, like I'm looking at a ghost. This version of my mother—smiling, happy, warm—was taken by a version of *him*.

She met my father a year later, at a frat party of all places. She'd been lining up for the bathroom with her friends when she saw this handsome boy in a toga. He noticed her, too, walked over, said something unmemorable. But, according to my mother, that's all it took. Six months later, she got pregnant with me and dropped out of college to move in with Dad. The rest, as they say, is history.

The photo behind it is my least favorite. It's of Mom, Minnie Mouse, and me during a trip to Times Square. I'm standing between them, one hand in Minnie's, one hand in Mom's as I grin at Dad behind the camera. Mom is smiling, too, but it's not her bright, *the world is my oyster* smile—it's her fake one.

We'd spent the day pretending to be tourists. It was my first ever visit to the touristy heart of New York, so of course I was immediately bewitched. It felt like I'd stepped onto another planet, one where screens lit the sky and people swarmed together like bees, moving and acting as one. I stopped and tilted my head at the buildings, suddenly feeling insignificant.

"Don't stop," Dad said, squeezing my hand, "or you'll be gobbled up by the crowd."

I clutched his hand tighter and quickened my pace. We walked a little farther, and when Spider-Man and Minnie Mouse greeted me, I nearly combusted with excitement. "Can I take a picture with one?"

"Of course you can," Dad said. He gently pulled us through the crowd and over to Minnie. Mom and I got into our positions, and afterward, Dad tipped Minnie and led us down the street toward the Disney Store.

It felt like we'd been walking for ages. My feet were begging for mercy, but my heart wasn't listening. There were millions of people and things to look at, and I didn't want to miss a thing.

We spent over an hour in the Disney Store, scouring

each shelf for the perfect toy to commemorate our trip. I'd narrowed it down to a handbag and a princess doll, settling on the handbag out of practicality. But as soon as we left the store, Dad knelt in front of me and pulled from behind him the princess doll I'd wanted.

"Happy birthday, my little ballerina," he said, and he kissed me on the forehead.

I could have burst into song as we continued down the street. My parents were holding hands, laughing about something as I cradled my doll, and for this brief moment, everything was perfect.

Then Dad stopped suddenly, right there in the crowd, and turned to Mom. Gone was the bright, gleaming smile I'd just seen, as if a switch had been flipped. "Are you really going to stare at every man we pass?"

My mother fell still. Her face seemed so calm in comparison to his, but her pulse thrummed and stumbled under my grip. "Henry," she said. "We're not doing this now."

"It's a simple question." He sounded calm, but something about his cool expression made me nervous. "Because if you are, I'd rather we just go home now."

I looked between them, panicked. "But I don't want to go home yet, Daddy."

"Come on, Maddison, honey," he said, holding out his hand, "let's give Mommy some alone time to think about what she's done."

Mom's eyes found mine, glossy with tears, but still warm as they regarded me. My dad, whose own eyes had hardened, beckoned me over. I clutched my doll harder, frozen with indecision.

Dad's expression closed down as he took a step forward. "I'm the one who got you that doll," he said softly. "If you don't want to come with me, then you'll have to give it back." He made it sound so reasonable, as though I should have known this.

"No," Mom said, stepping forward, but one look from him gave her pause.

Forever passed as I walked toward him, doll outstretched, tears flowing. He pried it from my clammy hands, kissed my forehead, then started down the street without us. I clutched Mom's hand tighter as we pushed through the crowd, no longer bewitched by the sights. Instead, it felt suffocating, the buildings twisting and pulsing like my heartbeat.

"What's wrong with Daddy?" I asked as we raced through the crowd. He hadn't yelled or raised his voice, but somehow I just knew he was angry, like I felt it to my core.

"That wasn't your daddy," Mom said as she squeezed my hand tighter. "That was Mr. Hyde."

But it wasn't until eighth grade, when I'd had to read *The Strange Case of Dr. Jekyll and Mr. Hyde* for English, that I finally understood what she'd meant. My father had two faces: one he showed the world, and one he kept for us; neither ever lasted.

As soon as we got home that day, I found the doll waiting for me in my bedroom, propped against the decorative pillows. I picked it up, clutching it to my chest as I thought about what had happened. I'd never seen Dad like that—at least, not that I could remember—and the change in him had been so subtle, so sudden, that it left me feeling dizzy.

Quietly, I tiptoed toward his office, knocking twice on the door.

"Come in," he called.

The door creaked open as I stepped over the threshold. He swiveled in his chair, saw me standing with the doll in my hand, and smiled. "You look like you've seen a ghost. What's wrong, honey?"

"Can I keep it now?" I asked, because I wanted to be sure. I wanted to be sure that he wouldn't take it again.

"Of course," he said, looking confused, "why wouldn't you be able to keep it?"

I stood there a moment, feeling small and out of place. His office was huge, covered in pictures of people's before and after surgery shots. He was a plastic surgeon, so there were countless photos of peeled-back noses and Frankenstein scars. "Because you said I couldn't if I didn't go with you."

"No, I didn't," he said, standing up. He walked toward me, running a hand through my doll's long hair as he gently kissed my cheek. "You must have misunderstood me."

Then he ushered me into the hallway, where I stood for the next ten minutes in a dreamlike state, as if a fog had taken over my brain. In some ways, that fog never lifted.

I pull on my clothes and fasten my sneakers to mentally prepare for my run. I joined track in junior year as a way to get Mom off my case about extracurriculars and ended up loving it. It's empowering when I'm pushed to my limit, knowing the only thing I have to rely on is my own strength and determination. And when I reach that limit, that point where it feels like I want to die, I feel stronger, somehow. Untouchable.

Grabbing my phone and headphones from the table, I

pause. The flyer from last night is still on the nightstand, the determined face of a boxer staring up at me. I should throw it away, but I'm reminded of the way Red Gloves fought the other night, and for a split second, the anger makes room for something I don't recognize. Instead, I throw it in the drawer and tiptoe downstairs, careful not to wake anyone.

The house is intimidatingly big, much like the others in this part of Granada Hills. It sits in a grove with four other houses, the front lawns perfectly pruned and trimmed, the driveways cobbled and edged with miniature hedgerows. The inside is just as seamless, each room lending itself perfectly to the next, with dark wooden floors that shine in the light, and wide but homey rooms.

Quietly, I slip onto the street, breathing in the warm spring air. With my headphones on and Red Gloves's fight still playing in my head, I select a song from my angry workout playlist and lose myself to the routine.

—

I'm showered and sitting at my vanity table before anyone wakes up. With a finishing touch to my makeup, I run my fingers through the ends of my hair, which started off wavy but now hang straight as a pin down my back.

I have a love-hate relationship with my hair. A combination it being frizz prone and me being in middle school—where kids are old enough to know how to hurt you, but are too young to understand the long-term damage—meant I'd had to endure the nickname Frizzy Head.

It was the first time I'd ever been stung by a word, felt

the cold, hard crack of its whip. I'd always hated that my hair wasn't as curly as Mom's, nor as straight as Dad's, and now this thing I disliked about myself had been recognized, confirmed, by somebody else. But somehow I kept it together. I bottled my feelings, wore that same smile that my parents both wore, and the bullies left me alone; it's how I've survived ever since.

By the time I'm ready, it's nearly six thirty, which means Jamie will be sitting in English right now, my desk beside him empty. I try to fit in a video call before he starts his next class, scared that the distance will have changed us already, but the moment I see him, there's this sense that I'm safe. Home.

"Hey, you." He smiles that bright, lopsided smile when he sees me. "Your hair looks nice."

He looks good right now too—even better than usual. His dark hair is styled into soft, messy waves, pushed away from his forehead. His eyes, which are a soft ocean blue, match the color of his heavy-duty jacket. It's practically still winter back in Brooklyn, a startling contrast to the early spring light that streams through my balcony doors.

That's the one thing about California that I hadn't been expecting. I'd banked on the pool (I'd read everyone has one), the palm trees, the sun, but nobody told me about the near-perfect view of the Santa Susana Mountains.

"How's life with the Applegates?" he asks.

"It's okay," I say, "but I miss you. It's weird that I'm not going to see you today."

There was rarely a day that went by where we didn't see each other back home. Everything about him is familiar to me—his touch, his warmth, even the thrum of his heartbeat from the hours spent leaning on his chest.

"I miss you too," he says softly as he takes a seat on the bench in front of the entrance. I can hear the familiar chatter of kids changing classes in the distance, but he doesn't take his eyes off me. "It's like I'm trying to function without a part of my body, like I'm missing an arm, or something." We laugh together, perfectly in sync, which makes me feel like I'm back home. "Hey, don't laugh, I'm vulnerable right now. Who's going to walk me to class? Who's going to help me study for finals?"

"Are you just using me for my brains, Mr. Parkinson?"

"Not *just* your brains." He says that, but Jamie and I have only ever made it to second base, so I know he's not using me for *that*. His friend, Tyler, walks up behind him, and he holds up a finger to him as if to say *one moment*, before turning to face me. "Just promise me that we'll talk every day, okay? No matter what happens."

"I promise."

"Good." He looks into the camera, his expression unusually serious. "We just need to get through the next few months. Come fall, you'll be back here, and we'll be getting ready to go to college together. We just have to survive until then."

"I know," I say. "I love you."

"I love you too."

As soon as I hang up, I check my schedule, then check it again. AP English is first, and if I can just get through that class, everything else will be fine.

I head downstairs, past the rows of pictures lining the walls. Lots of the twins holding various trophies, holidays shots with Grandma and Grandpa, snaps of them as a family. Even though Lilly never wanted kids, it's clear she treats Dylan and Olly as her own.

Our apartment back home is the opposite. Dad likes everything neat and orderly, so there are no trinkets or photos, nothing to show that we were there, we *lived*. It's the kind of home where you are careful not to disturb the polish on the floors or the perfectly plumped pillows on the couch.

My bedroom had a similar feel, but tacked to the inside of my closet door, hidden from view, was life: ribbons from recitals, honor roll, shots of me and Jamie ice-skating at the Rockefeller Center. There were a couple family photos too. One was from last Christmas, the three of us dressed in matching pajama sets, the picture-perfect snap. Mom sent it to Lilly as our holiday card—a *look how perfect we are* gesture—and now it's pinned to their fridge. Perfection, or at least the illusion of it, was the only way she'd found to survive.

Tim and Lilly are already in the kitchen, which is my favorite room in the house. It's got these huge French patio doors that filter in light and open up to the pool, which I've spent nearly every day in this week.

"Good, you're up," Tim says. He's bent over the stove with a spatula in his hand, wearing one of those World's Best Cook novelty aprons. Despite being in his forties, Tim has the bone structure of a model. Big dark eyes, warm brown skin, and the kind of cheekbones I've always been jealous of.

Lilly is at the table, the opposite of Tim in every way possible. She's wearing an oversized black hoodie, her dark curls poking in different directions, and she's clutching a Baby Yoda mug.

The great thing about Jamie is that we are so alike. We like the same food, the same books, the same movies—we even love the same TV shows. But with Tim and Lilly, it's like they don't have a single thing in common. Lilly, having had to work just as hard as my mom to get by, is every bit the confident, independent New Yorker I've always wished I were, while Tim is goofy and laid-back. Every time I look at them, I find myself wondering what twist of fate allowed someone so composed to meet someone so disorganized.

"Morning, Mushroom," Lilly says. "Have some breakfast."

I sigh at my unfortunate nickname, which I'd earned myself three Christmases ago. With Mom's family all living in different states, tradition looks a little different in our family. Instead of meeting up for birthdays and holidays, Lilly would gather her family, Mom ours, and we'd all jump on FaceTime for a catch-up. Even my grandparents would tune in from their new bungalow in the Florida Keys, though the camera was usually upside down as they argued over who got to hold it.

For everyone else it was a laid-back occasion, but for Dad it was an opportunity to show off how perfect we were. He didn't have a family—after going through a messy divorce, his parents abandoned him when he was just seven, leaving him in his grandma's care, so while his pride in our nuclear unit bordered on unbearable, a part of me understood why; he was terrified of being alone.

Still, last Christmas is when I finally put my foot down. He forced us to wear these ridiculous Santa hats that made my head itch, so I threw it off midcall, despite the twitching of his smile, not realizing my hair had flattened like a mushroom. Lilly found it hilarious—she's been calling me Mushroom ever since.

I take a seat at the table, which is barely visible under the pancakes, yogurt, and fresh muesli. "This is a lot of food."

"No kidding," Lilly says. "Tim's procrastinating."

Before I can ask what she means, Tim slides some funny-shaped pancakes onto my plate. "I have a bad case of writer's block," he explains. "Figured I'd get my creative juices flowing with some comfort food."

Lilly shudders dramatically. "Don't say creative juices ever again."

"Juices," Tim says with a devious grin, "juices, juices, jui—"

The pan Tim is holding suddenly clatters to the floor. The noise startles me, and instinct kicks in. My chin snaps forward until it's tucked into my chest. My arms rush to cover my face. Eyes closed, I imagine his large, clenched fist rushing forward, only to withdraw again last minute.

"Crap," Tim says, but he sounds far away. "The handle got too hot again. I thought you said you were going to throw this pan away, Lill."

When something brushes the side of my arm, I flinch. "Sorry," Lilly says, withdrawing her hand. "I didn't mean to startle you."

"It's fine." I smile in a bid to reassure her, but my heart's still throwing itself against my chest, trying to catapult out of it. "I think I'm just nervous about today."

Lilly reaches across the table and squeezes my hand. "The school is still fine with you starting next week if you need a few more days to settle in."

"No," I say quickly. Tim, who is best friends with the principal, had to pull a lot of strings to get me off the waiting list for Granada Hills Charter School. Not only would delaying my start look bad, but I need to keep busy. Distractions, goals, are what keep me sane.

"You'll never convince her. Maddie loves school."

Mom crosses the room and takes the seat opposite. She's made an effort as usual—fitted, pressed jumpsuit, dark hair carefully scraped into a bun—but her brown skin looks ashen, her dark eyes plagued by dark circles. They're partly hereditary—like mine—but have worsened from sleepless nights.

My hand extends to hers, squeezing it tight. Maybe she was happy and confident once, but if so, I don't remember it. I have only ever known this version of my mother, quiet and withdrawn, preferring to retreat inside of herself than contribute to discussion. Lilly and the others put it down to the split, but the truth is, my mother was like this long before we left.

"Like mother like daughter, then," Lilly says. "You used to make Mom drop us at school early just so you could be there before everyone else, remember?"

"I remember," Mom says. She grabs the pitcher of orange juice, pouring herself a glass. She pauses, then, "I've been meaning to ask how they're doing. It's been a while since I've, well—"

"They're both great. Can you believe they're in the Bahamas? Tim and I are thinking of traveling once the boys leave for college in the fall. Europe maybe, or the Caribbean. We're undecided."

Mom's expression clouds over. *We're going somewhere fancy this year*, Dad would say. *The Caribbean, or Turks and Caicos—somewhere hot*. He never meant a word of it, but the hard part was never the lying. It was knowing he was lying and wanting to believe him, anyway.

"How's the job hunt going, Lori?" Tim asks. "You're a photographer, right?"

Her eyes suddenly dart to her lap. "I was. I mean, I am." She's nervous, I can tell by the way she stumbles over her words. Dad might as well be standing over her shoulder, breathing down her neck. *Did you just look at him, Lori? Are you flirting with him*? "I haven't really done much lately. Henry worked so hard that he felt I didn't need a job, and looking after Maddie was pretty much a full-time job." She shoots me a playful look and adds, "I'm just going to get a job in a store, or something."

Lately is an understatement. Mom worked as a freelance photographer for a while but quit when Dad complained she wasn't spending enough time with her family. She turned it into a hobby instead, turning the fourth bedroom into her private studio, and she'd lock herself away for hours, flicking through the pictures she'd taken, editing them on her computer. It was rare that she'd let us in, so being in there always felt like a special occasion, like seeing a part of my mother she tried to keep hidden.

Then one night, as I worked on my homework upstairs, she screamed. I ran downstairs to see what was wrong, finding her in a ball in her studio, rocking back and forth. Her camera was gone from its stand.

For a split second, I wondered if Dad had something to do with it. While he was known to be controlling, impatient at times, he knew how much that camera meant to my mother, there's just no way he would have touched it.

When he finally came home, he peeled off his coat and hung it on the coat stand before placing his briefcase by his feet. Mom rushed to him sobbing, begging him to tell her what he'd done with her camera. Dad just looked at her, eyebrows furrowed, an innocent frown on his face. "I have no idea what you're talking about. What's going on?"

"Mom can't find her camera," I said. "We've looked everywhere." It was a running joke in our family that my harebrained mother would lose her head if it wasn't screwed on, but this was the first time she'd lost something so valuable—both in price and sentimentally.

"I haven't seen it," he said, and he pulled my mother into his arms, stroking her hair as he cradled her close. "I'm always telling you not to leave things lying around," he said softly. "Aren't I always telling you that?" But whatever she said was muffled by his cotton shirt. "We'll find it, Lori, I promise." But we never did find it, and Mom never went in her studio again. The camera was gone, just like the last of Mom's will to live.

Mom's still staring at the table in a trance, so I wave the breadbasket in front of her. "Make sure you have something to eat."

She snaps to attention. "Oh, I don't really have much of an appetite. I would love some coffee, though."

Tim rushes to the table with the coffee pitcher. "I'm not much of a breakfast person either, Lori." He pats his gut, which is slightly bulging beneath his T-shirt. "Breakfast is what left me with this little fella. Well, donuts for breakfast, specifically." He hovers a moment for some kind of response, but he's not going to get one.

"These pancakes are amazing," I say to fill the silence.

For as long as I can remember, I have been Mom's buffer to the outside world. The one who talks to the cashiers at the supermarket, or who thanks the delivery driver or answers the phone. I am the mouthpiece for a woman who lost her voice.

"I'm glad *someone* appreciates my culinary skills," Tim says. "Lill always sticks to that cardboard-tasting toast, and the boys are never up early enough to eat anything other than an apple on the way out the door. My potential is wasted."

Right on cue, the twins drag themselves into the kitchen, where they grab an apple from the fruit bowl. Tim gives me a look as if to say, *I told you so*, and I get to my feet, kissing my mother on the cheek.

"I love you," she says.

"I love you," I say back.

CHAPTER THREE

We pile into the Audi the twins share. It's warmer than I'd anticipated for this time of year, and I can already feel the sun burning my shoulders as it beams through the open window.

The trees fly by, broken up by the oversize homes with their landscaped lawns. Granada Hills is like any other gated community, and north of the freeway where Tim and Lilly reside are midcentury homes filled with hospitable neighbors. Lawn mowers growl over the bass of Dylan's music; the clockwork sounds of suburban life. In one of the front yards, a man is mowing his lawn in a flannel shirt and khaki green shorts. He waves as we pass, using his T-shirt to wipe the sweat from his forehead.

Back home, there was always this sense of freedom that came with knowing you could be anywhere you wanted in thirty minutes, but here, life has slowed to a crawl. There's no rush to get anywhere, no sense of urgency or purpose.

An old couple stops in the middle of the street, a move that would earn you a side-eye in New York, but here no one cares. Strangely, I like it.

I focus on the notebook in my lap, checking my list of things to do: join track, don't think, *breathe*. The last one is underlined three times, just in case I forget.

This is the first time in years that there isn't anything huge on my list. I have the perfect 4.0 GPA, I've been accepted to three out of four of my colleges, and while I've still got finals and graduation to think about, the hard part is over. The problem is, it's the hard part that stops me from unraveling.

After finishing up my checklist, I neatly rip the page from my notebook before putting it in my pocket. Jamie thinks I'm crazy for making lists, especially on paper and not on my phone, but there is something therapeutic about writing things down.

He messages now, his fifth one in ten minutes, but it's a relief to know he's thinking about me. I take a picture of my view from the window, then send it over WhatsApp with a heart emoji.

Can't wait to visit you in California, he messages back.

Dylan turns down the stereo to be heard above the noise. "You've gone quiet on us," he says. "You're not nervous, are you?"

He's looking right at me, waiting for me to confess. "Are there actually people who don't get nervous about their first day?" I ask. "Because to me, that makes you a psychopath."

He grins, and I'm surprised at how easily it settles my nerves. "You'll be fine," he says, "trust me." Like it is just that easy.

"What are you, omniscient?"

A snigger erupts from the backseat. "He thinks he is," Olly says. "You'll never meet a bigger know-it-all than Dylan, I promise you."

Dylan glares into the rearview mirror. "I think I know everything?" He shakes his head and says to me, "Trust me, it won't be long before you start to ask yourself how that skinny little body of his can carry around such a big head."

I laugh, and when Olly hurls an insult at Dylan, Dylan reaches back and thumps him. I watch as the pair of them go back and forth, not used to any of this.

"Look," Olly says, poking his head between the seats, "you look like someone who gets off on the whole school thing, unlike Dylan here, so I'm sure you'll do great. Just don't do anything to embarrass us."

I'm ashamed to say he's not wrong. Growing up, I was always the kid with my hand up in class, or who asked for extra work to do at home, and as a teenager, I'm even worse.

At first it was just my little way of making Dad proud. He loved to praise: his favorite thing to do was tell you that no one could paint like you or run like you or sing like you. He loved making you feel special. But when you were special, it meant someone else was not—usually my mother. Looking back, most of my memories are of her standing on the sidelines, watching us with what I'd always assumed was adoration, but instead was a hopefulness that one day, he'd look at her that way too.

Later, when I realized this, school became a goal to focus on, a way for me to distract myself. If I wasn't with the track team or hanging out with Jamie, I was studying to maintain my perfect GPA, or volunteering at care homes, or running homework clubs. Anything I could control, I would, and anything I couldn't, I ignored.

"If you really want to know the truth," Dylan says, making a left turn, "I was always kind of a bad egg. Can you believe that my third-grade teacher once told me she was wasting her time with me? She said I was never going to be able to write properly."

"I can," Olly says.

"That's awful," I say.

"Yeah, it is," he agrees. "I guess it all worked out in the end. Her comment was the reason I turned to music."

"Is that what you want to be?" I ask. "A musician?"

"Not quite that cliché. I don't really know where I want to go with it, but I got into Northwestern for music, so I guess I'll go from there. What about you—where are you going?"

I'm saved from having to answer when Dylan pulls into the senior parking lot. I step out of the car, about to get my schedule out to check it again when a noisy black motorcycle zips past me. It pulls into the space beside us, forcing me to jump back or risk getting my feet crushed.

"Hey!" I say.

The rider takes off his helmet and glances over. His eyes narrow, and I try to keep the surprise from my face. It's the same guy I'd met at the fight last night—the boy with the red gloves. Up close, I realize he has the manliest face I've ever seen on a high schooler, with a sharp-edged jaw and tousled black hair that seems to fall into perfect waves. The faintest shadow sits beneath his eye, a lingering bruise from his fight the other night.

"Yeah?"

For a second, I forget what I'm saying. Then I remember the peril I'd just been in. "I was walking here."

"That's what the sidewalk is for." Then he climbs off his bike, stuffs the helmet into the back compartment, and simply strides off.

Dylan opens his door and climbs out, stonily watching the boy's retreating figure. "Hayden Walker," he says. "Not very pleasant, right?"

"No," I say, staring after him. "Not at all."

We step onto the curb just as June's convertible pulls into the space beside us. She kills the engine, takes a quick look at herself in her sun visor, and throws the door open.

"Hey, losers," she says, pulling me into a hug. "Is anyone else still traumatized from last night?"

There's this second where Olly looks at June, and his expression changes completely. His eyes lighten a little, and there's a boyish bashfulness about his smile that makes me wonder if he likes her. "I am," he says, swinging his bag across his shoulder. He looks like a giant next to June, who barely comes up to my shoulder. "I'm traumatized that I lost two hundred freakin' bucks."

"Serves you right for gambling." She hooks an arm through mine as we start toward a long, yellow building with green pillars. Kavi joins us midwalk, accompanied by her boyfriend, Zion, and the six of us fall into step as we cross a courtyard filled with students. There's a quiet, hopeful buzz in the air. Other seniors walk past us with a spring in their step, gushing about prom and graduation. Everybody seems a little lighter, somehow, like we've all just caught a glimpse of the light at the end of the tunnel. If I can learn to relax, I can be that way too.

"You'll be fine," Kavi says, like she can sense my discomfort. I wonder if it's because she has four siblings—all younger, all girls—that she's so tuned in to others' feelings. "Everyone's already pretty much checked out. There's a serious case of senioritis going around."

"She's right," June says, "but there are a few things you need to know."

And in the two minutes it takes for them to drop me at the reception, she gives me a crash course on all things Granada Hills Charter: what food to order from the cafeteria, what rumors are currently making their rounds, what teachers are lenient with missing homework. By the time I'm walking up to the main desk, I feel like I somehow know everything and nothing.

The receptionist spends the next fifteen minutes going over my schedule before leading me down the corridor. We make a right, stopping in front of a door with its blind pulled down. She opens the door and steps inside, explaining to Mr. Shipman that I am the new student he's been expecting.

Heads swivel to look at me as Mr. Shipman, a tall, balding man with glasses, points to the table with an empty chair at the back, right behind Hayden Walker. Slowly, I make my way down the aisle, slip into the seat behind him, and try to make myself as small as possible.

When I'm no longer under a spotlight, I take a moment to look around the room. It's long and narrow, with eggshell white walls softened only by a canvas of inspirational quotes. *Be braver than you were yesterday*, one reads. *Always follow your heart*, reads another, like it is just that easy.

In front of me, Hayden is leaning so far back in his chair,

he's practically on my lap. He's looking ahead, tapping out a rhythm on his jeans with his pencils. I should be focusing on Mr. Shipman, but instead I'm repeating our encounter last night, over and over.

Apologies are free, Dad would say. *What have you got to lose*? It's true too; sometimes it felt like he never *stopped* apologizing.

By the end of class, I have gathered enough courage to apologize. It's clear I offended him last night, and I'd rather not make enemies on my first day of school.

As soon as the bell rings I'm out of my seat, making my way to his desk. I hesitate for a moment. Long enough to realize this is probably a mistake. Long enough for him to lift his head. Our eyes connect, and for a second he just looks at me before he grabs his bag, swings it over his shoulder, and walks right past me.

At lunch, instead of playing the age-old game of *where do I sit*, the decision is made for me. June waves me over, so I take a seat at an already-crowded table overlooking the courtyard.

"You're just in time to hear June start one of her mumbo-jumbo therapy rants about love languages," Olly says. For someone so skinny, he's managed to inhale his pizza and fries and is now helping himself to June's. "Her mom's a relationship therapist, so she thinks she's some kind of expert by default."

"It's not mumbo jumbo," June says, yanking her fries away. "It's, like, scientifically proven."

"Whatever. Just *once* I'd like to eat lunch without being psychoanalyzed."

"No one is psychoanalyzing *you*. I'd be done in two seconds."

He reaches for her fries again, dodging her attempts to slap him away. "And if I were doing you, I'd be done in *three*."

"You'll never be doing me."

Zion, who up until now had been fixing his dark hair in the reflection of a spoon, bursts out laughing.

Confused, I say, "What are love languages?"

June turns to me mid–smoothie sip. "The idea is that we all have a primary love language, a specific way we like to be appreciated or loved. I'm a words of affirmation kind of girl, which means I like people to tell me they appreciate me rather than show me. Olly, no surprise, likes gifts." Her eyes land on mine, and she tilts her head. "Obviously, I haven't worked you out yet, but I will."

The idea of being psychoanalyzed by June makes me nauseous. "Can't wait."

They start talking about senior week as I try to keep up. Hayden is over by the window, sitting on a table with his friends. He's more animated than I've seen him so far. The grin on his face is sweet and boyish, the opposite of how he'd looked at me earlier.

June follows my gaze. "Ugh."

My head snaps up. "You don't like them?"

"I don't like *him*."

"Sure you do," Dylan says. "Didn't you make out with him after Homecoming?"

For a moment, June doesn't say anything. She just finishes her smoothie, sets down the carton, and calmly says, "Olly, do you mind?"

"Not at all." He leans across June, his T-shirt rising slightly to reveal a sliver of taut skin, and punches Dylan on the arm.

To me, he says, "Ignore him. He gets mopey whenever Hayden is mentioned."

Dylan looks at Hayden, his body rigid, then turns to his plate. I can't help but ask, "Why?"

"Dylan made out with Hayden's ex, Caitlyn," Olly says. "She ditched them both, moved schools, and now they mope around shooting each other death glares every now and then." He looks at Dylan and innocently asks, "Did I leave anything out?"

"Yeah, you're a dick," Dylan says. "I realize I come across as the bad guy in this story, but it's complicated. He's not a nice guy."

I don't answer. Judging people on gossip has never been my thing, but something about Hayden sets alarm bells ringing. Maybe it's the piercing stare, or the fact that my mom has spent several years warning me about boys like him, but every time he looks at me, it makes me wish he wouldn't.

Conversation soon moves to prom. As relieved as I feel to be back in a routine, prom is the one thing I'm not looking forward to. The dress Mom and I had spent months searching for now hangs in my closet, a reminder of a night with Jamie I'll never get to have.

"Oh, you don't need to worry about finding a date," Kavi says. "June already asked Dylan to take you."

"You mean *forced*," Zion says, glancing at me. "No offense."

I turn to Dylan, who is trying to look anywhere but directly at me. "Are you okay with that?"

His eyes flit to mine, warm and intense. "Yeah. I mean, if you are. I figured it would be stressful moving here halfway through your senior year and then having to worry about prom."

For a brief moment, I worry what Jamie will think about me going to prom with another boy. But then I remind myself he won't think anything—I'm not my mom, and he's not my dad. "Thanks," I say. "That's really sweet of you."

The rest of the day passes in a blur of new faces. June insists we go shopping after school, followed by dinner. I hesitate briefly—I'd been planning on checking out the school's athletics facilities—but her and Kavi practically drag me to the parking lot.

We climb into her convertible and, with the top down, ride down a palm tree–lined street with the music turned up. Head back, I'm suddenly hit with this rush of adrenaline as my hair whips back and forth in the wind.

It's not long before we're pulling into the busy parking lot of West Hollywood Gateway mall. We spend the next hour rushing through stores, trying on clothes like in a bad teen movie before heading to Sephora.

"Oh my God," June pants behind me, closely followed by Kavi, "why do you walk so fast?"

"Why do you walk so slow?" I say, but I let her grab my hand and take the lead, pulling me down the foundation aisle.

"Here, try this," Kavi says, handing me a tube. "You're a similar shade to me, and it's the best I've ever worn. Doesn't make you look all ashy like some brands do."

June, who is looking between us like she's being left out, says, "I'll get it for you. It can be your Welcome-to-California gift."

My guard goes up, and I tell her I can't. Gifts come with a warning label, a fine print on the side of the box: *accept this and you'll owe me.*

"Okay," she says, handing it back, "gifts are definitely not your love language. I'll keep trying."

We settle on an Italian restaurant for dinner. I order spaghetti while they get ravioli, and we spend the next hour getting to know each other better.

It seems June is a movie buff. Anything I mention, she's either seen it or heard about it, and if it doesn't have at least a seven-star rating on IMDb, it's not worth her time.

"What's wrong with low-rated movies?" I ask. "They can be good."

Kavi looks up from her phone long enough to say, "Don't get her started," but I can tell from June's passionate expression that it's too late.

"Who wants to waste two hours on a movie that's got a bunch of bad reviews?" June asks. She leans across the table, eyes bright with expression. "I figure time is precious, and you should make the most of it." She stabs at her ravioli and pushes her side of garlic bread toward me. "Have some, it's nice."

I rush to take one of the slices. "You must miss out on a lot of good movies that way, though. Some have terrible reviews but turn out to be really enjoyable. Some of them might not be critically acclaimed, but does it matter?"

"I guess, but if the majority of people who watch a movie think it's bad, it's a good indicator that the movie is going to be bad."

"No, I know." This garlic bread is delicious. I eye the other slice for a second, and June laughs and says I can have that one too. "I'm just saying that even a bad movie can be fun to watch. I mean, I've watched movies with two stars before, not expecting much, and ended up loving them."

"What you should both be watching," Kavi says, "are murder documentaries. There are loads on Netflix. Zion and I have these murder marathons, and we try to guess who the killer is before it's revealed."

"Sounds morbid," June says.

The buzzing of my phone cuts through whatever Kavi's about to say. I glance at the FaceTime call from Jamie and hesitate.

Kavi peers over my shoulder and asks, "That the boyfriend?"

"Yep."

"Can we meet him?" June asks.

I hesitate, then click Accept and wait for Jamie's face to fill the screen. As soon as it does, my heart flips. "Hey," he says. "You home yet? How was your first day?"

"Not yet. I'm just having dinner with my—" I pause, because it feels strange to call them friends after only a week.

"—new besties," June says. "Quick, point it to me." She smooths down her curls, readjusts her sweater, and grins.

Laughing, I turn the camera to them both. "This is June and Kavi. They go to my school."

"Hey," Kavi says.

"Hey," June follows, then scrunches her nose. "Is that the weather in New York right now? It looks like you're in the Upside Down."

There's confusion in Jamie's voice as he says, "The Upside Down?"

"Yeah. You know, from *Stranger Things*?"

"Oh, yeah," he says, laughing, but Jamie has never watched *Stranger Things*, and it's not like him to lie, "I gotta get going, Madz," he says, so I turn the camera back to me.

"I'll call you later," I say.

"Can't wait."

As soon as the call ends, June leans across the table in excitement. "He is *so* cute. Have you guys had sex yet?"

I practically choke on my garlic bread. It's not that I'm a *prude*, it's just that I'm not used to talking about these things with people. The only other person I talk to is Jamie and it's not like we actually talk about it all that often. I've *thought* about sex a lot this past year, the reasons behind why Jamie and I haven't taken that step, despite having been dating nearly a year. We're not religious or anything, we aren't waiting until marriage, and while he's pushed for it a few times, I've never felt ready to give away that part of myself yet.

"No, have you?"

"I haven't," Kavi says. "Zion and I want to wait."

"I have," June says, and she leans across the table like she's about to tell me a secret. "I was with this guy, Lucas, for a year before his family moved to Kentucky. You should have seen me, Maddie. We were forever confessing our undying love for each other. Then a week after he moved, we didn't speak again. I was so distraught by it all that I ended up making out with Hayden Walker at a party. Can you believe that?"

For a moment, I'm silent. I take a moment to process her monologue. I'm not used to someone like June, someone who can just trust a complete stranger with such personal information. But maybe that's how we all start out. Maybe we just go around blindly trusting until one day, we learn why we shouldn't.

When I realize she's still looking at me for an answer, I say, "Is that why you don't like him?"

She scrunches her nose again. "I don't like him because he treated my friend like crap. I mean, I know she cheated on him, but before that he was a dick to her. All Caitlyn ever talked about is how much they'd fight."

"Bearing in mind that Caitlyn had a habit of exaggerating," Kavi says.

June rolls her eyes. "Whatever. He's a jerk."

"I don't get it," I say. "From what I've seen, Dylan doesn't seem like the kind of guy to steal someone's girlfriend."

She bites her lip. "You didn't hear any of this from me, okay?"

Kavi puts a hand out, as if to say *halt*. "Not your story to tell, June."

June ignores her and turns to me. "Dylan and Caitlyn were best friends, except Dylan was madly in love with her. Then Hayden and Caitlyn got together, which for Hayden was practically unheard of—he never went out with just *one* girl. But around the same time, Hayden lost his dad and started acting like a jerk. I guess the more Hayden spiraled, the closer Dylan and Caitlyn grew. Hayden turned into an even bigger jerk afterward and hasn't been with anyone since. Dylan and Caitlyn got together briefly, but when her family moved last year, she completely cut contact with everyone."

Even though I feel terrible for Caitlyn, a part of me can't help but feel bad for Hayden too. He lost his dad and his girlfriend at the same time. That had to have been hard.

"Moving on," Kavi says, "are you going to college? Which ones did you get into?"

My whole body tenses. While college is something to look forward to for most, it has always been a sore subject for me.

It's not that my parents weren't supportive of my choices, they were. They trailed around college after college with me, took me to my interviews, helped me to prepare. But as excited as they'd been for me, I could never mirror that same excitement back. The colleges I'd wanted to go to were miles away, which would mean leaving Mom for months at a time—I just couldn't do it.

In the end, most of the colleges I'd applied to were close to home. There were a few further afield, colleges on my *Never going to happen but a girl can dream* list. I knew even if I were accepted to one, I would never take it, but it was enough to know that they wanted me, that all of my hard work had paid off.

At least, that's how I'd felt at first. Then my acceptance letters came through, and I realized I'd been accepted to my dream college, UCLA. All of a sudden, it *wasn't* enough just to know that they wanted me; I needed more. Only now that I'm here, talking about it, do I realize that UCLA is no longer a dream, it's a possibility. California is our new start, and with UCLA being a stone's throw away, there is only one thing stopping me.

"I'm thinking about accepting my offer at UCLA," I say, "but my boyfriend wants us both to go to NYU."

The pair pull a face at this, so I say, "What?"

"Nothing," Kavi says, but she has a *something* face. "It's just, are you sure you want to go to the same college as your high school boyfriend? What if you break up? College should be about where you want to go."

Mom had said pretty much the same thing when I'd told her. *Don't you dare use me as an excuse not to follow your dreams,* she'd said, and *don't let Jamie keep you here either.*

Wherever you go, whatever you do, do it for you, no one else. Still, living for yourself and not others is easier said than done.

We finish up our meal, which June insists on paying for, and by the time she drops me home, it feels like I've known them for years. I head into the house and peer into the living room, where Lilly and Tim are watching TV. Tim has got his arms around her, holding her close, and she's resting her head on his chest. It reminds me of my parents on one of their good days.

"Hey," Lilly says when she notices me hovering. "How was your first day?"

"Good." I shrug. "Everyone's really nice."

She looks a little relieved. "I'm glad. Something came for you earlier, by the way. I've had to stop Tim opening it for you about five times."

I glance at the coffee table. On it is a crisp, white box with a pink ribbon around it, my name scrawled in gold calligraphy across the side.

"The suspense has been killing me," Tim says. "Open it, open it."

Briefly, alarm bells ring. My fingers tremble as I pull off the ribbon and watch it unravel. Inside is a beautiful thin-cut bracelet with several silver charms.

"Wow," Lilly says. "I wish *Tim* was that romantic. You'd think he'd be better at this stuff being a romance writer, but no, I get electric toothbrushes for my birthday, or snow tires. We don't even get snow, Tim. When would I need snow tires?"

"Hey, I got you the toothbrush *once*. Plus, you're always talking about driving up to Canada. It snows there."

The pair go off on a tangent as I study my bracelet. My

thumb gently traces the pieces of our history, a few of the charms winking at me as they catch the light. A sterling silver book to commemorate the first time we'd spoken in the library. A tiny Stitch, for the first Disney movie I ever made him watch. I pause on the most important charm, resting in the center of the bracelet. A pair of ice skates, identical to the ones we'd worn on our first date to Rockefeller Center.

"Do you know how to ice-skate?" he'd asked. It had only been a few weeks since we'd been talking—mostly through messages—but now he was leaning against my locker, wearing that cute, boyish smile.

"Not without falling on my ass."

Jamie grinned. He leaned in closer as other students hurried to get to class. "What if I took you ice-skating and promised to let you hold on to me?"

My heart pounded. I'd vowed to myself that I would never do boyfriends, but weeks of Jamie calling me beautiful, of making me laugh, made me want to make an exception.

"What if I fall?" I asked.

"Then we're going down together," he said seriously. "You fall, I fall."

I laughed in spite of myself, because it had only been last week that I'd made him watch my favorite movie, Titanic.

I still didn't understand how any of this happened. His attention baffled me, not just because he was popular, but because he was so handsome and social. He was the kind of guy who'd strike up a conversation with anyone, flitting between social groups like a butterfly.

I was the opposite. I had people I sat with at lunch and walked to classes with, but there was no one I'd hang out with after school. Between extracurriculars and pretending to be happy, there wasn't much energy left for anything else.

"Okay," I said. "I'll go."

When Jamie showed up that weekend, my mother seemed nervous. This was the first boy I'd ever been out with, and I could tell she was wondering whether Jamie was another Dad; whether I was destined to meet the same fate. It's what I kept wondering, too, but Jamie was the perfect gentleman. He politely introduced himself to my parents and spent the next ten minutes discussing the golden ratio with my father and photography with my mother. When it was time to leave, both my parents were smitten.

"Have fun," Dad said.

"Don't stay out late!" called Mom.

We headed to Rockefeller Center, making small talk on the subway. Jamie held my hand, and it felt warm and solid in mine. He chatted about his parents—his mom ran a makeup business and his dad was a lawyer—and his favorite films. I learned he loved Buffy the Vampire Slayer, which was my favorite series of all time, that he spent every weekend at Tyler's, because his parents were always out, and he hated being alone. The more he opened up to me, the more comfortable I felt, and by the time we got to Rockefeller Center, it felt like I'd known him my whole life.

"I feel like I don't really know you," he said as we climbed up the stairs to the street level. "Tell me something no one else knows. Something real." He noticed my hesitant expression and said, "I'll go first." He looked down for a moment at his hands, conflicted. "My ex cheated on me."

My eyes softened. "I'm sorry."

He nodded. "I was in love, and I thought she was too. Obviously not." He looked up then, something vulnerable in *his expression. "That's not the something real, though. The something real is that you're the first girl I've wanted to open up to since then."*

My heart swelled, like I'd somehow achieved something no other girl had. I thought for a minute about what I could tell him in return. I wanted to be as open and as vulnerable as he was, but there was a mental blockage that stopped me. Sharing your secrets never ended well.

"I like to make lists," I said. "With time frames that everything needs to be completed by. The girls in track saw one on my phone once and said I was crazy."

His face fell a little, but he tried his best to hide his disappointment. "They sound evil. Can I see one?"

Hesitant, I got out my phone, opened up my schedule app, and passed it to him. He scanned the list, not saying anything, and I began to wonder whether he thought I really was crazy. But then he scrolled to the bottom, typed something in, and handed back my phone. He'd written down a schedule that said Second date with Jamie.

I was still grinning when we got to Rockefeller Center, and the moment we got onto the ice was like something from a movie. Christmas music blasted from the speakers as I leaned into his side. He took my hand and turned to face me, sensing I was nervous.

"Do you trust me?" he asked.

The question caught me off guard. I'd only really known him a few weeks, so how could I trust him? And yet in that moment, as he stared at me with those trusting blue eyes, I did.

"Yes."

We moved slowly but steadily as I clung to him. I kept

expecting him to grow annoyed at my snail pace, the way Dad would have at Mom, but instead he was patient as little kids zoomed past us, spinning around on their skates.

"You're a natural," he said, and even though I knew it was a lie, it filled me with happiness.

He pulled me toward him, and I felt the heat flood my cheeks, as if I were blushing. He reached down, tucking a strand of hair behind my ear like he was going to kiss me. And it surprised me how much I wished that he would kiss me, so much so that I'd already imagined how soft his lips would feel on mine.

"You want to know something real?" I whispered.

Against my ear, in a low, soft voice, he whispered, "Yes."

I took a deep breath, my heart pitter-pattering in my chest. "I've never done this before."

"Skated?" He grinned. "That's kind of obvious."

"No, been on a date. Liked . . . someone."

His grin fell away, his serious eyes back. "I know it's not because you've never been asked out. Tyler said you turned him down a few months ago."

Nodding, I said, "It's just that—" I took a deep breath, because this was the first time I'd ever be saying this out loud. And it seemed crazy to do it—I'd only been hanging with Jamie a few weeks, but somehow he made me feel vulnerable. Safe. *"My parents have a toxic marriage. I guess I've been scared I'd end up that way too."*

He suddenly pulled me closer, his hand like a reassuring presence on my back. "Thank you for telling me," he said, and he lowered his mouth until it was right by my ear. "And just for the record, I'd never hurt you." He tucked my hair behind my ear then, looked in my eyes, and kissed me.

The bracelet is out of the box and over my wrist in a second. The gold color catches the light and glows as I gently finger the *J* charm. It's beautiful. I send Jamie a picture of it on my wrist, tell him I love it, and promise to call him after dinner.

Not as beautiful as you, he texts back.

"Where's my mom?" I ask.

"She's having a power nap," Lilly says, and I can tell from the way she quickly looks at Tim that there's something on her mind. "I'm a little worried about her—about both of you. I can't imagine how hard this split must have been, but therapy is a big thing here. If you want—"

"No." The word comes out quick, and Lilly stops dead. I know my mother, I know how she prefers to shut the world out, and forcing her to do something she doesn't want to do just pushes her further away. Already it feels like she's slipping through my fingers, fading away before my eyes. "We're fine," I say. "Or we will be, once we've settled in. She just needs a little time."

Lilly opens her mouth like she wants to say more, but Tim puts a hand on her shoulder, gives her a look, and my aunt backs down.

"You want to watch something with us?" he asks. "Maybe a third vote will help us actually decide on something."

I tell them maybe later and head upstairs. I pass my mother's room on the left and find her curled up on her side. I'm suddenly hit with the smell of Dad's aftershave, like she's spritzed it on the pillows. My first instinct is to lie down behind her and wrap an arm around her waist. "Hey," I say softly. "How are you doing?"

At first I think she's asleep, but then she curls a hand

around my arm, squeezing me tight. "I should be asking you that. How was your first day at school?"

"It was fine. Come on, Mom, it's just me now. How are you really doing?"

Her chest contracts beneath my hand. She takes in a breath, then quietly says, "I spent the morning working on my résumé, thinking I was fine, then out of nowhere I"—she pauses as though trying to find the right words—"I just started missing him." All of a sudden, this invisible thread snaps, and her body folds in on itself. "I know that I shouldn't," she says through sobs, "but I can't help it. It feels like I can't breathe."

Eyes squeezed shut, I pull her in closer, biting back tears. Ever since our first date, Jamie has been my anchor, the one person I know I can be vulnerable around, but for my mother, it's me; it's why I have to be strong. "It's okay to miss him," I say, but sometimes I'm not so sure. "I miss him too."

Mom turns in my arms until she's facing me properly. I'm always surprised by how different she looks without makeup. Growing up, it felt like she never went a day without wearing her bronzer or blush or eyeshadow. Not because she thought she needed it, but because she enjoyed it; it made her feel good.

Dad could never understand this. To him, makeup was a weapon Mom used to lure other men. It didn't matter how much she argued or tried to explain; she was never going to win with him. Eventually, she stopped wearing makeup at all.

"What if he's hurt?" she whispers. "What if he needs us?"

A familiar lump works its way up my throat. I close my eyes, repeating his words in my head: *I love you both so much. If I ever lost you, I'd kill myself.*

I pull her in closer, pressing my cheek to her face. "Whenever you start to miss him, just hold on to the bad stuff," I say, but even to my own ears, it sounds impossible. Over time, the bad memories fade, until all you are left with are the good parts.

Mom nods, and when her eyes take on a far-off look, I know she's thinking about everything it took to get here. It hadn't been easy to set aside money when Dad controlled the finances, so we'd taken to withdrawing small amounts at a time, stuffing it all into a Ziploc bag before stashing it into a plant pot. It wasn't exactly the greatest of hiding spots, but Dad had a habit of searching the house—cupboards, light shades, floorboards—and it was the one place he'd yet to look.

What he was looking for, I never quite knew. My theory is signs of my mother's *infidelities*: maybe he expected to find a male's phone number stashed in the light shade, or a secret phone beneath the floorboards, but even that's just guesswork. The truth is, nobody knew what went on in my father's head—least of all him.

The tiniest flame ignites in my stomach. I count to ten, working hard to extinguish it. "You can do this," I say, but I'm not sure of that either.

She nods and buries her face in my neck. I stroke her hair, over and over, knowing it's all I can do. I feel it, too, this loss, even though I've pushed it down. But there are moments when I let it in, when I let myself think, and it feels like I'm suffocating.

—

Later that night, once I've showered and written out a schedule for tomorrow, I fall onto my bed, sideways, and stare at the photos on my nightstand. Breathing heavily, I pick them both up, holding one in each hand. For so long, I've wondered why these pictures stood out to me, but I think I finally get it now. One is the person I wish I could be, the other is who I fear I'll become.

Exhausted, I turn off the light in an attempt to get some sleep when my Instagram pings. I open it up, expecting it to be Jamie, but it's a message request from an account with no picture. My skin prickles, like a faint warning bell. Breath held, I click the message.

I'm sorry, I love you.

Dad.

For about a minute, I think I'm having a heart attack. I focus on breathing: inhale, exhale, inhale, exhale. I think it will calm me, this rhythm, but then my breathing comes faster, until all I can feel is the weight of my lungs, expanding and contracting. There's been this dark, empty space in my chest since we left, and for a second, his apology filled it.

I can't take it when he apologizes. When he frowns and tells us how much he loves us. It's like I forget he hurt us, and Mom does, too, and we forgive him again. Because we love him. I hate him, and I love him.

Another message comes through before I can react.

I can't live without you.

Two seconds later.

I'll never hurt you again. I'm sorry.

One second.

Answer me or you'll regret it.

I jerk as if I've been slapped. The ease in which he switches between Dr. Jekyll and Mr. Hyde is terrifying. With trembling fingers, I block his account. Despite his threats, there is a part of me that wants to write back. That misses him so much, it physically hurts. But then there is this other part that is angry and hates him. Not just him, but myself. He hurt us, time after time; how can I want to forgive that?

That's when it hits me—I might be physically free, but I'm as emotionally tied to him as ever. His words still hurt, his messages have the power to unravel me in an instant, and until that stops, I will never be free.

I hate you, I want to scream. *I hate you, I hate you, I hate you.* I grab a pillow and punch it as hard as I can. In my head, I'm reliving that night, but instead of taking his abuse like I did, I'm fighting back. That's when I pull back, remembering the flyer, and grab it from my drawer.

Straightening up, I smooth it out, staring at the front.

Welcome to GymCon, the flyer reads. Where fighters are made.

Raise money.

Take control.

Push yourself.

GymCon White Collar Boxing is a unique opportunity for people with no boxing background to experience the world of boxing in a safe and enjoyable environment. With eight weeks of one-to-one training, you'll be ready to face an evenly matched opponent at a glamorous event in Vegas. Raise money for charity and push yourself to lengths you have never gone before. Are you ready to be brave?

I read those words over and over, turning them around

in my head. Are you ready to be brave? My heart pounds as I stare at the boxer on the front. He looks fierce, controlled, and for the briefest of moments, the anger I feel is replaced by something else: hope.

CHAPTER FOUR

The night we decided to leave started off like any other. We were going for dinner to celebrate Mom's birthday, and we spent the evening getting ready, using subtle makeup that Dad wouldn't notice, picking out an outfit that flattered but didn't show too much skin. Dad was never fond of dresses or skirts, so a fitted jumpsuit was perfect. I straightened her hair, taking the time to curl the ends as she watched in the mirror. When we'd finished, she looked just like the woman I remembered as a kid.

I was wearing a cute dress that Jamie had bought and had straightened my hair the way he liked. Then I spent ages putting on my makeup. Maybe it was wrong of me, but everything she couldn't do, I made sure I did. There was something in me that refused to succumb to the same restrictions, not that it mattered. Dad never imposed these rules on me, just her.

"Come on," Mom said softly. "We don't want to be late."

She was nervous as we walked down the hall. I could feel her behind me, readjusting her jumpsuit, rubbing her cheeks to take off the blush, and I reached out behind me and grabbed her hand, letting her know it was okay.

The second Dad saw us, he grinned, and the relief on Mom's face as he pulled her into a hug was unmistakable. "I'm the luckiest guy in the world, do you know that?" he said. He kissed her cheek, spinning her around before setting her on her feet. "Happy birthday, Lori."

Things only got better once we got to the restaurant. Dad was himself again, the version of him that made the most sense. He told us to order whatever we wanted and spent the whole meal gushing about how beautiful Mom was, how many colleges I was going to get into, how I was going to be the best teacher the world had ever seen.

By dessert, he'd promised to take us on vacation, somewhere fancy like Hawaii or the Maldives, places my mother had always wanted to visit. "We'll get you a new camera for the trip," he said, squeezing her hand, "and you can show off your amazing photography skills." Mom beamed as he showered her with compliments, reminding us of all the reasons we loved him so much, and everything was perfect again.

Then came the check. The waiter stood patiently while Dad got out his card and asked Mom about the meal. She smiled politely and avoided his gaze. "It was great, thank you."

Less than two hours later, his other side was back. "You were flirting with him right in front of my face," he said as I listened from the upstairs landing. "Admit it, Lori. You know him from somewhere, don't you?"

Silence followed. Once upon a time, my mother would

argue back, try to defend herself, but now she stayed quiet. Breath held, I hovered outside of the kitchen. I strained my ears to find the only voice I could hear was his. It was always his.

He stood hunched over my mother, gripping her phone in his hand. He was large enough that his body completely shielded her from view.

"Who else are you messing around with, Lori? Whose numbers have you been saving as women again?" He frantically scrolled through her contact list, then pressed a number and waited for it to ring. As soon as he heard what I presumed was a woman, he hung up and tried another.

"Stop," Mom whispered, reaching for her phone. "You're going to embarrass me."

"Then tell me," he pleaded. It was the calm, desperate tone that he always used with us, the kind you might use to whisper *I love you* or something sweet. It's what made things so confusing. "Are you still seeing that guy?" Silence answered his accusation, and I was afraid any moment, he'd be able to hear my racing heart. "Answer me, Lori, or I'll call every single person you know and tell them what you've been doing behind my back."

The defeat on her face was apparent. "For the last time, he was a client. He wanted to buy a photograph I'd taken."

He reached down with his other hand and gently cupped her cheek. "You're lying." His voice broke on the second word, filled with hurt. "If he was just a client, why did you save his number as someone else?"

"*Because*," Mom shouted, "I needed to be able to contact him, and I knew how you'd react if you saw his name in my phone! I just wanted to avoid *this*."

"You don't need to get hysterical," Dad said, scraping away her tears, "I'm just asking a simple question."

This was my least favorite version of him. When he yelled, it was easy to understand the hatred in my veins, but this version confused me, made something awful ache deep in my chest. His brokenness left doubt in my resolve, and as his eyes began to water, I didn't see his cruelty; I saw a man who needed help.

"I can't do this anymore," Mom whispered.

My father stilled. Behind his crazed eyes, I could see his mind turning, processing her words. The veins in his neck grew in size, and his pale skin reddened. Whenever his face turned like this, I knew we were past the point of reason.

"If I'm so awful, if I'm everything you say I am, then why don't you leave?" He reached toward her, and something primal propelled me forward, away from safety and into the kitchen, where I crouched in front of her. I didn't meet her eyes, I couldn't, but I shielded her the best I could, meeting my father's instead.

We have the same eyes. Green, with little flecks of yellow and brown, like the color of leaves at the beginning of autumn, just as they're beginning to fall from the trees.

He stepped forward an inch. A warning. "Go back upstairs, Maddison." It was his subtle way of giving me a way out. To turn and make my way back upstairs, the way I usually did. One last chance, before he turned on me too.

My mother was still crouched on the floor. Gone was the carefree girl from that photograph. All that remained as she lay across the tiles was a tired, broken woman. She had no friends now, no family besides us—if I didn't protect her, who would?

"She didn't do anything wrong, Dad."

My father raised his hand, then stopped. I jerked as always, but Dad rarely hit me, he just liked to see me flinch. I reached for my mother again. Dad's arm shot out, pushing me away, and something inside me snapped. I shoved him so hard, he lost his footing and fell to the ground.

Mom got to her knees, panicked. Dad straightened up, then took a step forward, slow and deliberate. "Come here."

His voice cut straight through me, twisted my gut into a tight, little knot. I could be perfectly calm, controlled, and this tone would ramp up my heart rate and make my palms sweat. Because I knew. I knew what it meant.

"I'm sorry," I choked out. "I'm sorry. I love you."

Mom moved in front of me. She reached behind her, hand outstretched, and allowed me to wrap my fingers around hers. "Henry," she warned.

He took another careful step. I held my breath, and from the way Mom stilled, she had too. He'd moved so close, his thin, narrow nose was pressed against hers.

"Is this how you show your appreciation for everything I've done for you?" he asked. "I put a roof over your heads, I spend all day working in a stressful job, I tell you I'm going to take you on vacation, and this is how you thank me?"

My breathing felt labored. Whatever happened next because of my actions, Mom would take the brunt of it; she always did. "It was an accident," I said. "I didn't—I just—"

"Stop. Stop lying." He pushed Mom aside and grabbed me by the wrist, pulling me toward him. "No matter how much I do for you, it's never good enough."

For a moment as he held me, I wanted to hit him, to hurt

him the way he hurt us, so I raised my hand. And then I froze. Fear took over, and I just stood there as he smirked at me, the same way Moby smirked at Hayden.

"What were you going to do, *hit* me?" he said. "That's not like you, Maddie. You're not a fighter."

What came next was almost too quick to process. He let go of my wrist, face almost purple, and in one quick motion, he slapped me. My skin burned hot with pain and embarrassment. Tears streamed from my eyes, not because of the pain, but because I was so shocked, so *angry*. It felt like he'd spent years establishing the rules, motioning to hit me but never following through. Then he went and changed them on me.

Suddenly, his eyes widened. "I'm so sorry," he said, his voice cracking. "I'm sorry, Maddie. I didn't mean to." He dropped to his knees in front of me, wrapping his arms around my legs. He reached toward Mom, taking her hand as he sobbed at my feet. "I'm just so scared of losing you both. I love you. I don't know what I'd do without you. You can't ever leave me."

My body was still as his tears sank into my skirt. My head screamed *Get away,* but my heart pulled toward him, broken by his tears. It felt like hours must have passed before we moved. Eventually he wiped his eyes and headed upstairs, leaving us behind in the kitchen. My eyes met Mom's, expecting her to be defeated, but instead she moved toward me, cupping my still-sore cheek in her hand.

"Get ready," she said. "When the time is right, we're leaving."

For a second, I just stared at her. This wasn't the first time we'd tried to leave Dad. Usually, we'd stay in a hotel until Dad had calmed down, and he'd feed us an apology and we'd be right back where we started. But the moment Mom contacted Lilly, I knew this time was for good. I suppose, in some ways, something good came from that night; it was the catalyst Mom needed to leave.

CHAPTER FIVE

Because of the LA traffic, it takes a while to get to the gym. The Uber pulls into the parking lot, and I notice the gym looks shabbier in the sunlight, wedged between a coin-op laundromat and a barber.

I walk up to the door, ignoring my nerves, and tug on the handle. A handwritten sign, duct-taped to the front, reads seven thirty a.m. to seven p.m. I glance at my watch. 7:03.

The lights are still on, so I lean against the wall and wait. The time gives the doubt a chance to settle in and for Dad's voice to bounce around my head. *This isn't like you, Maddie. You're not a fighter.* It had taken me three days to muster up the courage to come here, but now that I'm here, staring up at the gym, it feels like I'm making a *mistake*.

The door swings open and a figure walks out, his face half shielded by his black hoodie. He closes the door behind him, looks up, and freezes. The first thing I see is Hayden's pale eyes, which stare back impatiently.

"Can I help you?" Despite his words, he doesn't sound like he particularly wants to help me.

Briefly, as I take him in, I think about what Dylan had said. *Not a nice guy.* My mother would certainly agree, but then, she's suspicious of any teenage boy who isn't Jamie, especially if they happen to be tall, dark, and handsome. *That's a bad boy wrapped up with a neat little bow*, she'd say. *Don't be fooled by the pretty wrapping paper, Maddie. It just hides the ugliness within.*

I think about what Jamie would say if he knew what I was doing. Now that I've had a chance to calm down, me being here seems absurd, but I can't bring myself to walk away. "I'm fine," I say, squaring my shoulders. "I'm just waiting for the owner."

He ignores me, pulling a key from his hoodie and locking the door with it. I start to wonder if he even heard me when he says, over his shoulder, "That would be me."

I'm so surprised that I don't answer right away. "You own this gym?" He raises an eyebrow but doesn't say anything. Slowly, I say, "Well, I'm not sure if you recognize me, but—"

"Sure, I do," he replies. There is a glint of amusement in his eyes. "Are you stalking me?"

"No, I'm not *stalking* you. I was handed this flyer at the fight the other night. I want to do it."

Clearly, that is not what he'd been expecting me to say. He thinks for a moment, burying his hands in his pockets. "Do what?"

"This," I say like it's obvious. "White Collar Boxing."

The corner of his mouth lifts. "I don't think so."

I wait a second for him to elaborate. When he doesn't, I say, "But—"

"Look, this is our senior year. Between finals and all the other crap we're supposed to do, there's no way you're going to be able to commit to eight weeks of training." He reaches into his pocket and pulls something out. I jump back, startled, before realizing it's his car keys. He smirks and steps forward like he thinks I'll step back, but I don't. "Are we done here?" He goes to move past me without waiting for an answer, but I block his path.

"The flyer says it's a unique opportunity for people with no boxing experience," I say, pulling it from my pocket to show him. "Right here."

He doesn't look at the flyer. "At my discretion. Besides, the slots are already filled."

My shoulders slump, but I'm not ready to give up. I could walk away right now and join the track team, or find some other outlet for my anger, but I've known from the moment I watched Hayden fight that this is what I need. I want to fight back, even if it's too late now. Even if it no longer counts. I want to fight back.

"I was handed this flyer," I say, "and I'm not leaving until you say yes."

"Why? You couldn't *wait* to get out of this place the other night, and no offense, but you don't exactly strike me as the type." His eyes rake over me from head to toe, clearly unimpressed.

I straighten up, undeterred by his assessment of me. "I have my reasons."

"Give me one."

"How about 'cause I want to punch something, and if you keep saying no, it's going to be you?"

He almost smiles, but he must see something desperate in

my expression, because his eyes soften slightly. "You going to be eighteen by the time of the fight?"

"Turned eighteen on January nineteenth."

He runs a hand down his face. "I'm tied up this week, but come by Saturday night, all right? It's two fifty a month, up front, and don't be late."

"Thank you."

He nods and, to my surprise, insists on waiting until my Uber gets here. As soon as it pulls up and I'm safely inside, he flicks up his hood and walks off.

—

Lilly makes chicken parmigiana for dinner. Everyone is sitting around the dining room table, which is neatly set with jute woven mats, silverware, and wine glasses.

The table comes alive with chatter as we take turns sharing about our day: Lilly kicked ass at work, Tim finished a chapter, the twins enjoyed their after-school clubs.

When eyes fall to me, I say, "I joined a gym in Burbank. Figured it would be nice to get back into a routine." I don't mention the boot camp or the upcoming fight—there's no way they'd understand.

"Are you going to inquire about outdoor track?" Mom asks. "I think having the same routine as back home will be good for you."

"There are only a few months left," I say. "Can't I just focus on getting to graduation?"

Her lips purse. "You don't want to throw away all your hard work."

"She's right, Lori," Lilly says. "Let her enjoy these last few months before college. The boys already checked out months ago." She turns to me, smiling. "But there's no way you're getting to Burbank without a car. Tim and I were planning on insuring you on mine since I rarely use it. Do you have a license?"

I nod. Driving in New York isn't exactly a necessity, but I'd insisted on learning anyway. It was another thing I could control, a backup plan in case I needed to leave. *Independence.*

"That's really kind of you," my mom says, and it's clear she's obviously still annoyed about track. "We'll pay for the insurance."

"How many times do I have to tell you?" Lilly says. "We're happy to help. You both just need to focus on finding your feet now that you're not with Henry."

There's an awkward silence before Tim asks how Mom's job hunt is going. She grabs my hand beneath the table, using me for support. For a split second, my mind is back home.

The three of us are at the dinner table, laughing at one of Dad's elaborate stories. He was always so good at making us laugh until our bellies hurt, and that night was no different.

Mom was laughing too. It was like the real her came out when he did: confident and sarcastic and full of light, like his best side brought out hers. But then his phone, which sat beside his plate, vibrated. He rushed to flip it over so the screen faced the table, but not before my mother caught sight of it.

A brief silence filled the room, broken only by the ticking of the kitchen clock.

"Who was it?" Mom asked.

"It was no one," Dad said. "Just another one of those scam callers."

More often than not, Mom would leave it at this, but very occasionally, there was a fight within in her spoiling to be had. "I thought I saw the name Jess on the screen." But there was doubt in her expression. Uncertainty. She was used to second guessing herself.

"Come on, Lor," Dad said, "don't be paranoid." It was his go-to word whenever we said or did something he didn't agree with. You're irrational. Insane. Paranoid.

I looked between them, my food untouched, my appetite lost. I was an invisible presence during these conversations, rarely seen or heard. It was easier that way.

"It started with a J," Mom said, her voice even. Calm. "Scam callers aren't saved in your contacts."

Dad put his fork down and looked at her. "Do you know how crazy you sound right now? I don't even know *any other women. You get so irrational about any female friendships I make, I've stopped trying."*

My mouth fell open, but nothing came out. There were so many times when I wanted to defend my mother, when I couldn't see things the way my father saw them, but speaking out made me seen. Heard. I didn't want that.

"That's because I don't think it's fair you're allowed to be friends with the opposite sex but I'm not," she said.

"You know what I think? I think you're projecting." He looked up then, his expression cold. "You're probably cheating, and you feel guilty so you're trying to accuse me of something." He rose to his feet, knuckles to the table, and stared at her.

It felt like slow motion watching her face fall. My heart pounded like a war drum. It was impossible to know what would happen once the fuse had been lit. Sometimes it fizzled out, sometimes it exploded in our faces.

Mom grabbed my hand beneath the table, squeezing it tight as if it gave her the strength to speak. "Forget I mentioned it. I must have read it wrong."

Dad sat back down, slowly, and spent the rest of the meal talking to me while giving my mother the silent treatment.

During dessert, Lilly and Tim go over some of the house rules now that we've settled in, like chores and allowances. The chores work on a schedule basis, which can be found in the kitchen, and I will receive a weekly allowance, the same as Dylan and Olly. It's a welcome surprise—I'd been planning on paying for my lessons with Hayden using my savings from the ice cream parlor where I worked back home, but now I can use this, instead.

Curfew is one a.m. for the twins, but Mom is insistent that my curfew stays at eleven, the same as back home.

"Oh come on," Lilly says. "If she's old enough to enlist, get married, and have kids, she's old enough to stay out past eleven."

"It's fine," I say. I've never minded the early curfew, because it's not like I ever do anything to stay out past eleven, anyway. Jamie and I would finish hanging out by nine, and I'd be back in bed to start my Buffy marathon by nine thirty.

Besides, I know the early curfew, even if it is a little draconian, helps Mom to sleep a little better. She's always been under the impression that if I don't stay out late, I won't end up meeting and falling for a boy like my father. I don't have the heart to tell her that the kind of boys she's referring to don't just exist in the dark.

—

Later that night, when I'm getting ready for bed, I pass Dylan's bedroom—second door on the left—and see moonlight spilling in through the open doors leading to his balcony. He's sitting on his bed, eyes closed, quietly strumming away on his guitar.

"Hey," he says. He turns slightly, midstrum, and grins. "Do you play?"

When I nod, he offers me the guitar. It feels heavy in my hands, but right, somehow, like I've clawed back a little piece of home. I start strumming a melody, nothing in particular, just a concoction of chords that complement each other. I have never really been musically inclined, but I taught myself guitar from a YouTube video three years ago as a way to distract myself; I've dabbled ever since.

"How are you feeling?" he says after a while. "Must be pretty weird not seeing your dad."

I keep strumming, but my heart suddenly beats twice as fast. "It's hard."

"I get it," he says, and he leans back against the wall, hands clasped behind his head, and watches my fingers brush the strings. "My mom and dad split a few years ago. She lived close by for a while, but then she met her new husband and they moved to Alaska. Going from seeing her regularly to never seeing her sucked."

"Do you see her much now?"

"Never." His eyes darken. "I guess she's too busy with her new life to think about us." Maybe it's the way the bedside lamp reflects in his eyes, but I could swear they've started to water. He clears his throat, then nods at the guitar in my hands. "You can keep that one if you want to." He nods to the other side of his room, where several acoustic guitars are lined up against his wall. "I've got enough to keep me busy."

"Thank you." I get to my feet and head back to my room, where I spend the next fifteen minutes playing. The longer I play, the harder it is to find enjoyment in it, to forget about the times I'd be playing in my room, only to be interrupted by the screaming downstairs. Eventually, I put the guitar to the side and don't look at it again.

No matter how hard I try not to think of him, everything I love links back to my dad. Panic creeps up on me, a mix of anger and grief. This was *our* choice, *our* decision, so why does it hurt this much?

Olly barges in without bothering to knock. I'm not used to such a lack of privacy, but the twins don't seem to mind. Already Dylan has barged into the bathroom while I'm brushing my teeth, or Olly into my bedroom when I'm trying to get changed. It's like they have no understanding of boundaries.

He looks around, taking in the color-coded binders on the desk and the stuffed unicorn Jamie won for me at a funfair. "Is this what the inside of your head is like?" he asks. "All color coded and fluffy and—" he shudders like he can't bear to think about it any longer.

"Did you need something?" I ask.

He perches himself on the edge of the bed, grinning. "Yeah, I have something to ask you."

"Ask me?"

"Yeah." He takes a deep breath, and for a moment that easy, confident expression is replaced by what looks like nervousness. "I kind of need your advice on something . . . girl related."

"What is it?"

He nervously runs his fingers over the embroidery on my bed quilt. "Let's say you were single, and you've been friends with a guy for a year. Could it ever turn into something more, or is it too late? Like, what do girls think?"

"You know I don't have some kind of pass to speak for all girls, right?" Olly frowns a little, and I realize he's serious about this. "I don't know. I mean, it depends on if she secretly likes you or not. If she does and it's just a case of you both being too shy to admit it, then sure, but a year is a long time to be friends with someone. You don't want to ask her out and have it become awkward, do you?"

He thinks about this for a moment and sighs. "I never have this kind of problem, you know? Girls usually make it pretty clear they like me—I mean, look at me." He gestures to himself in a way that makes me think he's not joking.

"I'm sure they love how modest you are too."

He grins, and his eyes fall to my nightstand as he takes in the flyer. "You actually kept that?" He jumps off the bed and snatches it up. "Wait." His expression turns to one of surprise. "No way. Is this what you meant when you said you joined the gym? Hayden Walker's boot camp?"

"You don't have to sound so surprised about it. I happen to enjoy a challenge."

"Hey, I'm not hating. I think it's cool you want to do this—I'm just a little surprised."

I snatch the flyer from his hands. "It's just something I want to try, okay? But I'd like to keep this"—I gesture to the flyer—"a secret, so please don't tell my mom."

The grin on his face is adorable. "I won't. She kind of weirds me out, no offense."

I leap to her defense like a lioness protecting her cubs, even though it should be the other way around. "She's not weird. She's going through a painful split. Try showing some compassion."

He raises both hands like he's surrendering to the police. "I'm sorry, I was just kidding."

"It's fine," I say, glancing at the clock, "but it's getting pretty late, and I still need to call Jamie."

He nods and peels himself off my bed before walking to the door. "Night, Maddie."

"Night." I wait for him to leave before getting out my phone. Jamie's number is first on my call list as though, despite being three thousand miles away, nothing has changed.

"Hey," he says on the first ring. He sounds a little groggy, and I feel bad for calling him so late. "You forget about me?"

"I'm sorry. Things have been hectic."

"It's fine." He says it like he means it, which is what I love about him. He doesn't hold things against me like Dad would. He doesn't get mad. "What did you get up to today?"

Excitement courses through me. "This is going to sound a little out there, but I've joined this White Collar boot camp. It's where—"

"I know what White Collar is." The frown on his face makes me nervous. "That's a little . . . crazy. I mean, you're not really the type, you know?"

It's not exactly the reassurance I was looking for, but he's right. This is so far removed from anything I've ever done that I can't blame him for being concerned. "My dad messaged me on Instagram," I admit.

He suddenly leans forward, frowning. "When did this

happen? How did he even find your new account? What did he say?"

"Yesterday, and I have no idea. He just said he was sorry. I blocked him straight away."

"Good. Just try and forget about him, okay? You don't need someone like that in your life, and you don't need to box to prove some kind of point to him either. All we need is each other, Maddie."

"I'm not doing it to prove something," I say, "I just—" I stop, because I don't know why I'm doing it, I just know that I need to. "It's really regulated, and you wear a bunch of equipment. I'll be fine."

He runs a hand through his hair and sighs. "This is a big commitment to take on during your last few months of senior year. Are you even going to have any time for us?"

Doubt works its way through me. I'd known this was a little out there, but hearing someone else say it makes it sink in. "Of course I will. I'll *make* time. You're more important than anything."

"Okay." He says it gently, but there's a look in his eyes I'm not sure how to read. Is he annoyed? "We probably have time to watch something if you want. What are you feeling? Horror, rom-com, comedy?"

"Hmm," I say. "Hold on, June is a movie buff. She might know something good."

"I'm sure we can think of something without Jun—" but I'm already sending her a message asking for recommendations. She sends one back immediately with ten different movies, accompanied with their ratings and lots of emojis. I laugh and go with *Joker*, which has a rating of 8.4.

"We've already seen it," Jamie says.

Confused, I rack my brain for any memory of the film, but I'm certain I've never seen it. "No, we haven't."

"Oh come on," he says, his voice teasing, "who's the one with the good memory out of the two of us? Although I'm pretty sure we missed the end of it. You fell asleep, as usual."

He's right, I do have a bad habit of falling asleep halfway through a movie. I'm usually just so comfortable and warm when I'm snuggled to his chest that I can't help it. "We'll pick something different, then."

"What about the new Marvel movie?" he says.

"We've seen it."

His expression closes down as silence stretches between us. "You must have seen it with someone else."

"Who else would I have seen it with?"

"You tell me."

My head is racing a mile a minute. I'm racking my brain again, wondering whether I've confused Jamie for Dad, but no, I'm certain it was Jamie because of what happened after. His parents had been out, and I remember halfway through the film his hand crept up my thigh . . .

"It's not a big deal," Jamie says. "I don't mind if you watched it with someone else. We can pick something different."

I'm about to say *I didn't*, but I stop. Jamie's memory is much better than mine—maybe he's right.

It takes us so long to pick something that we're both too tired in the end. "I gotta get up early for practice," he says. "Love you, Runner Bean."

"Love you, Green Bean." I hang up the call and climb into bed. With Hayden's fight from the other night still playing in my head, I drift off to sleep.

CHAPTER SIX

Saturdays in the Applegate household start with some kind of home-cooked breakfast, and end up with us all at the beach. Nestled away in Malibu, Lechuza Beach is a combination of white, soft sand and turquoise waters—my own personal paradise.

I'm spread out on a flowery towel, stomach to the fabric, sunglasses on as I work on some homework. Most of the family are spread out in the ocean, except for Olly, who is snoring on the towel next to me. Every so often, I look over and see dried drool on his chin. I sit up a little, reaching over to whip off my sandals, so I can feel the grains between my toes. I scan the beach, spotting a few surfers and kids in the distance, but it's surprisingly not that busy.

In the distance, Tim and Dylan are standing talking, their surfboards tucked under their arms. With a short wave, they head toward the ocean. I know nothing about surfing—I doubt

I'd be able to keep my balance if I tried—but there's something calming about watching them hit the water. I focus on the way their arms move as they paddle out past the break, fighting against the current.

This is the first time since moving here that I've felt myself relax. I'm still checking my phone for any messages from Dad, but knowing I'll be starting my training today gives me this tiniest sliver of courage.

Olly lets out a snore beside me. Growing up without siblings means I never knew what it felt like to have brothers, but having the twins around—even if they can be annoying sometimes—has shown me how lonely I was before.

As the sun pours down on me, turning my warm, beige skin a golden brown, it feels like I'm in paradise. Jamie needs to see how amazing this is. I give him a call, but he cancels it and sends a message immediately after, telling me he's busy. I send a picture instead and put my phone away.

"Seriously," Olly says, "who brings homework to the beach?"

When I turn, I see he is awake and busy lathering his chest with sunscreen. He gives the bottle another shake, and a blob flies out and lands on my arm. I wipe it off, about to tell him to go back to sleep when my phone rings with a FaceTime from Jamie.

"Hey," I say. "I thought you said you were busy." He looks handsome as always in his new, fitted jacket, but it's hard to make out where he is. There's just a plain white wall behind him, so I know he's inside, but it doesn't look familiar. "I was," he says, "but I'm taking a break. You still at the beach?"

"Yep." I turn the camera to show him the ocean and the strip of white sand. "Doesn't it look amazing?"

His grin is easy as he says, "Not as amazing as you. Who are you there with? I thought I saw a hairy leg in the photo—it wasn't yours, was it?"

"Definitely not. That would belong to Olly." I point the camera at Olly as he plays with his phone. He looks at me from over his Ray-Bans, realizes he's on camera, and flexes his muscles like he's some kind of bodybuilder. Laughing, I say, "This nerd is Olly, and over there is my mom, Tim, and Dylan." I turn the camera so it's pointing to the ocean again. "Where are you, anyway?"

"My cousins'. They were struggling to build this new wardrobe they bought, so I offered to help. I should probably get back before one of them puts their back out. Love you, Jelly Bean."

"Love you, String Bean," I say before hanging up.

Dylan comes over just as I'm getting out the sunscreen. He takes a seat next to me, shaking his head so that droplets of water fly everywhere. Laughing, I lightly push his shoulder.

"You just missed the cheesiest FaceTime ever," Olly says, "and considering what I had to put up with last year with you and Caitlyn, that's saying something."

Dylan laughs, but I can tell the mention of Caitlyn upsets him. "He's just jealous because no one ever wants to FaceTime him anymore. All he ever does is stare at himself in the corner of the screen."

"Hey," Olly says. "I can't help it if I'm handsome."

"Yeah, the girls are lining up," Dylan says.

"They are," Olly insists. "I'm just not interested in them."

"Too busy pining after June?"

My eyebrows fly up. My suspicions were correct. "You like June?"

Olly glares at Dylan before thumping him on the arm. The two become embroiled in a fistfight, so I roll my eyes and look out at the sea, where Mom and Lilly are splashing around in the ocean like kids. Mom borrowed the turquoise swimsuit from Lilly, so it's a little—a lot—big around the bust area, but it looks good on her—so does the rare but genuine smile.

The rest of the afternoon is spent playing beach volleyball—something I'm apparently awful at—but spending time together as a family is just what we've needed. Mom is laughing in a way I've never seen before, and for the tiniest moment, it's like Dad doesn't exist.

Standing in the doorway, ignoring the stench of sweat and leather, I take it all in. It looks different in the daytime, and for the first time, I notice the small mural of golden wings on the wall. Beneath it, in a delicate scrawl that catches the light, reads City of Angels.

I'm twenty minutes early, so I take a seat on the bench and wait for Hayden to appear. Of the ten or so gym-goers, only three of them are girls. The rest are men, varying in age from about fifteen to twenty. At the end of the room, pounding on one of the punching bags, is the man who'd given me the flyer. His salt-and-pepper hair clings to his forehead in curls, and his undershirt is soaked through. I watch him for a moment, enthralled by the power he packs behind his punches.

"Hey, you new here?"

I turn around. The boy before me is tall and handsome,

with an Afro taper fade and the tiniest dimple in his chin. Everybody in California is *far* too good-looking.

"I'm here for the White Collar boot camp," I say.

His eyebrows fly up. "The old man actually got people to sign up to that? Damn. Guess this means we'll be seeing a lot more of each other." He wiggles his eyebrows. "Lucky me."

At the far end of the gym, Hayden walks out of a black door and crosses the room toward us. "Don't you have somewhere to be, Wiley?"

Wiley puts both hands up and grins. "Hey, I'm just being polite. I like to make the newbies feel welcome."

"Yeah?" Hayden nods in the direction of one of the gym-goers. "Where was Tyrell's welcome yesterday?" Wiley walks away laughing at the same time Hayden turns to me. "You're early."

"Sorry," I say, but I'm not. Being early is a million times better than being late.

Hayden makes me wait in his office until everyone else has left. The dark walls are covered in medals and various photos. There is one of little Hayden holding up a shiny trophy, one of him and a man I presume to be his dad at a competition, one of him and his dad on a fishing trip; I'm sensing a theme and can't help but wonder where his mother is.

In the far corner is an old oak desk covered in papers and books. Next to it is a single bed, the blue sheets tucked smoothly between the mattress and box springs like it hasn't been slept in. To the left, a door leads into a small en suite. I leave my stuff in the corner and pull back my hair.

Hushed voices travel through the gym. Hayden and Flyer Guy are standing across the room, arguing. Hayden's got his back to me so I can't see his face, but from the way he is standing, he's tense.

"You should have run it by me," Flyer Guy says. "*I'm* supposed to be running this boot camp, not you. All of my one-on-one slots are already filled. I don't have time to train her."

"Which is why *I'm* doing it," Hayden says, "in the evening."

"*You*," he says, poking him in the chest, "are not qualified."

"Would you relax, Jenson? It's quick money. She'll get bored after a few lessons, and we'll have some spare cash to buy some equipment. Win, win."

Jenson's jaw moves back and forth in frustration. "You're more trouble than you're worth, you know that?"

Hayden turns a little, revealing the grin on his face. "That's not the first time I've heard that."

Shoulders back, determined to prove him wrong, I walk toward them. Jenson spots me first, then excuses himself. Hayden motions for me to follow him to the bench. He holds out his hand, and for a moment, I think he wants me to take it.

"Up front," he says.

I reach into my pocket to pull out my money but end up finding another folded to-do list. Hayden stares at the cursive words on the front and says, almost disbelievingly, "You carry a handwritten to-do list around with you?"

Ignoring him, I pull out my money and hand it over. "It's all there."

He flicks through the bills in his hands, counting each one. "You sure you want to do this? I'm not giving you your money back if you quit."

Clearly, this boy has no filter. "Has anyone ever told you that you're really rude?"

He finally grins, and I'm taken aback by how beautiful it is, all white teeth and dimples. "All the time. Are you going to answer the question?"

I hesitate. This is my way out, my chance to turn around and stop pretending to be someone I'm not. Instead, I say, "I'm sure."

He shrugs a little. "All right, this first session is just to ease you into it."

He has me sign a waiver, then sits me down and proceeds to go through the process. The fight camp is an eight-week training package that consists of technical and fitness drills, cardio, and sparring sessions, which are held in the ring and carefully supervised. I'll learn to hit without getting hit, with both technical and body sparing alongside tactical coaching. He's pacing back and forth, his hands clasped loosely behind his back; he's enjoying playing the role of teacher a little too much.

"Is what Jenson said true?" I ask. "That you're not qualified to teach me?"

He frowns at the interruption. "No. Well, kind of. I'm not registered with USA Boxing like Jenson. I've got a level two certificate, but a long way to go before I reach his level. The only difference it makes to you is that when it comes to your fight, it'll be Jenson standing in your corner, not me."

None of what he is saying makes sense. But I do know that even without whatever qualifications Jenson has, I want to learn how to fight like Hayden. He'd shown control the night Moby smirked in his face; he'd stood fierce in the face of his opponent—I want to be that brave too.

"Diet is key," he continues as if I'd never interrupted. "I'll provide regular nutritional advice throughout the process.

The event is held in Las Vegas in the first week of May—accommodation is free." He stops to look over. "Your parents gonna be okay with you going to Vegas?"

I pick at a loose thread on my yoga pants. "I'm actually going to keep this to myself." When he smirks, I add, "I'm eighteen, so I don't have to tell anyone."

"Hey, you can lie to your parents all you want. It just better not jeopardize the fight."

"It won't."

Hayden leads me over to the scales and talks about the different weight categories, how I need to make sure to maintain this weight, how I need to keep up with my cardio even when I'm not in the gym. I hang off his every word, able to feel the adrenaline already working its way through me. He shows me the various equipment on offer, from punching bags and dumbbells to resistance bands and jump ropes. When he's finished, we move to the mats so he can show me the hamstring stretch.

"How did you and Jenson end up running a gym?" I ask.

He's quiet for so long that I'm forced to look over. His eyes are closed, his body hunched over as he grips the back of his legs. "It used to be my dad's. Jenson pretty much runs the place on my behalf."

"Used to be?"

He pauses, then says, "He died last year of a heart attack."

"I'm sorry." I can't imagine how it must feel to lose a parent. As difficult and complicated as my relationship with Dad is, I don't know what I'd do if he died.

Hayden straightens up and starts his triceps stretch. "That's what, your fifth apology tonight?"

"Sor—" I stop just in time, hating the smirk that crosses his lips.

A couple of stretches later, he digs into an equipment box and hands me a jump rope. I pull it from his hands, surprised by the jolt I feel when his fingers brush mine.

"Now what?" I ask.

"Start jumping."

It doesn't take me long to realize how different jumping feels from running: the pain in my muscles return, my heart pounding with every jump, and the anguish in my chest slowly releases.

I stop jumping to catch my breath and notice Hayden is playing on his phone. If I didn't know better, I'd think he's just running down the clock. "I've been jumping for, like, an hour," I say. "How is this teaching me to fight?"

"It's not, it's helping you to get in shape."

My cheeks burn. "I'm already in shape."

His eyes travel over my chest and stomach, lingering on my hips. They shift to my thighs, making their way down my calves before settling on my feet. He doesn't even attempt to be subtle about the way he's assessing me. I am silent until he's finished. "A nice body doesn't mean you're in shape." His eyes flit to mine; I have failed to meet his approval. "You need stamina. Endurance."

"Listen," I say, holding the rope loosely between my fingers, "I was on the track team back home. I've been running three miles every day for the past three years. I know all about stamina and endurance."

"Rule number one," Hayden says, leaning in close, "don't question me, and you should be running at least four."

I ignore him and resume my jumps until he tells me to stop. Finally, when I'm hot and covered in sweat, he motions for me to follow him to the mats.

"Your body's gotten too comfortable with one form of exercise," he says. "It's why you find running easy but not this."

Spread out on the mat like a starfish, I wait for my heart rate to settle. Hayden sits next to me, watching me with an expression that sits somewhere between amusement and distaste. When my phone pings with a message, I'm so tired that I don't even check it. "I'm dying."

Hayden takes a long, slow swig of his water before placing it between us. "Ready to quit yet?"

"I'm not a quitter."

"You know, a lot of people say that." He gets to his feet before offering out his hand. I clasp my fingers around his own, letting him pull me up. "Very few people mean it."

"Well, I do."

"Come on," he says. "Let's focus on some breathing techniques before you give yourself a heart attack."

He shows me a series of techniques to slow down my heart rate and after a few minutes, I copy him. Clearly, from the way he's watching me, I'm not doing a very good job.

"Breathe from *here*," he says, pointing to his chest.

"I am." In, out. In, out. I think I am finally getting it, but then Hayden sighs in frustration and slips behind me so my back is to his chest. I flinch as he rests his palm on my stomach and suck in a breath, surprised at the little jolt that travels through me.

"Now you've stopped breathing completely. You're not so good with instructions, are you, Maddison?"

I swallow hard. "Don't call me that."

"Okay, *Maddie*."

I close my eyes. I've never been this close to another boy besides Jamie. It's hard for me to concentrate on anything else.

"Is that a kidney on your necklace?" His warm, deep voice jerks me from my thoughts. He's staring at my necklace, head tilted, an incredulous look on his face.

"It's a bean."

The way he bursts out laughing is both endearing and infuriating. "I just don't get it." He shakes his head, and something tells me he's not talking about the necklace. A remnant of a smile still graces his lips, revealing the dimples in his cheeks. "What are you doing here, Maddie? Seriously."

"Training," I say like it's obvious.

"No, really," he says. "You just got to California, it's your senior year, and the first thing you do is join a boxing boot camp. Ninety-nine percent of the people who sign up for a White Collar fight do it for validation, or because they have something to prove. If no one even knows you're doing this, what's your motive?"

"You wouldn't understand."

"Try me."

Finally, I look at him. His eyes are dark, but for once they aren't mocking or sarcastic. Just like the night of the fight, I find myself wanting to be honest. "I'm tired of people walking all over me. For once, I just want to be different. I want to do something no one would expect of me."

He looks at me for the longest moment. I think he's going to laugh at me or call me a freak, but instead, he nods. "I get that."

"You do?"

"Yeah." He shrugs. "I was pretty messed up for a while, but whenever I got to the gym, it felt like a mental reset. I got to leave the old me and the bullshit at the door."

There's this moment of relief at being tuned in with someone else, like we've chosen the same radio frequency. I suddenly remember his hand is still on me and quickly step away.

Hayden's eyes flit to my lips, then up again. "We're going to focus on a basic stance and do a little bit of shadowboxing. Which hand do you write with?"

"My right."

He nods as if this confirms something and tells me to stand with my left foot forward. He moves in front of me, feet slightly apart, and shows me how to stand: feet a little wider than shoulder-width apart, elbows tucked in, hands against my cheeks. I mirror his stance, but he frowns and steps forward, curling his palm around my wrist. He positions it lower, then steps back to assess me.

I catch sight of myself in the mirror behind him. Standing like this, I look focused and sure of myself; controlled.

Hayden slips behind me so his chest is to my back. "This is the stance you always need to find your way back to." Gently, he takes my lead hand and shows me how to throw a straight punch. My arm extends fully, elbow tucked tight as my fist connects with air. "Your punch hurts more when it hits the full extension." He lowers it back to its starting position, right near my cheek. "After every move, you should end up back here."

I'm acutely aware of how close he's standing, but he doesn't seem to care. He has me add in a right cross after the jab, in a combination called the one-two. He demonstrates a few times until I get the hang of it, then steps back to watch me. "Step into the punch just a little bit with your lead foot," he says.

I do as I'm told, but he complains that I'm stepping too forward, then not enough. Eventually, I snap, "Why don't you just *show* me?"

He breaks into a boyish grin. "You really don't like getting things wrong, do you?"

"Does anyone?"

Still smiling, he kneels in front of me like he's about to propose and gently moves my foot into position. We spend the next thirty minutes switching between a straight jab and a one-two, until Hayden's phone alarm rings to signal the end of the session. I hurry to my bag, pulling out my phone to check the message I'd gotten, but there's nothing. This phone is as temperamental as my dad.

I turn to Hayden, who's busy looking at his own phone. "How did I do?"

He starts to pack the equipment away without looking at me. "Color me impressed."

My face lights up as I gather my stuff. The whole drive home, I replay the session in my head on repeat, thinking about how strong I'd felt when I'd looked in the mirror, how brave, and any doubts I'd had melt away.

CHAPTER SEVEN

Sunlight falls through the slatted windows, coating the room in a pale shade of gold. I've gotten so used to these silky sheets that I don't want to move, but the clock on my nightstand reads five thirty a.m.—time for my morning run.

I've been religiously checking my phone for any messages from Dad, but it's been radio silence for the last two weeks. I want to take it as a good sign, like maybe he's finally got the message, but I'm not that naïve. There are several texts from Jamie. One tells me he misses me, another is a picture of him and Tyler, making heart symbols at me with their hands. I laugh out loud, filled with this overwhelming sense of love. I'd been worried that the distance would ruin us somehow, but we're stronger than ever.

I'm sluggish as I throw on my clothes. My body aches in ways I never thought possible, but already I feel calmer than I did two weeks ago—more in control. The key is to distract myself, to focus on anything and everything but *him*; that's when I can relax.

Hayden's giving me some information on what foods to eat, or what cardio to do, and then has me jumping rope or doing tactical drills until I nearly throw up. Then we'll focus on footwork and shadowboxing, with some basic combos thrown in. He says I can't work with an opponent yet, but if we've only got six weeks, I should be sparring *now*, not doing cardio.

Still, the feeling I get when training is better than any feeling track gave me. I'm breathless and hurting and wanting to quit, but beyond all of that is a sense of relief. My chest isn't tight with anger. I'm not on the verge of losing control; if anything, it's the opposite.

I shadowbox in front of the mirror for the next few minutes, practicing my one-two. Even just standing like this gives me a sense of power.

Mom meets me at the bottom of the staircase, and we step out onto the street just as the sun is starting to rise. We start off slow, a nice, easy jog that transitions into a steady run. My feet burn with every slap of the sidewalk, but it's the good kind of pain. I force myself to steady my breathing in time with my steps.

"I've missed this," Mom says. Back home, she'd regularly accompany me on my morning runs. It was the one time she could leave Dad and not have him question her whereabouts. "I don't know how you do this and keep up with the gym, though. You're not on drugs, are you?"

My watch pings with a congratulatory message to say I've hit my target steps. I press the screen. "No drugs. I just want to keep busy."

It's silent while we pick up speed down a leafy, suburban street. It's hard to tell—my mother has always kept her feelings locked away—but I think she's doing better than she was when we got here. In between searching for a new job, she's taken to puttering around the garden or swimming laps in the pool, nothing life changing, but a sign that it's different this time, that maybe, if we keep ourselves busy enough, we'll forget ever missing him.

"Have you decided which college offer you're going to accept?" she asks.

"It's down to UCLA and NYU."

She frowns and stops running, forcing me to stop too. "I'm not going to tell you what choice to make," says, "that's up to you, but you need to do this for you, Maddie, don't make a decision based on a boy. Where do *you* want to go?"

With a deep breath, I say the first thing that comes to my head. "UCLA."

She nods like she'd expected as much. "Then that's what your heart is telling you to choose. Jamie is a wonderful boyfriend—he'll understand."

We carry on jogging, and I feel lighter somehow. I've had this choice hanging over my head for weeks now, and finally knowing what I'm going to do lifts this weight off my chest.

The second I get home, I start preparing to accept my offer from UCLA. It's a long process that involves establishing my California residency status, filling out forms, and paying a deposit. The deadline isn't until June, but the earlier I get started, the less time I'll have to question my decision.

At breakfast, Lilly asks Mom if she'll take some pictures for her online nature blog. "You can use my camera," she says.

"I'd love to," Mom says. "I mean, they probably won't be any good . . ." Her face falls, and I imagine Dad's words ricocheting in her head. *Don't you think messing around with a camera is a waste? Don't you want to spend time with your family?* For all the times he was your biggest fan, there were times when he wasn't. When his words were like heavyweight chains around your ankles, and every time you tried to stand, he'd pull them from under you.

Lilly waves her hand dismissively. "Don't be silly. They'll be great."

Outside, Tim is standing on the patio, hands behind his head, staring at the sky.

Lilly watches him, her forehead crowded with worry lines. "God, I hate seeing him like this."

"What's wrong with him?" I ask.

"His last book was such a success that he's afraid this one won't match up, so he's kind of in a panic."

Hearing this surprises me. He's usually so cheerful, but right now it's easy to see the panic in his expression. The doubt. I guess he's learned to fake it too.

I kiss Mom on the cheek and tell her to have a good day before following the twins to the car. I'm not as nervous about school anymore, mostly because June and Kavi go out of their way to make me feel included, but I still miss New York: I miss the versatile weather and the track team. I miss Jamie, and even though I try my best not to, I miss Dad too.

It's why I spend most of the day looking forward to my training. When I'm busy jumping rope or learning combos with Hayden, I don't think about back home. I don't think about Dad; I just focus on my goal. Nothing else.

At lunch, when I tell June about my college decision, she's thrilled. "That's only a five-hour drive from Stanford," she informs me, "and five from Santa Clara, which is where Kavi is going. It's going to make our long-distance friendship so much easier."

I'm surprised by the *F* word, mostly because the last time I had a friend—a real friend—was in middle school. I turn to June, remembering she's a words-of-affirmation kind of girl, and say, "You know, starting at a new high school would have sucked if it wasn't for you. So, thank you."

Her face lights up as she pulls me into a side hug. "You're welcome."

We grab our trays and head out to the courtyard, where the twins are sat near a picnic table under a tree. They're in the middle of a heated discussion about MMA when Olly lets it slip that I've joined Hayden's boxing gym.

Dylan's eyebrows fly up. "Why? Isn't that going to make the next few months really stressful?"

"I just like having something to work toward," I say, "and it's barely even boxing."

Olly gives me a sheepish look and mouths the word *sorry*. June puts her hand out. "Wait. So, you're learning to box? Like, punching-people kind of boxing?"

"Yes."

June looks both impressed and alarmed; I don't blame her. "Aren't you worried about getting hurt? Or breaking your nose or something? Nose jobs are expensive here in LA. You're talking ten grand, minimum."

I laugh and steal a couple of her fries. "I guess I'm a little worried, but it's for a good cause, so that makes me feel better."

The truth is, though, when I'm training is the only time that my thoughts switch off. I don't think about how broken Dad must feel without us. I don't imagine him curled up on the sofa, alone; I don't imagine him at all.

Dylan's mouth pulls down into the tiniest frown. "I take it that means Hayden is the one training you for it?" But it's not a question.

"Yeah."

The three of them look at me with varying expressions of concern. "Just be careful," Dylan says.

"It's just training."

This seems to relax him, but not by much. I make them promise that they won't tell Mom or Lilly, and June spends the rest of lunch relaying everything she's learned from Rocky Balboa films.

Across the courtyard, Hayden is sitting with his friends. Two girls join them, Larissa and Amara, and when Larissa leans forward to speak to Hayden, he smiles. It's one of those award-winning smiles he always gives out. The kind that can momentarily stun you. The kind that he never gives to me.

Outside of the gym, Hayden and I don't speak. We don't make eye contact. We don't acknowledge the other's existence. It's like we've made an unspoken pact to compartmentalize our sessions, so we only exist in the gym.

It's why, when he turns, I expect him to look right past me, but he doesn't. This time, he looks at me. For a second, I stop thinking. Stop breathing. I don't know why, but he has such an intensity to his stare that as soon as it's on me, it's like I can't think straight. Then, just as quickly, he's turning back to his friends as if we've never even met.

—

Mom invites me to a trip to the farmers' market after school, which isn't exactly my idea of fun, but it's the most excited I've seen her in ages, so I can't say no. I'll pretty much do anything if it helps her to get her mind off Dad.

"Lilly says you should go for the vegetables at the bottom," she says, thrusting her hand into a crate full of peppers. Tim is cooking his famous fajitas for dinner, which means we're looking for fresh bell peppers for the filling. "They're juicer that way."

I pretend to be interested. We never went to farmers' markets back home, but I can see the appeal. There's a sense of community about it, which is exactly what Mom needs right now.

I'm reaching for a bell pepper when I spot Hayden over by the fruit section, standing next to a woman who looks so similar it has to be his mother. She's pretty, with long dark hair and the same brilliant green eyes as Hayden's.

He looks over and smirks, and my mother conveniently notices.

"Do you know that boy?" she asks.

"No. I mean, not really." Her stare has the power to rip the truth from my lips. "He goes to my gym."

Hayden's attention has already moved to the box of fresh apples in front of him. He picks one up, throws it in the air, and catches it before putting it in his basket.

I finally give in and glance up. Mom's dark eyes chastise me. Even though I've done nothing wrong, my cheeks burn as if I have.

"You don't want boys like that smiling at you," she says. "You might think he's just doing it to be nice, but he's not. He's trying to get you to let your guard down. The second you do, he'll change."

I open my mouth to defend myself, but nothing comes out. It's not as if I'd ever be interested in Hayden, but that's not the point. "Not everyone is like Dad."

Her eyes darken. "More than you think." She heads to the fruit section while I'm left to stare after her. There are times when I see flashes of him in her, like he's poisoned her. Flashes of distrust or paranoia. Sometimes I see it in me too.

When I've composed myself, I join her by the fruit, where she's paying the man behind the booth. He's trying to make small talk, but Mom's eyes are on her shoes as she waits for her change. Even though I'm angry right now, I move beside her, grab her hand, and squeeze it tight. When the fruit man says, "Here's your change, ma'am," Mom turns her head, takes a deep breath, and looks him in the eye.

"Thank you." She says it so softly that he probably doesn't hear her, but I do.

The moment we get home, I phone Jamie. I hate to admit it, but Mom's words have forced their way into my head, so now I can't stop wondering if I'm some terrible girlfriend. Jamie is the one person I trust: he won't cheat on me, or lie to me, or steal from me. He won't go through my purse or read through my texts. I think of how my mother ended up with someone like Dad, and I realize how lucky I am.

By the time I've made it home, changed, and head to the gym, my excitement from earlier has waned. Hayden is in the corner, half-hidden in the shadow of a heavy bag, late for our session as usual. There's a kid who can't be older than thirteen in front of him, and he's got his hand wrapped around the kid's arm as he shows him how to hold his fist. My heart does this tiny little flip. I'm not used to seeing him like this.

"It's you again." Wiley stands before me with a white towel around his neck. "You're still here." He takes a slow but deliberate sip of his water before screwing the lid back on. "That's a good sign, by the way. Showing up is half the battle."

"What's the other half?" I ask.

He grins. "Not getting hit."

The bruise Dad left the night that he hit me plays on my mind. Why does it feel like I've lost the battle before it's even begun?

"How's it going, anyway?" he asks. "Hayden says you're a quick learner."

I raise my eyebrows. This is news to me. "He did?"

"Yep."

"Are you guys friends or something?" Why is Hayden talking about someone he'll happily ignore at school?

"Yeah, but not by choice," he says. "We've been next-door neighbors since we were kids. He was the scrawny kid who loved getting naked." He notices my horrified expression and grins. "Yep, as soon as their front door would open, he'd run outside, strip off his clothes, and start running around his lawn butt naked."

I laugh at the mental image, about to say something along the lines of, *I hope he doesn't do that now*, but Jenson comes up behind Wiley, clips him round the ear and says, "This isn't speed dating. Move."

Wiley grins and saunters off. Jenson sits next to me, using the towel to wipe the sweat from his brow. "Ignore that buffoon," he says, shaking his head. "Spends more time standing around talking than training." He turns to the ring, watching the two boys inside of it spar. "Your feet!" he yells at one of the boys. To me, he says, "I'm going to observe some of your training today, if that's all right with you. Need to make sure that bonehead is doing something right for once."

"That sounds good."

Right on cue, Hayden looks over. He finishes showing the kid the technique before walking over. "Hey." His voice is low when he speaks. Warm. He turns to Jenson, who shows no signs of moving. "Auden needs your help in the ring. His footwork is all over the place."

Jenson nods and gets to his feet. He rests a comforting palm on Hayden's shoulder, then hurries toward the boy in the ring. I expect him to chastise me for being early, but instead he leads me over to the weights. He picks a set of dumbbells for me, shows me the correct form to use, and picks up his own.

His eyes are on mine as I try to lift my weights. I mirror his movement, curling my biceps the way he curls his. Every so often, his eyes flit to mine. They darken, and the corner of his lip lifts as though he's on the verge of smiling.

My breathing is controlled as I focus on my reps. It's when I am in this state, focusing on something physical or enduring, that my mind feels the clearest. UCLA might be my long-term goal, but training for this fight is what is going to keep me sane until I get there.

By the time the gym closes, we've moved on to shadowboxing. As promised, Jenson comes over and watches a moment, but I don't feel self-conscious. If anything, I'm excited to show off what I've learned.

"Good form," he says.

Hayden grins as though proud of himself—and *me*. "She's a natural."

Hearing this surprises me. It seems Hayden goes around complimenting me to everyone *but* me. Jenson waits a moment longer, his fingers to his chin. "Don't look at your hands. Punch toward an invisible opponent."

I nod and do as he says. After a minute, he tells us to keep up the hard work, gives Hayden a quick hug, and heads out.

Hayden steps back and heads to the equipment box. When he comes back, he's holding some pads and boxing gloves. He puts them on the floor by our feet and pulls a long strip of soft, black cloth from his pocket.

Carefully, he takes my hand, looping the tape over my thumb and between each of my fingers. His hands work quickly, making a pad over my knuckles and weaving *X*'s across the backs of my hands. His own hands are large, soft, with tiny white scars across his knuckles. Every time his fingers brush across my palm, I shiver.

"I heard you're living with Olly and *Dylan*," he says. "What's that like?"

Heard from who exactly? Has Hayden been asking about me? "Nice, I guess."

"But?"

"I don't know," I say. "I guess everything is a little *too* happy. I feel like they've got to be hiding a dead body in the basement or something."

He shakes his head, still smiling. "I thought *I* had trust issues."

"I heard what happened with your ex." I wait for his reaction, but he refuses to give one. "I'm sorry. I know how it feels when someone breaks your trust."

"Yeah?" He looks skeptical. "You ever been cheated on?"

I shake my head. Thankfully, Jamie cheating on me is something I never have to worry about. He made it clear when we first started dating that he wasn't—and never would be—interested in anyone else. "No, but people can betray you in other ways."

Up close like this, I can see the little flecks of yellow in his eyes, can smell the vanilla and pinewood on his skin. It's such an odd combination that the two can't be from the same aftershave, but it works.

"Thank you."

"For what?"

He shrugs. "No one's ever said that before. Everyone's always been quick to blame me—like I drove her to it."

I'm silent as I take in his face. Behind his tough exterior is a boy who is hurting. It makes me wonder if maybe we're all just faking, and some of us are better at it than others.

When he's finished, he hands me a pair of black sixteen-ounce gloves, and helps me to slip them on. We go through some boxing pad drills, which gives me a chance to work on my footwork as well as my jabs.

"Chin down," Hayden says.

I keep going, and it's nice, in a way, to be here with Hayden.

It's silent as we train, calm, just the sound of my punches as they crash against his pads.

The sound of my phone makes me jump. I peel off my gloves and hurry to my phone, where Jamie's name flashes across the screen. "Hey, Jamie." I sink onto the mat, barely able to stand. "Everything okay?"

"Hey, you." He frowns and adds, "You haven't replied to any of my texts."

"Sorry." I'm acutely aware of Hayden listening to every word. As much as I want to come clean about college, now is not the time. "I'm just at the gym."

"I can see that."

Embarrassed, I dab at the sweat on my forehead. He's right, I can see myself in the corner of the screen, and I do not look pretty. "I can't wait to go home and shower."

He flashes a devilish grin. "You should go and do that. In fact, I'll join you over video."

"No way." I laugh, "I'll call you when I get home, okay?"

His easy expression doesn't falter. "Can't you leave now? I gotta get up early to fit in practice, so I'm probably going to have an early night."

"Even if I leave right now, it will take me a while to get home. If it's too late when I get back, I'll just FaceTime you tomorrow."

"Traffic can't be that bad this late, right? You'll probably be home in thirty minutes, tops."

Sighing, I say, "Okay, I'll leave in a second."

"Okay, love you, Runner Bean."

"Love you"—I glance at Hayden, dropping my voice—"Green Bean."

I hang up and turn to Hayden, who is watching me. "What?" I ask. His mouth lifts slightly, but he doesn't say a word. "Seriously, what?"

Finally, he says, "*Green Bean*?"

My cheeks grow warm. Calling your significant other a cheesy pet name is the kind of thing you vow not to do but then end up doing anyway. "He's a vegetarian," I feel the need to explain. "On our first date, I stupidly pretended to be vegetarian, too, and ordered this weird bean salad that I hated. It's kind of a running joke now to refer to each other as beans."

He looks at me like this is the stupidest thing he has ever heard before pulling me to my feet. His hand feels warm and solid in my own. I'm certain he feels the way my pulse is pounding through my wrist.

"Is he always that controlling?" he asks.

"He's not *controlling*, he just misses me."

"You're right, telling you what to do isn't controlling at all."

I'm suddenly irritated. If only he knew how much Jamie has been there for me over this past year. If only he knew what controlling *really* looked like, then he wouldn't be so quick to judge Jamie. "I'm sorry, am I paying you to train me or be my relationship therapist?"

He raises his hands like he's surrendering to the police. "I'm not trying to be a dick; I'm just saying you can say *no*."

But he's wrong. Saying *no* leads to *why*, and *why* leads to confrontation. I've seen it happen with my parents more times than I can count. Giving in is just easier.

By the time I get home, it is late. There was an accident on the freeway and it took ages to get back across town. Too late to call Jamie. Dinner is cold on the stove, but I'm too tired to heat it up. Instead, I get out a mismatch of snacks that would make Hayden proud: cucumber, carrot sticks, water, and a banana. Then I carry them back to my room and nibble away to Netflix.

Without meaning to, I think about my dad. This is the longest we've ever spent away from him. I can't help but see him propping me on his shoulders as we walked through the city, or staying up late with me to study for a test. My chest squeezes, a mix of anger and grief rolled in one. This was *our* choice, *our* decision, so why does it hurt so much?

When the pressure gets too much, I think about Jamie. But his face doesn't calm me—all I can think about is what Hayden had said. It's ridiculous. I've seen controlling, and Jamie is the opposite. In a world where people like my father exist, Jamie is sweet and uncomplicated. I don't have to worry that he's got an ulterior motive, or that he's going to suddenly blow up. From the day we first talked in the library until now, he's stayed exactly the same; it's why I love him so much.

Giving up on my program, I pull up the covers and try to get some sleep. The lights are off and my eyelids feel heavy when my phone starts to ring on the nightstand.

Slowly, I sit up. Heart pounding, I glance at the screen to find a number I don't recognize. Even though there's no way he could have my number, it's Dad, I'm sure of it. I gnaw at my nails as I let it ring out. When it stops, I scramble to turn off my phone, but it rings again.

Those doubts start to work their way in. What if he's hurt? What if it's an emergency and something has happened? In the seconds that pass, I convince myself that I'll answer this once, that I'll hear his voice and know he's okay, and I'll never ever answer again.

My fingers snatch it from the nightstand quicker than humanly possible. "Hello?"

"Maddie," he says, sounding relieved, "I'm glad you answered. I've missed you."

Tears burn my eyes, but I fight to keep them back. Just the sound of his voice can take me back to my childhood, to all the times he cuddled me and made me feel safe. Sometimes, in my head, his dark side is a completely different man altogether.

"What do you want, Dad?"

"I'm here," he says, "in California, but I can't find the house."

I almost drop the phone. "What?"

"I need you to come out," he says. "I've been walking around for ages, and I'm exhausted. All these damn houses look the same."

My heart is pounding a mile a minute. This isn't happening. "Dad—"

"Please," he says, his voice shaking, "I just want to talk to you. I won't come inside—I won't even tell your mom I'm here, if that's what you want. I just want to see my girl."

My girl. It's like my heart is tearing at the seams. The thought of him wandering the streets at night, lost, is enough to force me to my feet. "Two minutes," I say. "That's it, Dad."

He lets out the longest breath. "Thank you."

I tiptoe down the stairs, out onto the dimly lit street. The warm evening air makes my skin prickle, but I ignore it and search the street for movement. "Where are you? I can't see you."

"I'm at the very end of the street."

I squint through the dark, but all I can see are shadows from the leafy trees above. I start to walk the length of the street until I make it to the end. "I can't see you anywhere."

"I'm standing right here," he says, sounding frustrated. "Are you sure you're even out here?"

"I'm out here, I just can't see you. Are you sure you have the right street?"

"I'm sure," he says. "You must be at the wrong end."

Irritated, I sprint to the opposite end of the street, breathless. Not because I'm tired from running, but because I'm so anxious that I can barely catch my breath. Hunched over, I lift my head to scan the trees and the beautiful homes lit up like dollhouses. "Dad, I'm telling you. I can't see you anywhere."

"You're not even out here, are you?" he says. It's that tone again, the calm, clipped tone that terrifies me. "You're lying to me."

Frustration builds inside me. Any moment, I'm going to explode. "I'm *here*," I shout into the dark. "I'm *right here*. I can't see you." My heart is pounding, this pressure building and building and building. I want to scream, but instead I sink to my knees as the first tear trails my cheek. "I swear I'm out here. I can't see you." My voice cracks, and I hate that I'm crying, hate that he can make me feel this bad.

"Just give me the address of the house," he says. "I'll come to you."

My mouth falls open, then closes again. There it is. This has all just been a game to him, a way to trick me into telling him where we are. I'm so stupid I almost fell for it.

"You know you want to see me," he says. "You wouldn't have gone looking for me if you didn't. You still care, and if you still care, it means there's a chance for me to fix things."

I pull my knees to my chest and let out a slow, shaky breath. Cradling myself in the middle of the street, I feel foolish. Weak. *Crazy*. "Good-bye, Dad," I manage, and then I hang up.

I toss and turn for most of the night, the same dream playing in my head on repeat, except it's not a dream, it's a memory I'd somehow suppressed—the week Mom began her new job.

It was the first time she'd had a stable office job since getting pregnant, so she was excited about going back to work. She'd wake up extraearly to iron her clothes, make us breakfast, and then she'd totter down the hallway in her shiny black heels and we'd hear the door click shut. She'd come back much later, gushing about all of the things that happened at work, and Dad would sit there smiling, as if he loved hearing about her day.

She was four days in when things started disappearing. She'd always lose something important right before she needed to leave, like her phone or her keys. She'd search the house in a panic, swearing that she'd left her phone in her bag or her keys in the bowl on the table by the door, but they were never where she said they were.

Eventually, Dad and I would help her look, and we'd find them upstairs by her makeup or in the bottom of her bag, as if she'd placed them there in a daze. She'd head off to work, flustered, late, shaking her head at her forgetfulness, and the same thing would happen again the next morning.

"There's something wrong with me," she said to Dad one night, when they thought I couldn't hear them. I tiptoed toward the living room door, pressing my ear to the wall. I could hear it in her voice, the worry, the brokenness. She was on the verge of tears. "Do you think I should go to the doctor and get checked out?"

"Shh," Dad soothed, and I imagined him pulling her into a hug, the way he always did whenever we were upset. "You're just stressed out from work, that's all. Maybe you should think about quitting and see if you feel better."

"I don't feel stressed, though," she said, but she didn't sound certain. She didn't seem certain of anything lately. "I like my job. I just don't understand why my memory is getting so awful. *God*." I put my eye to the gap in the door and saw her sitting on the sofa, head in her hands as Dad gently stroked her hair. "I feel like I'm going insane."

Backing away, I headed upstairs and closed the door to my room. I was seven years old, pacing back and forth the way I'd often seen Dad do. I'd noticed it, too, this forgetfulness of hers, the way her mind always seemed to be elsewhere. It scared me. Why couldn't she just listen to Daddy? Why didn't she want to get better?

Then one night, when I was in the kitchen sneaking ice cream, Dad came downstairs. I hid immediately, knowing I'd get in big trouble if Dad caught me up this late, but the way he moved around, shuffling his feet against the cold kitchen tiles, it was clear he was still half asleep.

He disappeared into the hallway and came back a second

later, Mom's keys in his hands. He opened the cupboard, which creaked on its hinges in the silence, and stuffed the keys inside. Then he half turned, his face lit up under a pool of moonlight, and I caught the small smirk on his lips. I stood there long after he'd headed back upstairs, trying to make sense of what I'd seen, but I couldn't. Instead, I tiptoed to the cupboard and took out the keys, placing them back in the bowl.

The next morning, my mother walked to the key bowl again, slow, defeated, as if she'd known before she even got there that the keys would be missing. She looked at the bowl, hesitant, staring at the keys as though she didn't quite believe they were there. Then, slowly, she picked them out, kissed me good-bye, and went to work.

Mom got fired that day for being so late, and I never told anyone what I saw, but in the back of my mind, I'd known something was very wrong. Just like with his silent treatment, Dad had found a way to inflict pain without bruising.

CHAPTER EIGHT

I'm jerked awake from a nightmare by a strange rolling sound. I sit up, the duvet pulled close to me as though I'm little and afraid of the dark. I can feel my heart pounding. Dad would sit with me when I was little and read me stories until I was no longer afraid. Now he's the thing I'm afraid of.

The noise comes again, and this time, I'm certain it's Dad. I throw the duvet off me so hard it slides to the floor, switch my lamp on, and jump out of bed, then yank the curtains open in time to see something hit the window and bounce away. I peer out and then stop, heart pounding. One of the knobs on the balcony furniture has fallen off and is rolling back and forth on the floor.

Relieved, I grab my phone to check the time and see a text waiting from Dad. I grip the phone tightly as I reread the words from today's message, over and over.

I can't wait to see you.

I settle back down on the bed. When I was little, Dad used to take me to the fairground to ride the teacups. We'd climb into a teacup and he'd spin the wheel faster until the world was a blur, and all I could see was Dad laughing, out of focus. That's how I feel now, staring at this message. We're back on those teacups, spinning around, but this time I want to get off.

The first thing I do is message Jamie and ask him to check in on my apartment. I have no idea whether Dad is really in California or not, or how he even *knew* about California, but if Jamie can find out for me then at least I can prepare either way.

I quietly pick at my fruit at breakfast, debating whether to tell Mom about Dad. It's becoming too hard for me to keep this to myself anymore, but the thought of springing this on her in the thick of healing might ruin everything.

When the doorbell rings, Tim puts down his coffee cup and moves to the door. I hold my breath as the door creaks open. Tim's body shields the visitor from view. Eyes shut, I scream in my head, *Please don't be him*. The visitor says something that causes Tim to laugh. He closes the door behind him and walks back in with a parcel for Lilly.

Lilly, unaware of the fact I'm on the verge of a heart attack, spoons some more yogurt into my bowl. "I hope you've got an appetite. We've got waffles too." She moves to the waffle maker and pulls three out, stacking them high on a plate. "Ah, you're awake, Lori. Want a waffle?"

Mom walks into the kitchen and hovers in the doorway.

Her hair is scraped back, and I notice her cheeks are bronzed and her lips a shiny pink; she's wearing *makeup*.

My resolve falters. If I tell her about Dad, everything changes. This woman she's become, this easy, relaxed version of herself, will be replaced with the other version, the one that won't be able to stop herself from going back to him. It's why, when she takes a seat and asks me what's wrong, I say *nothing*.

There isn't a moment during the rest of the day when I'm not checking my phone. By lunch, it's obsessive, and I try to keep my phone in my pocket and act like I'm fine, but the harder I try, the less convincing I seem to be.

"Earth to Maddie," June says.

"Hmm?"

"We're talking about the most effective ways to hide a body," Kavi says.

"Oh." I think for a moment, but it's hard to string together a coherent thought when I'm obsessing over Dad. "Chop them into pieces and feed them to an animal."

Everyone laughs, and for a second I'm hit with this sense of belonging, like I've finally found my place.

Olly leans in closer to June, his eyes briefly flitting to her lips as he says, "What about you, June? I bet you've thought about killing me more than once. What would you do with my body?"

The rest of us eagerly await her response. June leans closer, resting her hand on his leg. Olly looks like he's about to kiss her right here in the courtyard. "Nothing," she says, dropping her hand. "I'd pay someone else to do it."

Olly's jaw moves back and forth as he tries to compose

himself. As arrogant and cocky as he sometimes is, I'm starting to think he really likes her.

"Nah," Zion says. "If I'm gonna go through the hassle of murdering someone, I'm gonna go big. You bury them vertically so the grave isn't too long, fill it in, then you kill an animal, then bury the animal on top to throw off the sniffer dogs."

Kavi frowns. "You've given this too much thought."

Under the table, Dylan nudges my foot with his. I look up from my lap as he mouths *Are you okay?* at me. I nod, hoping it's enough to convince him, but it isn't.

He waits until we're over by my locker before resting a hand on my arm. "Is everything okay?" he asks. "You've been kind of quiet."

I'm surprised he's even noticed. Either Dylan is more observant than I thought, or I'm seriously off my game. "I'm fine, I'm just feeling a little homesick," I say, so the whole ride home he plays Alicia Keys's "Empire State of Mind" to make me feel better; I don't have the heart to tell him it doesn't.

Jamie still hasn't messaged, so I phone him several times in a bid to get an update, but his phone goes to voicemail. I start to feel out of control in a way that I haven't felt since I started boxing. My palms sweat, shaking as I ball them into fists.

The time before the gym is spent going back and forth, debating whether to tell Mom about the fact Dad might be here. But when I peek in the living room and see her talking to Lilly, I realize I can't. They're curled up on the sofa together, drinking white wine and laughing about something. *Laughing.* It's been a while since I've seen or heard Mom do that.

She leans forward slightly, her curly hair down for once and bouncing around her shoulders. Despite years of living in different states, of communicating only through FaceTime, it's like they've picked up where they've left off. How can I ruin that?

I get to the gym at exactly six thirty, counting down the minutes on my watch. As soon as the number flicks to seven, I'm running up those steps and throwing open the door, making my way across the gym.

Hayden is shirtless by one of the punching bags, in the process of taking off his gloves. On the left side of his chest is a serpent tattoo: its head is etched directly over his heart, while the rest of its body coils around thick, muscled arm. For a moment, my eyes are glued to his chest as the thin sheen of sweat on his abs reflects under the light. His body is like a work of art, all sharp angles and edges, like he's been carved from stone.

Heat pools where it shouldn't as he slowly lifts his head, letting his hair gently fall across his forehead.

"Teach me something already," I say, walking up to him. "Let me *hit* someone. Because if you ask me to jump rope one more time, I'm probably going to hang myself with it."

His eyes darken in a way that makes me step back. I don't mean to take it out on him, but the words are out of my mouth before I can stop them. If he's shocked by my outburst, he doesn't show it. Instead, he grabs some tape from the equipment box before walking toward me. "Put your hands out."

With a brief hesitation, I hold out my hands. He gently wraps the tape around my knuckles, brushing my skin with his hands. The tiniest goose bumps spread across my arms at his soft, gentle touch. There is something sensual about the way his fingers work around the tape. I force myself to look away and think of something else.

When he's finished, he leads me over to a heavy bag. "Make sure your knuckles of your index and middle fingers are hitting the bag first," he says. Then he steps back, nods at the bag, and says, "Start hitting."

As soon as I turn to the bag, I start punching, lightly at first, still feeling unsure of exactly what I'm supposed to be doing, but it feels good to be hitting something, even if it's only a bag.

"Harder," Hayden says.

My punches come harder as *his* face fills my head. Before much longer, I am punching so hard that I'm struggling to breathe.

Hayden grabs the punching bag to stop it from moving. "That's enough."

Collapsing against the bag, I lean on it for support. When my heart is no longer pounding, I wipe away beads of sweat from my forehead.

Without a word, Hayden moves toward the equipment box, pulling out a helmet and mouthpiece. He throws me the helmet first, then the mouthpiece, and tells me to meet him in the ring.

This time, I don't hesitate. I don't know what game he's playing, but right now, I don't care. My body is being dictated by anger, and all I want in this moment is to hit him. I step into the ring and slowly turn to face him. He's not wearing a helmet or his mouthpiece, just the same cherry-red gloves I'd first seen him fight in.

I step forward and swing, expecting to land a punch to his face, but he blocks my attack. I clench my jaw and try over and over, but he's too fast for me. And he knows it. Then, without warning, he hits my helmet. It's not a hard hit, but it's enough to momentarily jolt me. He hits again when I don't react, causing me to scowl.

"That anger that's driving you, it's not helping, is it?" he says. "You haven't landed a single punch."

It's obvious that he's trying to make me mad, and it's working. I swing wildly, desperate to land at least *one* blow, but he's too fast. My hands are all over the place, like I'm forgetting everything he's taught me so far—all I want is to hit him.

"Your feet are all over the place," he says. He lands another hit to my helmet, not to hurt me—he's doing it so lightly that I barely feel a thing—but to annoy me; it's working.

"I want to stop," I say.

"But I thought you weren't a quitter," Hayden says, knocking my helmet again. "Isn't that what you said when we started?"

I'm glad this helmet is covering my face, because my cheeks feel bright red. He looks like he's going to hit me again, but I pull off my helmet and throw it to the floor, letting it bounce against the mat. He drops his hand instantly and pulls off his gloves; I catch a glimpse of his tanned, scarred knuckles.

"I've been where you are," he says, his voice low against my ear. "When my dad died, I had the same rage living inside of me, which is how I know it doesn't just go away because you've decided to box. Whatever it is, you need to let it go."

My heart is pounding as I try not to focus on his mouth near my ear. He's standing so close that just another inch, another tilt, and our lips would be touching. For a split second, I wonder how it would feel to kiss him, to have those strong arms wrapped around me and his hands tangled up in my hair. His eyes are on my lips like he's thinking the same, and he starts to lean *closer, closer*, and . . . I step back suddenly, hating myself for letting my mind go there, for doing that to Jamie.

"This was a stupid idea," I say, backing away. I am a terrible person. "This whole thing. You're not even a qualified *teacher*."

As soon as the words leave my mouth, I want to take them back. But I can see by his face that it is too late for that. Quick as a flash, he closes the remaining distance between us, putting his face in mine. When he speaks, his voice is dangerously low. "Get your shit and get out of my gym."

I flinch at the sharpness of his tone. "What about my money?"

His mouth hovers somewhere near my jaw. "Call it compensation for wasting my time."

I want to scream or punch him or both, but instead, I grab my bag and storm out.

I'm so furious when I get home that the first thing I do is head up to my bedroom, grab a pillow, and scream into it the way I used to as a kid. I hate that I lashed out at Hayden when he was only trying to help. I hate that I'm so messed up. I hate, full stop.

My phone vibrates with a message. I throw away the pillow and stumble over my own feet to grab my phone off the nightstand. Jamie's sent a picture instead of a message, and it's of Dad about to walk into the apartment building. Relief hits me like a tidal wave. He's not in California, he's still in New York. He's not here.

And suddenly, the weight of what I've just done hits me. I'd let the anger I'd felt take over, let it ruin my training with Hayden, and he's not even here. Once again, he found a way to get into my head and ruin my life without having to lift a finger.

—

The next few days are a whirlwind of regrets. My pride tells me to walk away from Hayden, but the longer I go without training, the more out of control I start to feel. The tight knot of anger is back, my thoughts all completely consumed by Dad.

My head suddenly flips through memories like pages of a book: us staying up late to finish off school projects, us singing as loud as we could to the radio, us baking chocolate fudge brownies on the weekend. The memories flip faster, each turn of the page like a sharp, mental paper cut: Dad hiding Mom's shoes when he didn't want her leaving, him giving us the silent treatment, him threatening to tell Jamie all sorts of lies about me.

That last one stamps out what's left of my grief and replaces it with anger. I'd been so terrified that he'd go through with this threat that I'd immediately apologized, because Jamie is the only thing that has ever made sense, and what if he believed Dad's lies?

I text Jamie, desperately overcompensating for wanting to kiss Hayden, but for once he doesn't text straight back. I put my phone away and sit here, feeling weird, like there's this space I've got so used to being filled and suddenly it's empty.

I try to catch up with Hayden at school, but he's avoiding me like the plague. Every morning, as soon as the bell rings, he's out of his seat and shoving past students to get as far from me as possible. It's why, when the twins invite me to a party on Friday and tell me everyone is going, I say yes in the hopes I might see him.

June comes over to get ready at our house. Kavi and Zion have a date night planned tonight, so it will just be the four of us. I think Olly is half expecting this to be his first date with June, not that she knows, and I plan to do some serious investigating tonight to find out if she actually likes him.

We spend most of the evening trying on different outfits to old nineties music. June empties the whole of my closet onto my bed, sorting through clothes before she pulls out a silky black top.

"Ooh, wear this," she says. "It's gorgeous."

Hesitant, I take it from her. Jamie has hated this top ever since I wore it to dinner once. He said it was too much, that it wasn't really me, but I must have scooped it up by mistake when I was packing for California. As soon as the top is on, I remember why I bought it. It fits perfectly, and the material feels soft and delicate on my skin.

"We have a winner," June says. "The twins' jaws are going to be on the floor."

"Ew." I shudder, because they're practically brothers at this point. "Speaking of the twins, what's going on with you and Olly?"

"I don't know what you mean."

"Oh come on," I say, laughing, "the tension with you guys has been insane lately. Do you like him or not?"

She tries to keep a straight face, but an actress she's not, and suddenly she collapses onto the bed beside me. "Fine, so he's hot. I like flirting with him, but I don't see the point in starting anything when we're going off to college soon."

"Maybe that's exactly why you should start something. Aren't you the one who told me life is too short?"

"What if he doesn't like me?"

"Of course he likes you," I say. "Who wouldn't?"

She jumps on top of me, pulling me into a bear hug. "I'm so glad you moved here."

"Me too."

When I'm ready, I turn to the mirror. I grab my pallette, softening my cheekbones with some pale peach blush and a smidge of highlighter. It's about the only makeup I usually wear, but tonight I add some lipstick.

My hair is down for once. I'm so used to having it pulled back that my wavy hair looks wild, somehow. Less refined. But strangely, I like it.

Jamie calls me just as we're finishing up. He takes in my hair first, then my face, before letting his eyes wander to my top. Something feels strange to me, an unsteady feeling like before lightning strikes. He still has his eyes on this top, looking at me the way Dad would look at Mom when she wore something offensive.

"You look pretty," he says. "Is that what you're wearing?"

June watches me in the mirror as she applies her mascara. "I was just trying it on. I'll probably wear something else."

His eyes soften. "Good. Are there gonna be guys there?"

"No, it's a party for nuns," I tease.

"Just be careful, okay? I'm not there to protect you anymore."

I nod, but something about his comment rubs me the wrong way. "What are you doing tonight, anyway?"

"Nothing, just gonna watch something and head to bed. Have fun, okay?"

"Okay, I love you." I hang up and turn to June, whose dark eyes feel like laser beams through my skin. I pull off the top and throw it to the side, picking something a little more me.

June watches me slip it on. "I know it's not my business, but you shouldn't let him decide what you wear."

"He didn't," I say. "It was my choice."

She doesn't say anything else, just finishes applying her mascara. When we're ready, Tim drops us outside of a house in the Palisades and tells us to be responsible. Olly throws an arm around him, flashes an innocent grin, and says, "Are we ever anything else?"

Tim clips him around the side of the ear, then swivels to Dylan. "I'm relying on you to keep him out of trouble."

Dylan rolls his eyes. "Don't I always?"

Tim looks at me now. "What did I do to deserve these kids, huh?"

His easy expression reminds me of how Dad would act

during one of his good moods. I close my eyes, remembering the way his face would light up whenever he was proud of me, which was often. *What did I do to deserve a daughter like you*?

June hooks an arm through mine as we climb out of the car, taking our time to stroll through the front garden. Water shoots from fountains on either side of the lawn, and sculpted rose bushes coiled in fairy lights line the walkway. I scan the Spanish-style balconies overhanging the top floor, where several people are grinding to music.

Olly throws an arm around me as we walk. It's nice, in a way. It's how I imagine a brother would prop you up when you felt nervous. "Make sure you stick with June," he says. "Don't drink anything that looks funny, and definitely no drugs, got it?"

"Got it," I say.

"Good, because if you die on our watch, I'm going to be grounded until graduation. Possibly until college."

Frowning, I duck from under his grip. As soon as we're inside, the twins disappear. I follow June into the open-plan living room, where I'm handed a beer by someone I've never met. I'm about to decline with a polite, "No, thank you," but it is already being shoved in my hand.

June's face lights up at someone in the crowd, and as she makes her way over to say hello, I take it as an opportunity to slip away. I wander around the house in search of Hayden, but this house is so huge that I can't find him anywhere. Defeated, I try to find June again but it's impossible with this crowd.

At some point, the beer I'm gulping starts to take its toll. I make my way upstairs in search of a bathroom. By now I've downed three cans in a bid to look less awkward, and I'm left with the sudden urge to pee.

Finally, one of the several doors lining the hallway opens. I glance inside, expecting to find a toilet, but it's the bedroom. Maybe if these shoes weren't killing me, and if the world wasn't spinning, that bed wouldn't look so tempting, but it does. I hurry inside, collapsing onto it like a starfish.

"Hey."

Something hard shifts beneath me. I lift my head, but it's so dark in here, it's hard for my eyes to adjust. I blink a few times, just about able to make out the outline of a hard, rippled chest. I pull back farther, allowing his face to come into view. Sharp jaw, pillowy lips. My eyes make their way up to his eyes—green, piercing, and all too familiar.

"Oh no," I whisper.

Hayden sits up with me still on his lap. I almost roll off, but his hands grab my hips to keep me steady. For a second, even though I know I should move, all I can focus on is the warmth of his hands as they lock me in place. I'm about to say something, to offer some kind of explanation as to why I am straddling him, but when I open my mouth, the words fall away.

He just looks so beautiful, sitting here in the dark. His features are softer when they're dusted with shadows, his gaze less intense. We sit like this for what can only be a second but feels like forever.

"What the hell?"

I'm shaken into action at the high-pitched voice. A girl stands near the window, in the process of stripping to her lacy underwear. I glance at Hayden, horrified, but he just raises an eyebrow like he's waiting to see what I'll do.

I pull from his grip and stumble out of the bedroom,

running back into the safety of the hallway. Oh God, that was bordering on a threesome. Stumbling back downstairs, I use the wall to steady myself.

I'm about to leave when June berates me for disappearing and pulls me into the living room. We take a seat on the already-crowded sofa while I try to forget what just happened. As much as I want to turn around and go home, the only thing keeping me from snapping right now is the thought of training again.

"I'm going to the bathroom," June says, getting to her feet. "Can you save my seat?"

I nod and watch as she pulls down her dress before disappearing into the hall. After a few minutes, Hayden walks in with a glass of something in his hand and occupies June's seat. Unable to help myself, I say, "That was quick."

He takes a sip from his drink before turning to look at me. "Having someone stumble in halfway through kind of ruins the mood. Shouldn't you be home FaceTiming your boyfriend?"

"Normally, I would be, but I need to talk to you."

"Are you saying you came here for me?"

"Yes. Can we go somewhere to talk?"

He avoids my gaze as he raises his glass. "I'm a little busy."

"Fine. I need the bathroom, anyway." I stumble into the kitchen, feeling rejected. When I turn back around, Hayden is standing so close to me that I practically turn into his chest. Tripping again, he puts his hands on my waist to steady me.

"This is where you're going to the bathroom?" he asks.

"What?" I can't think straight with his hands touching me. "No."

"Then what are you doing?"

"I want you to train me again."

"Why should I?" He suddenly steps forward. "You said some pretty hurtful things to me, Maddison." The way he says my name sends a shiver down my spine. "What was it you said? I'm not qualified?"

"I'm sorry. I was having a bad day and I took it out on you. I shouldn't have done that."

"While I appreciate the sentiment," he says, "this isn't going to work."

"Whoa, are you breaking up with me?" When his face remains blank, I sigh. "Look, I already apologized. What more do you want?"

He pushes himself off the counter and steps toward me, forcing my breath to hitch in my throat. "You know, we're a lot alike."

"We are?"

"Yep." His breath is warm and smells of alcohol, a sign he's probably drunk. I tell myself that's why whatever he says next, I won't hold it against him. "You act like you're so perfect with your boring boyfriend, and your to-do lists, but I see the real you, Maddison. Deep down, you're as angry and as messed up as I am. That's why you want to fight, isn't it?" He leans in closer, positioning his mouth by my ear. "See, I don't think you're as straightedged as you pretend to be."

My cheeks burn. It feels like I've been opened up, my worst fears laid bare; deep down, I am just like my father. "You couldn't be more wrong," I say, "and my boyfriend is *not* boring."

Hayden laughs before leaning in closer. "Yeah, I'm sure *Green Bean* really does it for you."

My cheeks grow hotter than they've ever been. "What do

you know about anything, anyway?" I snap. "From what I just saw, I'm guessing you haven't been in a committed relationship for a while."

"Maybe you've been in one too long."

His mouth is far too close to my face. I'm terrified that the slightest of movements will make our lips touch. I turn around, about to walk out of here and never see, never speak to Hayden again, but then desperation takes over, and I turn back to face him.

"Please," I say.

The second the word leaves my mouth, it's like his whole demeanor changes. Maybe he can smell the desperation on me, or see it on my face, because his features suddenly soften, and he gently bites his lip. "Fine."

It feels like a turning point between us, a moment of truce. I thank him and head back to the party in search of June. I've had enough of this night and want to go home, but I want to check she's okay first. I end up finding her in the coat closet, making out with Olly. The pair don't see me, and I slowly close the door behind me, send her a text to let her know I'm leaving, and then text Lilly to come and get me.

It's my mother who picks me up, which surprises me. She doesn't say anything about the alcohol on my breath as I climb into the car, and I'm glad. It's quiet as I stare out the window, surprised by how familiar this place feels now, so much so that I can look out the window, see people stopped in the middle of the street, and my first thought isn't, *No one does that in New York.*

"How was the party?" Mom asks as we fly around a corner. It's been a while since she's driven anywhere, so I'm half tempted to grab the armrests and hold on for dear life.

"It was fine." As relieved as I am that Hayden has agreed to train me again, it's not something I'm eager to share with my mom after what she had said at the farmers' market. "How come you came to pick me up?"

She shrugs as we make a sharp turn. "I haven't driven anywhere in a while. I kind of miss it." She suddenly glances over, studying my face as though this is the first time she's seeing me. "You don't know how glad I am that you're settling in," she says. "I know it's not easy starting somewhere new near the end of your senior year. You've had to sacrifice a lot, and I'm sorry."

My heart squeezes at the guilt on her expression. "It's not your fault, Mom. None of this is. You know that, right?"

Her fingers clench the wheel at the same time she nods, but she doesn't look convinced. Her eyes are on the road again, and I notice her shoulders are no longer slumped forward like she's trying to make herself small. They're pulled right back, her curly hair hanging wildly around her face as though the old her is trying to break through. As we pull into the drive and cross the lawn to the house, I find myself praying she does.

As soon as I'm tucked up in bed, I call Jamie. It's almost out of routine and comfort than a genuine missing him. He answers on the first ring, but the shuffling and loud music makes it clear he's answered by mistake.

I'm about to hang up when a girl's voice rings out. It's hard to make out through the music and noise, but the high-pitched laugh that follows is unmistakable.

My phone starts to shake. Why is he with a girl if he said he was staying in tonight? I hang up and call again, surprised when he answers. "Hey, you," he says. "How's the party?"

"Awful," I say. "Are you at home?"

Tyler's loud voice fills the background. "No, I'm over at Ty's."

My heart beats faster. "Who else is there?"

"Just a few of the guys." He frowns and adds, "Why, what's wrong?"

"No girls?"

"No, just the guys. What's wrong?"

"I could have sworn I heard a girl laughing." I'm acutely aware of how jealous I sound, but I don't mean to be. I don't even *mind* if Jamie is hanging with girls, I just don't know why he'd lie about it.

The phone goes silent. He switches on video, and when his face fills the screen, he looks hurt. "Why would I lie?" He pans the room to show Tyler and some of the guys on the sofa.

"Jamie, you don't need to—"

"No, I do need to," he says, "because clearly you don't believe me. I thought we trusted each other."

Tears burn my eyes. Arguing with Jamie always somehow feels like the world is ending, like I'm one word away from losing everything. "I do trust you."

"It doesn't sound like it," he says.

My heart is pounding the way it used to when Dad would accuse me of something I didn't do. "I was asking because I called you a few minutes ago and heard a girl."

He laughs, and it's so sudden and loud that it makes me jump. "That was the TV, Maddie."

"I don't know why I didn't think of that."

"Look, I get it." He sighs. "You're just stressed out because of all the stuff with your dad, but you have nothing to be paranoid about, okay? We're nothing like your parents. I love you. *Only* you."

The last remaining sliver of doubt dissipates. Hearing those words makes me feel safe, special, and I hate that I nearly caused an argument. "I love you too."

As soon as he hangs up, I crawl into bed without even taking my clothes off. My phone pings with a message from June.

WE KISSED.

I send back congratulatory emojis. When my eyelids feel heavy, I curl on my side and try to sleep, but my head is filled with images of Dad, of Jamie, of Hayden, until they all blur into one.

CHAPTER NINE

The next week falls into a steady routine, and it's like I can breathe again. There are only four weeks until the fight, and in a bid to make up for lost time, Hayden has me training nonstop, starting with drills and weights before moving into the ring. Even Jenson comes over a few times to give me some pointers before he hurries out again.

Our sessions spill over into the first few days of spring break. While June, the twins, and the others spend every day at the beach, I'm in the gym with Hayden, more determined than ever to win this fight.

I stand opposite him in the ring, feet slightly apart, hands to my face. It's in the seconds before we start sparring that my heart starts to drum, and I forget about the world. The only thing that matters is me and him, him and me.

The second he swings, I'm ready for it. My body moves for me, dipping to the left as his fist flies over my shoulder. I circle him, throwing a one-two. He blocks the jab with his elbow, slips to the left, then hits me on my helmet.

This is what I love about boxing: I know what to expect when I slip through these ropes. The odds, the outcome: I either leave this fight a winner or a loser—no surprises. This kind of stability is what I have lacked my whole life; it's what keeps me coming back.

I try my best, but Hayden parries and hits me with a short right hook. It hits my helmet, jolting me slightly, but I'm undeterred. The helmet is snug but not too tight—it makes me feel safe.

"I'm so going to win," I say, despite the fact I've yet to win a fight against him. Still, I have a good feeling this time: my footwork has improved, and I'm building up speed; all I need is to land the perfect hit.

My fist flies out in what I think is going to be a perfect jab. Hayden ducks, then switches the rules on me by flipping me onto my back. The look on his face as he stares at me is pure innocence. "What were you saying?"

"Cheater."

He grins and pulls off my helmet, letting it drop to the floor. "Looks like I win." He bites his lip, and there's this moment where he looks like he's contemplating kissing me. For about half a second, I wonder what *that* would feel like, maybe it would shock him, make him think he doesn't know me so well after all. His lips are red and full, with a perfect Cupid's bow. I imagine myself taking his bottom lip between my teeth and gently nibbling it.

Common sense kicks in. I drop my hand and watch his eyes cloud over.

My heart pounds. Around Hayden, it's like everything else dims. I shift out from under him and head over to a punching bag, needing to put some space between us.

Hayden follows me, and for the next few minutes, it's silent as we snap out some combinations, sometimes in the same rhythm. I don't think about anything as I punch, just the rhythm of the bag as it echoes around the room.

Just as we're wrapping up, my phone rings. I hurry to my backpack and pull it from the side pocket, glancing at Jamie's name. "Hey, Jamie."

"Hey," he says. "What are you up to?"

"I'm just at the gym. Do you want me to call you when I'm home?"

Silence. Finally, he says, "You've been going to the gym a lot lately. We hardly have time to talk anymore."

My chest tightens. I glance at Hayden to see if he's listening, but he's busy packing away the equipment. "I know, I'm sorry—it's just been really hectic lately."

"Can I at least see your face?"

I laugh and say, "I look disgusting right now."

"Come on, Maddie, it's me. I've seen you after a four-mile run before."

I glance back at Hayden. This time, he's watching me. In a low voice, I say, "Fine." With my free hand, I wipe away the sweat on my forehead and answer his video call. "Happy?"

He nods, but he's not quite looking at me, he's looking behind me at the row of machines. "Much better," he says. He tells me he loves me and that he'll talk to me later before hanging up.

The rest of the lesson has this strange cloud hanging over it since my call with Jamie. As soon as I get home, I climb into bed and call him back, hoping it will untwist the knots from earlier, but when he answers, my heart sinks.

"Hey," I say brightly, glancing out of the window. "Sorry, I know it's late there."

For the first time since being here, I miss rain and the way it lightly patters on the glass, leaving a trail in its wake. Jamie thinks I'm crazy for this, but it's my favorite type of weather. There's just something about a downpour that gets me all excited.

When I was little and it rained, I'd beg Dad to take me out onto the streets so I could splash in the puddles. He hated getting wet, but every time there was a thunderstorm, without fail, he'd take my hand and he'd lead me just a little past our apartment, where we'd spin around in circles, getting absolutely soaked. That was my favorite version of him, the way he'd go out of his way to do things for you, even if he hated it.

We spend the next few hours watching movies together, and for a while, it's just like old times. He's cracking jokes about the plot holes and the characters, and I'm laughing until my belly hurts, because that's what he's good at, making me laugh and happy. By the time we hang up, things feel a little better, like the distance between us has closed a little.

I start to get ready for bed, but my phone buzzing stops me. I've come to dread the sound, and there's a part of me that wants to ignore it or toss it out the window, freeing myself from its control.

Strangely, my screen says the message is a WhatsApp from myself. I have to check the number three times, because it doesn't make any sense that a WhatsApp would be from me, but that's what it says. I click the chat, still feeling confused but also on edge, and read the message.

I miss you.

Dad

For about a minute, it feels like I'm suffocating. My mind turns, trying to process what's happening right now, but it can't, because it doesn't make sense. Dad is messaging me. From my own number. And if he can message me, does that mean he can read my messages?

I spend the next fifteen minutes scouring the internet for answers. I'm pulling up articles about scam messages and phishing and a bunch of other terms that don't quite fit, and then I finally find something useful. You can send and receive Whatsapp messages from any computer so long as you're logged in.

I read that part over and over, trying to recall when I might have logged into my WhatsApp on a device Dad uses. I can't recall, but then he'd have found a way around it anyway. He was good at finding passwords, at taking your phone when your back was turned and retrieving whatever information. He's been reading my messages and possiby deleting them, too, and I'd never even noticed.

The thought makes me sick. I feel like my privacy has been violated, further proof that he has no respect for anyone around him, despite demanding respect from *us*. I change my account details and log out of any and all devices before deleting WhatsApp altogether, not that it matters. He already knows we're in California, and he'll have already read conversations between me and Jamie discussing Granada Hills—all there's left to do is wait.

CHAPTER TEN

The first thing I do when I get to school the next day is find Hayden. He's standing by his locker with some of his friends, but the second he's alone, I make a beeline for him. He turns as I get there, looking surprised. I'm breaking all of our unspoken rules by being here, but this is an emergency.

"Hey," I say. "I need to talk to you."

He straightens up and pulls me closer. "What's wrong?"

"I know it's not a training day, but I need the gym."

He frowns a little. "It's not good to train every day. Your body has to have a day of rest in between."

"Fine." I'm about to walk off, but his hand shoots out and grabs my own, turning me to face him.

He grins again. "Your heart is racing. I can feel your pulse."

I pull away. "That's because I'm mad."

"Why, because I'm trying to look out for you?"

"I'm not mad at *you*," I say. "I'm just mad, okay?"

He raises an eyebrow. I think this is possibly the longest conversation we've ever had at school. And he's being nice. Kind of. The bell rings, and he rolls his eyes before looking at me. "Look, meet me after school. I want to show you something."

I'm about to tell him I'd been planning on getting some work done in the library, but he's already halfway down the hallway. Instead, I make my way to my next period and spend the rest of the afternoon wondering what it is that Hayden wants to show me.

"He's probably taking you off to chop you into pieces," June says, but she's just being dramatic. *I hope.*

"We need a code word," Kavi says, forever the sensible one, "so that if he does murder you, he can't dispose of your body and pretend to be you to stop us from worrying."

"Have you been watching murder documentaries again?"

She grins. "That's beside the point. It could happen."

We settle on the code word *squashed lemons*. If I don't say this with every text I send, the pair of them are sending out a search party.

When school lets out, I'm nervous. June and I hurry to the parking lot to meet the twins, and I spot Hayden leaning by his car. Turning to them both, I say, "Don't get mad, but I'm going somewhere with Hayden today."

Olly wiggles his eyebrows as he slips an arm across June's shoulder. "Don't let us stop you," he says. "I was just thinking about how nice it would be to actually sit in the front seat of my own car. Come on, Dyl—" he pats Dylan's back, attempting to guide him over to the door, but Dylan doesn't budge.

"You guys are friends now?" Dylan asks.

"Kind of. I think."

He narrows his eyes at something behind me. I make the mistake of looking at Hayden and see his arms are folded as he leans against the lamppost, the biggest grin on his face. He's enjoying this far too much.

"You don't have to go with him if you don't want to," Dylan says. His eyes find mine, almost pleading, like they're begging me not to go.

"I'll be fine," I assure him. "See you guys later?"

June gives me a hug before heading over to her convertible. Dylan, after a brief nod, climbs into the car with Olly.

The inside of Hayden's car smells like leather and pinewood. I relax in my seat. Outside, the school building is disappearing as the sun sits behind it, casting a glow through the back window. The farther we get out of Granada Hills, the more cars and trucks traffic we encounter. I rest my eyes for only a moment, tuning into the drone of the motor. The drive to wherever we're going is silent. At some point, Hayden turns on the radio, and some old-school song blasts from the speakers. After a while, a song I love comes on and I can't help but quietly hum along.

Maybe I should be more concerned about the fact Dad most likely knows where we are and is coming to find us, but for once, I don't want to worry about what *could* happen. I want to be in the moment.

"Where are you taking me?" I ask.

"Do you really want to know, or can it be a surprise?"

"A surprise," I say, "as long as I'm not home too late. I have to—"

"FaceTime with your boyfriend."

"Why are you saying it like that?"

"Like what?" He looks at me, the picture of innocence.

"Like I'm just so predictable," I say.

His smile is teasing. "Because you are."

"But I'm not."

"I've never met anyone as predictable as you, Maddison. Except the wanting-to-fight thing—I'll admit, that's a little out of left field."

I scowl a little and look out the window. "Fine, so I'm predictable. It's better than being unpredictable."

"Says who?"

"Says me. No one wants to end up with someone who's unpredictable. They want someone who's dependable."

"Someone who's boring," Hayden says. The look he gives me suggests he's talking about Jamie.

He suddenly reaches over. I jump, thinking he's going for my thigh, when he raises an eyebrow and turns on the stereo. I swallow hard and try to settle my nerves, suddenly regretting this detour. When we finally park up, we walk down North San Fernando Boulevard to a funky little diner on the corner. "This is where you're taking me?"

"For now," Hayden says.

I follow him in, where we take a booth near the back. It's pretty inside, with checkered floors, a red ceiling, and photos and vinyl records on the walls. I flick through the menu's milkshake selection while Hayden watches me from the seat opposite.

"I bet you'll have vanilla," he says.

I bite my cheek and quickly change my order. "Then you'd be wrong, as usual. I'm having the caramel-and-popcorn milkshake."

Hayden lets out the quietest laugh. It's the first one I think I've ever heard. "You can get the vanilla, you know. I won't judge you." The thought of Hayden judging me strikes me as funny, so I let out a laugh.

"What's so funny?" he asks.

I'm saved from answering when our waitress comes over to take our orders. Hayden orders a chocolate brownie milkshake with extra whipped cream. I hesitate for a second before sheepishly whispering, "Vanilla milkshake, please."

"I'm sorry, honey," she says. "Could you speak up?"

I clear my throat. "Vanilla milkshake, please, and a Smokin' BBQ burger."

The dimples are out in full force. "I'll take one, too, as well as some hot wings and nachos."

The waitress takes our menus before saying she'll be right back. Hayden must notice my expression, because he leans forward slightly and rests his arms on the table. "Hey, I didn't get this body through luck—I got it through protein."

When the waitress comes back with our milkshakes, things fall quiet. I glance across the table, finding it weird seeing Hayden slurping milkshake through a straw. It's weird that I'm here with him, period. He's so reluctant to be seen with me at school, but he's happy to take me out for food. It doesn't make sense, but then again, nothing about Hayden Walker makes sense.

"Do you miss home yet?" he asks.

"Not really," I say, and then I feel guilty. "I just mean I like living with my aunt and her husband. They're like a real family, you know?"

Hayden's eyebrows furrow. "And yours isn't?"

I play with my straw so that I don't have to look at him. "My dad is a . . . complicated man." Just like the night we first met at the gym, being honest with Hayden feels like the most natural thing in the world.

Hayden leans forward now. "He hurt you," he says, but it's not a question.

I nod. "Mostly mentally, but he hit me once—it's why my mom and I moved here." The truth is spilling from my lips before I know what I'm saying. Whenever I'm around Hayden, honesty doesn't seem like such a battle anymore.

"Is that why you wanted to train?" he asks. "So you could learn how to fight?"

"It was more about control," I say. "Or a distraction. I don't know *what* it was, but I know it's more than that now. When I train, it's like everything else is stripped away, leaving just me. Maybe that doesn't make any sense."

"It does." He reaches out slightly, his fingers brushing mine. "When my dad died, I lived and breathed training. It was the only thing I could still make sense of. The only thing that made me feel good."

I nod, because that's exactly it. He gets it. Gets me. I realize his fingers are still touching mine, so I quickly retract them. Hayden asks me a few more questions, like if I've been to the beach yet or if I'm going to college.

"Yes to the first, no to the second," I say. "Are you going to college?"

He shakes his head, which surprises me. Hayden is in most of my AP classes at school, so I know it's not because of his grades. "I want to focus on the gym," he says. "It hasn't been making much money since my dad died. A lot of the kids he used to train have grown up and moved on. I want to focus on turning it into a successful business, you know? It's why Jenson agreed to the boot camp. We figure if it can bring some newbies in, we can start expanding."

He continues to tell me about his plans, and I watch the way his eyes light up as he talks. It's nice that he has something he's so passionate about. When I try to think of what my own passions are, nothing comes to mind.

"What about you?" he says. "What do you want to do after college?"

"Teach," I say automatically. I hadn't known it was what I wanted to do until my sophomore year, when my favorite English teacher pulled me aside and asked me what was wrong. Dad had been giving Mom the silent treatment for coming home late, so I'd been quiet and withdrawn, thinking nobody noticed, but she did. She sat me down and told me she was there for me whenever I was ready to talk. I never ended up telling her what happened, but just her concern was enough to get me through that day; I'd like to do the same for someone else.

My muscles tense. It's the first time I've thought about my dad since being here. "I like the thought of being able to make a difference in someone's life."

His forearm is pressed against mine. It is warm and tanned and about three times the size of my own. "Same reason my dad first opened the gym. He gave out free memberships to all of the kids, wanted to give them a safe space. I still get guys dropping by every now and then to tell me how much of an impact my dad had on them."

Something has shifted between us, and I'm starting to see

that behind his prickly exterior, Hayden has an exceptionally big heart.

"Are you looking forward to prom?" I ask.

"I don't do proms," he says.

I'm horrified. "Prom is a milestone. It signifies the end of an era. You can't seriously be thinking about missing it."

He grins through a mouthful of fries. "Prom is a money-grabbing machine under the illusion of a good time."

"More like you couldn't find a date," I tease.

"Hey, I had plenty of girls ask me; I just don't want to go."

I don't bother arguing, because it is obvious that Hayden is as stubborn as I am. Instead, we talk about his mom and dad, and how their relationship was like a fairy tale before he died.

"My mom still sticks to her side of the bed," he says. "She kisses his photo frame every morning."

My throat stings. It hurts to think you can love someone so hard, so deeply, only to have them suddenly pulled away from you. It makes me wonder if love, in the end, is even worth it at all.

When we're finished, Hayden gets the check for both of us. "It's fine," I say, "I can pay for my half." I don't want him thinking this is some kind of date, but my pleas fall on deaf ears.

"If it bothers you that much, I'll think of a way you can pay me back."

"The way I'll pay you back is with my half of the check." I pull on my jacket and follow him back to the car. It's not that I'm opposed to guys buying me food, but I don't want Hayden to feel like I owe him.

The rest of the drive is mostly silent, but it's nice to be able to relax. I don't let myself focus on anything but the sight of the sun peeking down through the palm trees from the passenger window. The longer we drive, the closer the strip of ocean gets until finally it's stretching across the horizon.

We drive through an archway, above which reads: SANTA MONICA. YACHT HARBOR. SPORT FISHING, BOATING, CAFÉS. "What are we doing here?" I ask.

"Taking a much-needed break."

The second I get out of the car, the familiar beach smell rushes on the wind to meet me, a fresh tang of seaweed. We swerve through bodies and walk the boardwalk together, taking in the ocean and cafés and rides. The beach and coast are picturesque, with mountains and the skyline of buildings on one side and the blue-green waters of the Pacific on the other.

Hayden takes my hand and pulls me through the crowd, leading me over to the pier. I want to let go of it, to feel bad about holding another guy's hand when I'm in a relationship with Jamie, but as we weave in and out of people, I find myself holding on tighter.

We walk along the rest of the pier, passing one of those caricature-drawing stalls. The man behind the table asks if he can draw a picture of the lovely couple, and a pang of guilt floods my body.

"Oh, we're not a—"

"Sure," Hayden says.

We take a seat at the table opposite. Hayden throws an arm around me, pulling me into his side. It's hard having to sit still for so long and with Hayden beside me. He keeps wiggling his eyebrows in an attempt to make me laugh, and the artist frowns in frustration. When he's finished, he spins his easel around so that we can see the end result, and I'm horrified at my fish lips.

Hayden laughs. "I love it. I'm going to hang it in my bedroom."

"If you even think about it, I'll kill you."

He laughs again and takes my hand as we weave through the crowd. "Stay close," he says. "I don't want to have to make a trip to the lost and found."

We continue to stroll down the rest of the pier, talking about all sorts of things. He tells me about his favorite movies, which are almost always horror films, and about his mother, who's a doctor. I learn he and Wiley have been friends since they were five, and when I mention what Wiley had said about him being naked, he says, "Hey, sometimes you gotta just be free."

Conversation moves onto his relationship with Jenson, whom he's known since he was a baby. He was his father's best friend, and ever since Hayden's dad died, he's been helping to run the gym and continue his father's legacy.

"He's like a second dad to me," Hayden says. "He comes over every Sunday for dinner, brings Mom some shopping, even though she insists it's fine, and then we sit and watch a movie or the game, or something."

"That's really nice of him," I say. "He seems like a good guy."

"He is," Hayden says. "Better than me, anyway."

"Hey," I say, and he turns his head to look at me. "That's not saying much."

He breaks into a wonderful grin, then asks me about my own dad. I can tell he wants to know about his *complicated* side, but I'm not ready to share with him that part of me yet, so

I tell him about the good times: Dad taking me to ballet every week, how we'd go to the park and for milkshakes, how he'd help me to make a costume every Halloween, even though it took forever. How he cried on my birthdays, because he was losing his little girl so fast. I feel my eyes well up, so I have to stop before I do something embarrassing like cry.

"Anyway," I say, needing to change the subject, "you should really change your mind about prom. There's probably not enough time to find a date, but you can still find a suit."

"No way," he says as we wander down the beach. "I don't do prom, I don't do suits, I don't do dates, I don't do relationships."

"Fine, whatever." In the far distance is the Ferris wheel, and I tug on Hayden's arm like a kid and say, "That's my favorite ride. You want to go?"

He studies my face for a second or two, looking apprehensive. "Okay."

We wait in line, Hayden's hand still wrapped around mine. Since when does holding his hand feel so normal? And why is it that he is doing it here and not at any other time?

Once it gets to our turn, we slide into a carriage. Things are quiet as the Ferris wheel ascends, elevating us into the air. Part of the reason I love this ride is that it feels like nothing can touch me up here. Not my dad or my old life or the girl I used to be—up here, I feel safe.

Every so often Hayden looks at me, studying me in a way that makes me feel nervous. When we get to the top, he closes his eyes, his tanned skin considerably paler.

"Hayden?" I say, peering into his face. "Are you okay?"

"I'm fine," he says, but his eyes remain shut.

"Are you scared of heights, or something?"

"Terrified."

"Then why did you come on the Ferris wheel?"

He opens his eyes now, the cutest little half smile playing on his lips. "Because you said it was your favorite. How bad would I have looked saying no?"

His words surprise me. Because I wanted to? Since when does Hayden do things he doesn't want to do just to impress me? When he closes his eyes again, I grab hold of his hand, entwining my fingers with his.

"Just think happy thoughts," I say. "Pretend your favorite author just released a new book, or a new documentary just came out, or someone left you the last piece of cake."

Hayden raises an eyebrow. "Those are your happy thoughts?"

I smile and glance out the window again. It's strange—holding hands is so juvenile and innocent, but with him it feels intimate. "Fine, then tell me your happy thoughts."

He's silent for a moment, eyes closed as his thumb traces circles on my palm. "The gym, my family, Spider-Man."

I almost splutter. "Spider-Man?"

"Yeah, Spider-Man was like my childhood hero. Whenever I got angry or upset, I'd pull out the comics my dad got me, and I'd feel better."

This is just so cute that I can't handle it. "Why him?"

He shrugs, finally opening his eyes. "I was a weedy little kid. Got bullied pretty bad for having *girly eyelashes*."

"But everyone loves long eyelashes on boys," I say.

"Yeah, *now* they do. I tried to snip them shorter a few times with scissors, before my mom started hiding them."

I hold his hand tighter, imagining a little Hayden being

bullied for his eyelashes, and it makes my heart hurt. Kids can be so cruel—not just kids, but adults too.

By the time our carriage is back on solid ground, Hayden has forgotten all about his fear of heights. We wobble off together to the end of the pier, window-shopping and snapping photos, and at the end we find not just seagulls, but a pair of sea lions playing near the local fishermen.

"Go and stand near one," Hayden says, pushing me toward them. "I'll take a picture of you."

I laugh and grab his arm, not wanting to get any closer to them. "No way, they look hungry."

He tries to push me closer, so I latch my arms around his waist, causing him to laugh. The wind sweeps a curtain of hair across my face, and there's this second where he gathers it in his hand, and it looks like he's going to kiss me. He leans in closer, and our noses almost brush. For a moment as he looks at me, I swear I see panic in his eyes.

An image of Jamie forces its way into my head. I drop my hands from around his waist, ripped with guilt. As strained as things have felt between us lately, he's still the best thing that happened to me, and here I am on what feels like a *date* with Hayden.

"Do you think they mate for life the way penguins do?" I ask, and when I glance at Hayden, I see he is watching me and not the sea lions.

"Penguins mate for life?"

"The male penguin offers the female a pebble and if she likes him, she puts the pebble in her nest."

The corners of his mouth curl upward, but there is something less playful in his eyes now. Something more serious. "Is this a hint?" he asks. "Do you want me to offer you a pebble?"

"You don't strike me as the pebble-giving type," I say, but inside my chest is pounding. "Come on, let's go."

At some point, when it starts to get late, I head to the bathroom to freshen up while Hayden waits outside. I glance in the mirror to see my cheeks look flushed, and my skin feels tingly and warm. This is not how someone with a boyfriend should be feeling. Not at all.

Hayden parks at the end of my street and kills the engine, turning to face me. "So, did you have fun?"

"Yeah," I say, "I did."

He leans over now, pushing a strand of hair behind my ear. I swallow hard, torn between wanting him to drop his hand, and wanting him to lean closer. "See? Not everything has to be about training. There are other ways to make you feel good, you know?"

I nod, but I can barely concentrate with his hand near my face. "Thank you," I say, pulling away, "for taking me. I should probably head inside."

His eyes grow dark, and he drops his hand. "See you at training."

As soon as I'm in the house, I slip on my bikini and head for a swim, needing to burn off some energy. I wade into the water, enjoying the feel of cool water on my skin. We never had a pool in New York, but if we did, I'd have lived in it. Luxuries like this are just wasted on the twins.

I swim a few laps before turning onto my back. The air is

dark and clear, so I can see a few stars in the sky. I close my eyes and hold my breath, dipping below the surface. Down here, it is peaceful, so I let my thoughts drift. I start off by thinking about Dad, as always, but then my thoughts shift through the different combinations I've learned, to the feeling I get when I'm standing in that ring. Finally, I think about today and how much fun I had on the pier with Hayden.

"Maddie."

I break the surface at the calling of my name. Dylan stands by the door, his head tilted slightly as he looks at the sky. "Where did you guys go?"

My heart skips a beat. For some reason, I want to keep the trip to the pier to myself. "The gym," I say. "Hayden wanted to show me some new equipment he'd ordered."

He finally looks at me. His eyes are usually bright and sincere, but tonight they are dark. He steps forward now, into the moonlight, and crouches beside me. "You should be careful around Hayden. He's not a good person."

Maybe it's the breeze or the fact that I'm wet, but a shiver runs down my spine. "You're the one who kissed his girlfriend, Dylan."

Hurt crosses his face, and I immediately regret what I've said. "I'd had a crush on Caitlyn for *years*," he says quietly. "We were both in music club and had a lot in common." I tense in the water, not sure if I want to hear the rest of this story. "He barely acted like a boyfriend to her. One day, she came over after they'd had an argument, and we ended up kissing." He must notice my horror, because he adds, "I stopped it straight away, but I guess she felt guilty about it, because she told him. He's been threatening to get back at me ever since." He stops for a second to shoot me a look. "I guess he's found a way."

My heart rate quickens. "Me?"

Dylan nods. "It's too much of a coincidence otherwise." He shakes his head. "Just promise me that whatever line he feeds you, you won't fall for it."

I turn to Dylan, who is still staring at me like he's waiting for an answer. "I promise."

No longer in the mood for a swim, I climb out and get ready for bed before calling Jamie. We haven't spoken in a while, and after going to the pier with Hayden—which had started to feel like a date—I'm feeling like the worst person in the world.

"Hey," he says after the first ring. "Long time no hear."

"I know, sorry. I've just been superbusy."

He shuffles around, and I know it's because he's getting ready for bed. "How's the gym?" He says *gym* like I'm doing something offensive.

"It was fine. How's lacrosse?" I stretch out my legs, only now just feeling the dull ache in my limbs from our session last night. It's like the pain becomes easy to ignore, but the moment you're aware of it, you can't think of anything else. I think of Hayden and wonder if he lies in bed with sore muscles or if his body is used to this by now.

"It was fine," he says, and then he starts talking about some project he's working on, and I can't help but feel the distance between us. He's made some new friends outside of school, so he's bringing up names of people I've never even met. I try to talk about the gym, but I know he's not happy about it, so it leads to dead ends. We both grasp at straws, trying to keep the conversation going, but eventually, we run out of things to say. When we go to sleep, it feels like the end. All that's left is for one of us to actually say it, and maybe that needs to be me, but the thought is too terrifying.

Leaving Jamie means leaving behind safety and stepping into the unknown. It means figuring out who I am when I don't have his love, his support. And what if I leave him and I realize that actually, who I am when I'm without him is no one?

Panic sets in as I feel him slip away before my eyes. Right now it feels like there's more than just physical distance between us, and I'm racking my brain for a way I can fix this, a way I can hold on to him that little bit longer, because the thought of being without him is impossible to comprehend. I just want to cuddle him, to lean my head on his chest and feel the familiar thrum of his heartbeat under my ear.

This can't be the end.

CHAPTER ELEVEN

Jamie is the one to end it. He calls me the following week, much later than usual, so I know there is something on his mind. It takes a little bit of small talk to coax it out of him, but he finally admits it: he doesn't want me anymore.

The first thing I feel is relief, followed by panic. I'd known it was coming, that long distance wasn't working, but I've been too scared to admit it. How do you say good-bye to two years of your life? How do you give up on something you thought that you wanted? I'd spent every day with Jamie back in New York; the thought of never seeing him again feels like I can't breathe. And yet there is the tiniest part of me that feels this relief, like a weight has been lifted off my chest. My relationship with Jamie feels like one step in the opposite direction, and growing closer with Hayden, loving training, finding a new life here, well, that was the other.

I lower myself onto the bed, phone to my ear, and wonder what I could have done differently. If this was all because of me. Did I put in enough effort? Did I make him feel special? Why doesn't he want me anymore?

The phone call is short. We spent nearly two years together, and it only takes two minutes to end it. We both say good-bye and promise to stay friends, but I know, deep down, this is the last I will hear from him. I can just feel it in his voice, thick with emotion, like this is something he's been contemplating a while. If I'm being completely honest, I think that's what hurts the most, the fact I've been going along as normal, blissfully unaware that the person I love has been planning to leave me after promising me forever. I guess even forever must end.

My mom knocks on the door in the thick of my crying to ask if I want some food. She sees me crying, and just like I'd done that night she'd cried over Dad, she curls up behind me and wraps an arm around my waist.

"Do you want to talk about it?" she whispers.

I shake my head at the same time my lips say, "Jamie broke up with me." And then, just like that, the invisible thread inside *me* snaps, and my body crumples like paper. For some reason, I expect her to convince me to get Jamie back, that to my mother, nobody will measure up to him, but she doesn't. She just holds me and strokes my hair, looking after me the same way I'd looked after her, repaying the favor. And for a moment, even though I'm heartbroken, a part of me is grateful this happened just so I could have my mom back.

—

I wake up Saturday morning in a human burrito. Kavi is on one side, snuggled into my shoulder as she gently snores away. June is on my other, one arm across my torso and the other tucked awkwardly under my pillow.

For the last two days, June and Kavi have tried every trick in the book to help me forget about Jamie, including a movie marathon, but I can't shake this funk I'm in. Not just because of Jamie, but because prom is in two weeks, which means soon I'll be graduating and going to college, and I don't feel ready for any of it. Not graduation, not my fight, not anything. The thought of Dad showing up one day casts a dark glow to everything.

The smell of breakfast fills the air. Whatever Tim is baking, it seems to involve cinnamon. I stretch out my legs into the little room I have and glance over at Kavi. "You talk in your sleep," she mumbles, her eyes half-closed. "Really bad."

"You snore," I say.

"Do not." She sits up in bed, her straight hair sticking up in different directions. We both look at June, who is not only snoring and murmuring, but drooling too. Kavi turns back to me, running a hand through her hair before giving up and lying back down.

"You're not still thinking about him, are you?" she asks.

I snuggle deeper into the pillows of the fluffy comforter and let my body relax. I've been training so often now that I don't wake up with that *hit by a bus* feeling I did in the beginning, and I like that. It makes me feel like all the hard work I've been putting in is actually paying off.

"You better not be," June mumbles. "He didn't deserve you anyway. I mean, I didn't want to say anything in case you hit me or something, but he was so controlling. What was with him telling you what to wear that one time?"

Kavi lifts her head a little. "He did? When?"

"The night Olly and I made out," she says, and the biggest grin crosses her face. Ever since the party, June and Olly have taken their fling to a whole new level. I'm constantly coming home from training to find June in Olly's room, *studying*.

"He didn't tell me what to wear," I say, but now with both her and Hayden bringing it up, is there some truth to what they're saying? I have never thought of Jamie as controlling, not when I've grown up with a man like my dad, and the two are not comparable.

"Whatever," June says. "Now you're free to find someone else. Not Hayden."

My heart does this weird, tiny flutter. "Why on earth would you say Hayden?"

She shrugs. "You guys spend a lot of time training together. Close contact plus sweaty bodies can make people start to develop . . . a thing. Plus, hello, I kissed him, remember? I know how charming he can be."

The thought of Hayden charming June makes me queasy. "No one is developing anything," I assure her.

"Good." She sits up properly and reaches for my laptop, switching the horror film we'd started last night back on. Kavi groans and snuggles into my shoulder in an attempt to cover her eyes. Despite her penchant for murder documentaries, she can't stand gore. We settle back down under the duvets together, and I realize I was wrong before—I'm not alone.

At six, when it's time for my session with Hayden, I'm unusually nervous as I drive to the gym. A part of me had wanted to cancel and just veg out in bed, but training has become such a staple part of my routine, it didn't feel right.

Instead, I walk into the gym with the plan to get through my session as quietly as possible, but ten minutes into the lesson, Hayden stops stretching to examine me.

"What's wrong with you?" he asks.

"What makes you think something is wrong?"

He reaches into the equipment box and pulls out my gloves. Slowly, he takes my hands and wraps them up before sliding on the gloves. "You're weirdly quiet and scowling."

"I don't scowl."

"Yeah, you do." His eyebrow arches. "You're not so good at hiding your emotions."

"Or maybe you spend too much time examining me."

He takes a step back and folds his arms, nodding at the punching bag. "Ready when you are, then."

There's a brief hesitation as that familiar feeling of self-consciousness hits, but then I decide I don't care. I turn to the bag, take a deep breath, and start punching. It's not just Jamie I'm punching for, it's mostly my dad. I picture his warm grin and his stupid eyes and I punch harder than ever, like maybe if it's hard enough, he'll be able to feel it. I'll be able to hurt him the way he hurt us.

Anger consumes me until it burns at my throat. I hit harder to get rid of it, but it just grows and churns around in my chest, refusing to die. So I punch and punch, and it's only when I'm struggling to breathe that I realize it's no longer my dad I'm imagining: it's me.

I suddenly start to feel light-headed. The next thing I know, Hayden has got his arms around me and is pulling me to his chest. I'm breathing hard, inhaling, exhaling, inhaling, exhaling, but it doesn't seem to be working.

"Hey, it's all right," he says, gripping me tight. "Just take a deep breath. I've got you." His arms feel heavy and strong around my body, keeping me grounded. I lean in slightly, letting my body relax into his.

It takes several minutes for me to finally calm down, and when I do, I am mortified. Hayden is still holding me like he's afraid to let go, so I shift out of his arms before turning to face him.

"Sorry," I say. "I got a little dizzy." I look at the wall, at the floor, anywhere but his scrutinizing eyes.

He steps into my line of vision, forcing me to look at him. "What's wrong?"

"Nothing, I'm fine."

"I'd say you're the opposite of fine." His eyes search my face, impatient and demanding. "Tell me."

I'm not sure what to say, so I don't say anything. I'm mad at myself for getting like this. I'm usually great at keeping it together, but with him, it's harder to pretend. "Look, can we just forget about this? I don't feel like talking about it."

I can tell by his face that he isn't going to drop it, and I'm right. "I've been where you are," he says, and when he steps forward, it takes everything I have not to take a step back. "I was angry for a long time."

"About your dad dying?"

He nods briefly. "I kept thinking the anger would go away one day, but it didn't." His eyes cloud over. In them is a layer of vulnerability I have never seen before. "I was sparring with this guy I didn't get along with too well. He said some stuff that riled me, and I let my emotions get the better of me." He looks away, like he can't bear to look at me. "It was bad—I could have killed him."

Hearing this causes me to flinch. "Is that what you meant when you said you let your emotions get in the way?"

He nods again, and I can tell this is hard for him. "That's the reason everyone thinks I'm some weird, dangerous guy. I brought my demons into the ring, thinking it would help make me a better fighter. The only thing it did was help destroy me."

I'm quiet for a few moments as I study his face. I have never seen this side of him before, this vulnerable, nonscowling side. This human side. "Jamie broke up with me."

Another tear trails my cheek. I haven't cried in front of someone in years, but for some reason, my body thinks now is a good time to start. Another tear slips out before I can stop it. Just as I'm reaching up to wipe it away, Hayden does it for me.

"Good," he whispers. His thumb still lingers on the curve of my cheek, soft and warm. I wish he would keep it there. I wish I could have this version of him forever. "He didn't deserve you."

His words sink right into my soul. My heart flips, I shift away from him, needing to do some damage control. "I'm not usually a crier," I say, fiddling with my necklace. It's the one Jamie got me; I have no idea why I'm still wearing it. "I mean, unless I'm watching a sad movie or something. Then I can't stop." I'm babbling, and I know it. It seems whenever I'm around Hayden, I turn into this bumbling idiot. From the look in his eyes, though, he doesn't seem to mind. "Thank you."

His eyebrow arches. I can tell he's surprised. "For what?"

"For not laughing at me, I guess." As I say it, I reach out and touch the side of his arm. I do it because I've been dying to touch him, and I need an excuse. "You're not as bad as I thought you were."

Something electric passes between us. His eyes burn through mine, intense, scrutinizing, but I find I'm not embarrassed this time; I want him to look at me. He feels it, too, this heat between us. I know he does. I can tell by the way he watches my lips that he's thinking the same thing I am.

I'm thinking about prying his lips apart to discover how he tastes. I don't know why I imagine this specifically—it's not like I've ever done it before. I'm used to innocent kisses, to kisses with lips slightly parted but never with tongue; kisses that are easily forgotten. The kiss I'm thinking about having right now is the kind you want to replay.

He must know this, too, because his eyes flash with something suggestive. I take a step closer, an innocent step, leaving the tiniest space between us. We're close enough that I can smell the fabric softener on his clothes and the hint of mint on his breath. Close enough that I can make out the fine, pink lines in his lips. His eyes are dark as they search my face, daring me to move.

"Come on, Maddie," he whispers. "Shock me."

His voice is low, deep, and the slight plea in his tone does something strange to my insides. Heat burns through me, igniting a flame that only he can put out; I'm certain of it. I don't think about all of the reasons I shouldn't. I don't think about the countless other girls he's been with. All I can think about as I stare at his lips is how badly I want to kiss him, so I do.

The moment our lips touch, I feel his sharp intake of breath. I've finally done it, I've finally shocked him, but it doesn't last long. He grabs my waist and pulls me toward him, kissing me back.

My breathing is ragged and out of control. His mouth

leaves my lips, and I let out a whimper as he moves to my neck, kissing near my jaw. I have never ever felt like this before: desired and excited and alive.

He brings his hands to either side of my neck, his lips back on mine, pushing and pushing, like he can't get enough. Like he needs to take more. "Maddie." He says it with his mouth still on mine, so his voice is all muffled. I don't bother replying. I can no longer form anything even slightly coherent; every thought is consumed by him.

He takes me by the waist, pulling us back onto the mat without breaking our kiss. He's got me pinned to the floor, his chest rising and falling as quickly as my own, his teeth nibbling my neck. I never want this moment to end. I want it to keep going and going, but I know where we are headed.

I put both hands on his chest. I mean to push him away, but I don't apply pressure. I'm too distracted by the way his hand is creeping up my thigh, sending shivers through my body. I need to stop this. *Stop, stop, stop, don't stop*. His fingers reach the waistband of my yoga pants, and I gasp.

"Wait!" My hands apply pressure now, enough to keep him still. When I look into his eyes, they are dark, his lips red and swollen from my kisses. There are love bites on his neck, pink and fresh. Did I make those?

"I'm sorry," I say, staring at his chest. "I need to go."

For a second, he doesn't move. Then slowly, he lifts himself off me and gets to his feet, readjusting his sweatpants. I continue to stare at him, breathless and nauseous. Hayden looks down at me and offers a hand, which I reluctantly take. He pulls me to my feet until I'm standing right in front of him.

"I really need to go," I say, grabbing my stuff. "I'll see you on Wednesday."

"Wait," Hayden says, his voice low and rough, but I am already gone.

I end up spilling my guts to Kavi and June in the courtyard. It's strange, the old me would *never* have divulged something so personal, which means wanting to tell them, being almost excited, means I must trust them completely. The thought makes me happy.

"I *knew* it," June says as she leans across the picnic table. "I knew something would end up happening. My Spidey sense was tingling." She turns to Kavi, who is clearly still trying to process this information, because her mouth is still shaped like the perfect O. "If you kiss him, too, we can start some kind of club," she says. "The three Kissateers. The Hayden Diaries. Three girls and a Hayden."

"Stop," Kavi says, turning to me. "How do you feel about it? Do you like him?"

I shrug as I pick at my sandwich. I should be focusing on my fight, which is in just a few weeks, or the fact that Dad could turn up at any moment. I have enough on my plate without adding Hayden to the menu, but I can't deny that there's this warmth in my chest when I think of that kiss, and as the pair of them stare back at me, I can't help but grin.

"Oh my God," June says. "You *do* like him!"

I raise my hands in defeat. "I don't know, okay? I guess I'll just see how it goes, but please don't tell Dylan."

"We won't," Kavi says as we finish off our lunch, "but just be careful, okay?"

"I will be," I say, and I mean it.

I arrive at my next training session two minutes early. I'd been obsessing all night, wondering how this session would go after what happened last night, whether it was going to be awkward. As much as I'd enjoyed that kiss, I'm not an idiot. Getting involved with someone like Hayden would just be setting myself up for heartache.

Music blears from the stereo speakers as Hayden pounds a punching bag. He turns when he sees me, his chest rising heavily as he tries to catch his breath. Sweat drenches the front of his T-shirt. His hair is damp, clinging in curly tendrils to the top of his forehead. It shouldn't excite me to see him like this, but it does.

He smirks like he can read my mind. Without warning, he pulls off his T-shirt and uses it to wipe the sweat from his face before he throws it by his feet. I'm about to make a comment when I realize that's what he wants, so instead, I gear up and meet him in the ring.

We circle each other for a little while, allowing me to practice my combos. The way Hayden moves is always so graceful, like this is part of a dance; I haven't quite mastered the skill. Still, the closer it gets to fight night, the more prepared I feel. If anything, my dad learning we're in California has only made me more determined to throw everything I have into this fight. I can't control if or when he shows up, but I can control this.

"Listen," he says. "I'm sorry about last night. I shouldn't have kissed you like that."

My heart beats twice as fast as I land another jab. He regrets it, of course he does. "It's fine, it was a mistake." He raises an eyebrow but doesn't say anything. I expected as much. "I was upset about the breakup and I wasn't really thinking."

Hayden steps closer. His hand brushes my face, catching a tendril of hair in his fingers. "Did you feel anything? When you kissed me, I mean."

"Yeah, shame," I joke. This is all just too much. Last year I was in a committed relationship with a boy I was madly in love with. Now I'm standing in a boxing ring with a notorious womanizer.

"I'm serious," he says. "Did you?"

I swallow hard. "Why are you so obsessed about one kiss?"

"You're a good kisser." His voice lowers and takes on a husky tone. "I mean, I was surprised, considering what a princess you are. Maybe it was a fluke."

I narrow my eyes. "It wasn't a fluke."

"Prove it." His eyes gleam back, daring me to shock him again. For a second, I want to. But I know why Hayden wants to kiss me again—it doesn't take a rocket scientist to figure it out. He's already told me he doesn't do relationships, and guys like him are all about the chase. The second he gets his way, he'll be gone.

"Like I'd fall for that," I say, landing another jab.

He doesn't see it coming, so he stumbles back an inch. Briefly, I see what looks like hurt in his eyes, but it doesn't last long. Without warning, Hayden swings, but I duck before he can hit me, swooping behind him as quick as a flash.

"You're getting fast."

"Thanks."

He goes to hit me and I do the same thing, dipping before

he makes contact. We dance around like this, him trying to jab me while I dip and dive, avoiding being hit.

When he starts to grow agitated, I swing. My jab gets him right in the throat. I physically see the air leave his lungs, and he drops to his knees. I throw off my helmet and sink to my knees, holding either side of his face. "I'm so, so sorry," I say. "Are you okay, Hayden?" His chest rises and falls in quick succession. His eyes are shaky and watery as he rubs at his throat. I feel absolutely terrible. "Please tell me you're okay," I say. "I'm so sorry."

He looks at me through my hands, his eyes wild and childlike. "You're not . . . supposed . . . to punch in the throat."

"I know," I say, stroking his cheek. "It was a bad aim. Are you okay?"

He takes another minute to catch his breath before looking at me properly. "A move like that in the ring and you'll be in serious trouble. You could have broken my larynx." He pauses, then, "I think you should kiss it better."

I'm about to say no and let go of his face, but I can tell that's what he expects. Instead, I lower my head and press my lips to his Adam's apple. I feel him take in a sharp, quick breath. He's still beneath my touch as though he hasn't prepared himself for me actually doing this. I deepen the kiss, lightly brushing my tongue against his skin.

My heart races the way it always does around him, and I run a hand along his abs. It's like my thoughts switch off, and I'm being controlled by my body instead of the other way round, but instead of fighting it, I let it happen.

I reach up to kiss him, and it feels different this time. His kisses are hard, but it doesn't feel like lust. It feels hot, and raw;

it feels like he needs me. His arms lock around me, solid and warm. I can't imagine another body fitting better with mine. It's like our bodies were made for this, right down to the way my face sits comfortably in his neck.

"What are you doing to me?" he says softly.

I don't stop kissing him. I like this power that I seem to have over him, it makes me feel special. I know it's not true—Hayden has been with countless girls who probably felt the same thing—but right now, it's easy to pretend.

His mouth catches mine before he moves to my ear, the warmth of his breath sending shivers down my arms. I had no idea kissing could make me feel like this. I've felt that slight tingle with Jamie before, that desire to continue, but this—this is something else entirely. His hand slowly moves from my waist to my stomach, resting on the waistband of my jeans. His eyes search mine, intense, and impatient, waiting for permission. Briefly, I nod.

His eyes don't leave mine as he takes my hand and leads me into the office, closing the door behind us. He lowers me onto the bed without breaking our kiss, moving on top of me. With one hand, he props himself up to take off some of his weight and uses the other to lightly brush my pants.

My heart is pounding. I wonder how it's possible to feel this scared and this excited. "Why is there a bed in here?"

He laughs a little, like he can't believe this is what I'm thinking about. "My dad used to stay so late that he'd end up falling asleep at his desk, so he converted his office into a bedroom."

His mouth finds mine again, warm and demanding. His fingers slip beneath my pants, resting on the hem of my underwear. I suck in a breath, unable to stop myself. He must like this reaction because he smiles against my lips.

He pulls back a little to look at me properly, his hand slipping into my underwear. His fingers feel warm, and I shiver against him. Hayden breathes sharply, his green eyes on fire. It's the way he's looking at me that turns me on more than anything, like I possess the ability to make him lose all restraint.

His fingers move slowly in circular motions. I let out a moan, and he buries his face directly in my neck, letting out a growl of his own. Every nerve in my body seems to pulsate at once. His touch is soft, gentle, and it causes little electric sensations to shoot through my skin. It seems impossible to fathom that I'm doing this with Hayden, but it doesn't feel wrong.

Hayden moves his mouth to my neck, leaving a trail of kisses down my chest. His fingers continue to rub and pinch, forcing me to arch my back as the feeling in my stomach intensifies. It grows and grows, filling up my belly and thighs until I'm ready to burst, and then it feels like I do.

Slowly, Hayden's lips move back to my mouth as he pulls his hand away. He's still for a second or two before he pushes himself off me and lies on his side. Briefly, he looks at me, and my heart sinks. I feel vulnerable, exposed, and any minute, I expect him to get up and tell me to leave like I'm just another conquest. But he doesn't. He throws an arm around my waist and pulls me in closer. I remain stiff in his arms, too afraid to move or do something wrong—too afraid to breathe.

A million thoughts start to race through my mind, half of them incoherent. I don't know what this means or what will happen after this, but one thing is certain: after tonight, there is no going back.

"Hayden?"

"Hmm?"

I pause, and then, "Why don't you do relationships?"

He shifts his focus to the ceiling. "I just don't."

"There must be a reason." Something tells me it has to do with Caitlyn cheating, but I want to hear it from him.

"There isn't." He slips out from under me and gets to his feet, so I do the same. His reaction annoys me. If this is how he reacts to a simple question, how is he going to react to literally anything else?

He must sense my mood change, because he takes a step forward and brushes my cheek. He leans in to kiss me, but I dodge it.

"Okay," I say, "well, I'm not really the kind of person who does casual."

His eyes burn back with a strange intensity. Every nerve in my body tells me to look away from those eyes, but they're holding me in position. "I'm not trying to be an asshole, but if we dated, one thing would lead to another and—"

"Isn't that what's supposed to happen?"

"Not with me."

Those words send chills down my spine. I fold my arms and wait for him to elaborate, but he doesn't. "What are you saying?"

He steps forward, closing the sliver of distance between us. "I'm not good at being a boyfriend. I'd only disappoint you."

"We don't know that because you haven't even tried."

His chest is rising and falling as fast as my own. His jaw

is still clenched, his bright eyes as defiant and unwavering as ever. "I'm not changing my mind."

Rejection burns through me, but maybe it's for the best. My mother once told me that fireworks always fizzle out in the end. What feels good in the moment never lasts beyond it. Real love isn't passion and fireworks, it is safety and comfort; it is being accepted even on the days when you can't accept yourself. It's something she never got to experience with Dad, something I'd had—and thrown away—with Jamie.

"Fine, then I'm not kissing you anymore. From now on, the rest of our sessions need to stay professional. There's less than a week until the fight, and that's what I need to concentrate on."

His jaw contracts, and for a moment I think he's about to give in. But then he takes a step back and shrugs a shoulder, refusing to be challenged. "Fine." He doesn't say anything else. I wait for a second, hoping he'll tell me he's changed his mind, but he doesn't. I tell myself it's for the best.

CHAPTER TWELVE

The morning of prom, June comes over early so that we can get ready together. I should be happy, but I can't get rid of this feeling in my chest, like everything I'm doing is just taking me one step closer to a life of uncertainty.

After lunch, we go to the hair salon. As I sit in the chair, staring at my reflection while she tames the wild frizz in my hair, I keep thinking about how much has changed in such a short time. I've gained things, like friends and a family and a less uptight attitude, but I've also lost things, like Jamie and my comfort zone.

By the time the hairstylist is finished, my hair has been pulled into a high bun, similar to the one I'd wear for ballet, except more sophisticated.

For the tiniest moment, I wish Dad were here to see me like this. We used to talk about what prom would be like. He'd tell me that I better be ready to have a million pictures taken, because there was no way I was leaving the house until his camera roll was full, and now he's not going to get to see me in my dress, my hair all fancy and pretty.

Jamie was going to FaceTime me tonight too. His prom isn't until May, but he was going to wear the suit we bought together while holding a corsage to the camera. It's hard to believe that it's over. Everything is changing so fast.

Jamie must be feeling it, too, this loss, because a message comes through from him telling me he hopes I have a good prom. I stare at the words for what feels like forever. Even though I still love him, something feels different. *I* feel different. I text him a thank-you and put my phone away.

"You're not thinking about Hayden, are you?" June says. "The guy's a loser, especially if he doesn't want to lock down someone like you."

I roll my eyes. I'd told her all about what happened with Hayden and him not wanting a relationship. I half expected her to say, *I told you so,* but June isn't like that; she just listened without judgment.

"I'm not, I'm thinking about how fast everything is changing," I say. "Don't you think it's fast?"

"Definitely," she says, "but I'm excited, you know? It's like starting a new movie, where you don't know the plot or the characters, but you just know you're in for a wild time. I can't wait."

The way she explains it, I kind of can't wait either.

When June and I are ready—her in a floor-length, pale pink dress, and me in my champagne slip dress—we flip a coin about who will make our grand entrance first. It lands on heads, me, so as soon as I'm ready, I start my descent.

Dylan is standing at the bottom of the stairs, where Lilly and Tim are busy fawning over him. His fingers are tapping a rhythm on his leg, so I know he must be nervous too. As soon as he sees me, he stands up. He raises his eyebrows.

"Wow."

"Thank you. You look nice too."

His tux fits him perfectly, equipped with a little bow tie that he keeps readjusting. When I get to the bottom of the stairs, he slips my corsage on my wrist and we wait to the side for June.

Olly jumps to his feet when June comes down, and the way he looks at her, it's clear he's in love. He pins a corsage on her, and her face lights up as she kisses his cheek.

Mom, Lilly, and Tim spend the next twenty minutes snapping pictures of us in different positions, until finally Dylan says, "Okay, let's go," and we all breathe a sigh of relief.

I still can't quite believe it. This night was supposed to be mine and Jamie's, but I don't feel as sad as I thought I would. If anything, I'm glad that I'm here with the twins and June; it feels right.

As soon as we get to prom, we get in line for our prom pictures and then join the rest of our class on the dance floor. Kavi and Zion are already here, and the moment she sees us she pulls me and June into a three-way hug. It's all so emotional, so raw, like we're coming to an end of an era. Deep down, I wish Hayden were here too.

After several upbeat songs where we dance as a group, a slow song comes on. Dylan and I look at each other awkwardly, wondering if we should sit this one out, but then he offers his hands and we join Olly and June on the dance floor.

It's wrong, but even though I came here with Dylan, I keep scanning the hall, expecting to see Hayden show up, and when he doesn't, I'm disappointed. I shouldn't care—I don't.

They announce the homecoming queen and king, which fills me with a sense of nostalgia. It's the kind of thing I'd care about back home—being homecoming queen—but between moving to California, Dad, and training, none of that stuff seems to matter anymore.

One last dance. It really feels like the end now, not just of high school, but everything. In a few months' time, we'll all go off to college and these memories will fade and fragment with time, just like my memories of Dad.

"Are you nervous about your fight?" Dylan asks. His mouth is ridiculously close to my ear, and I can feel the warmth of his breath on my cheek. "I mean, do you feel prepared?"

"I don't think you ever really feel prepared," I say, "but I've done all I can do."

He nods as his hands clutch me tighter. "I don't get why you're doing it," he says slowly, "but I'm proud of you. It takes a lot of courage to go through with something like that."

My eyebrows fly up, because *courageous* is never a word I'd have used to describe myself, but hearing it from him makes me want to believe it. As the long song plays through the speakers, I lean my head in his shoulder and look over at June, who is doing the same with Olly. For so long it feels like I've been living in the future, worrying about things that haven't yet happened, but right now I'm content with the present.

CHAPTER THIRTEEN

The night before the fight, I barely get a wink of sleep: a combination of nerves and embarrassment has me tossing and turning, which means I end up sleeping in until midafternoon. When I finally wake, it's to a text from Hayden. I hold my breath and open the message, not knowing what to expect.

Jenson booked us two rooms at the MGM Grand.

It seems absurd to lie about going to Vegas when I've always told my mother the truth. But this is something she'd never understand, and the last thing I want is to make her worry when she's doing so well.

I message back a simple "okay." The past week between us hasn't felt *strained* per se, but ever since we swore to each other that neither of us would cave, our sessions have been strictly platonic. A huge part of me is still mad that we'd done what we did and he didn't want more, even though I have no reason to be. I've always known Hayden doesn't do relationships—he'd made it clear from the start—and who I'm really mad at is myself.

Feeling exhausted, I sit up in bed and get ready. Despite getting nearly ten hours of sleep, it feels like I've hardly even slept. I spend the rest of the day thinking too much. Then thinking too little. Then thinking about thinking. My head starts to hurt, and I know if I don't snap out of this funk, I'll stand no chance tonight. But I can't seem to pinpoint what's causing it all: my father? The fight? My declaration to Hayden? Or more than likely, all three.

A text comes through from June not long after. *You're going to kick ass tonight, literally. Send me a selfie when you're there!*

I send a fingers-crossed emoji back. When I'm ready, I head into the living room where Mom and Lilly are watching TV and remind them I'm heading over to June's. Mom tells me to have a good time, which makes me feel guilty for lying, but for once I'm excited to do something that's just about me, and I refuse to let guilt ruin that.

Hayden is waiting at the end of the street in his car, and I climb in without saying anything, throwing my bag in the back before looking straight ahead.

"Aren't you a ray of sunshine."

"Just drive."

"Yes, ma'am," he says.

The journey is quiet for the first half an hour until finally, he cracks. He turns up the radio and shoots me an agitated look. "How long are you going to stay mad at me?"

"I'm not mad."

"We've already established that you have a bad poker face."

"I'm not mad."

He looks at me again, a wicked gleam in his eye. "Sure."

We get to the hotel around five and meet Jenson and his crew in the lobby. I have never been to Vegas, but the hotel is exactly as I expected. The lobby is huge and made of marble, from the floors to the walls to the ceiling. Everywhere I turn there is the pinging of slot machines, and before me is a fountain of flowers, in the middle of which is a gold brass lion.

"About time you two showed up," Jenson says. "I've already checked you in." He reaches into his pocket and pulls out our keys, handing them to us. "You better stick to your own room," he says, giving Hayden a look. "I mean it."

Hayden rolls his eyes. "I will."

"Good," Jenson says. "Those of us who are old enough are going off to gamble. Stay out of the casino, kids."

I follow Hayden into the elevator. The mirror opposite shows me what we look like together: he's three heads taller and built like an action figure—I look like a toothpick.

Our rooms are on the fifth floor, three doors down from each other. He follows me into mine, and we stand in the hallway for a second as I take it all in. It's spacious, with a dark patterned carpet, a large double bed, and an incredible view of the Las Vegas strip. I take a picture of the view and send it to the girls, who both immediately reply.

OMG, so jealous! June says. *Don't even think about having sexy time with Hayden.*

Good luck! Kavi says. *Make sure you stay safe over there.*

Suddenly nervous, I tell them I'll be fine, but it feels like I'm convincing myself more than them.

Hayden sits in the armchair and turns on the TV. I try to focus on the show on the screen, but with the fight getting closer, it's hard to concentrate on anything else. Nerves get the best of me. I run into the bathroom and drop to my knees, throwing up into the bowl.

Hayden is right behind me in seconds, pulling my hair back. "Let it all out," he says, his voice soothing, so I do.

When I'm finished, I wipe my mouth and turn to face him, utterly horrified. Like it's not bad enough that I made a fool of myself the other night—now he's seen me throw up too.

He sits back on his knees, looking at me, but he doesn't look disgusted. "Are you okay?"

I shake my head, able to hear my heartbeat through my ears. "I don't know if I can do this."

He reaches out, pushing a strand of hair from my face. "If you don't want to do it, you don't have to—but you can do this. I know you can. Remember why you wanted to do this in the first place. Don't let your nerves get the best of you."

I close my eyes and force myself to remember. "Okay."

Hayden gets to his feet, helping to pull me to mine. "That's my girl."

Turning to face the mirror, I try my hardest not to look at him. "I'm going to take a quick shower."

As soon as he's gone, I strip and step under the water, allowing it to loosen my muscles. It feels like heaven, and I start to wish that we could just hole up in this hotel room and watch movies all night.

It's almost time. I climb out and quickly blow dry my hair, plaiting it into two French braids before studying myself in the mirror. I look ready and strong, sure of myself, not like a girl who's spent the past few years feeling lost. I like this girl I see in the mirror—I want her to stay.

Hayden is ready to go when I'm finished. He stands up and pauses, taking me in. "Your hair looks good like that." He crosses the room until he's standing right in front of me, then touches the end of my braid. It's unnerving standing this close to him, especially after last night, but I can't step away.

"Wish me luck?" I ask.

He lets my braid go, brushing my cheek with his thumb, instead. I tense a little and his eyes search mine, dark and concerned. "Remember to keep yourself protected," he says. "Hands high at all times."

I swallow hard. "I'll be fine," I say. "We should probably get going."

With one last look, Hayden nods and steps back. I turn on my heel, following him out of the hotel door. Jenson and a security guard lead us through the lobby and casino, which is packed. It feels like I might throw up with every step. At one point, when I think I might actually do it, I feel Hayden's fingers entwine with mine.

We're led into the back room of the venue, which the security guard says is just for me. Another man walks in and explains that there are several different fights tonight, with my fight being the first, and then leaves me to get myself ready.

Jenson pulls me into a fatherly hug. "I'm sure you'll do fine," he says. "As much of a knucklehead as this guy is, he knows what he's doing."

I breathe in deep, then release it slowly. "I'm so nervous."

"Everyone is before a fight," Jenson says. "Just don't let it control you."

I'm about to ask him how exactly I stop myself from doing that, but he's already hurrying out.

Hayden gets me to take a seat on the stool and hold out my hands, allowing him to wrap them. He does each hand slowly, letting his fingers trail my skin in soft, gentle brushes. It calms me, this movement, and I close my eyes, focusing on his touch.

When he's finished, I unzip my hoodie, revealing the cropped black sports top beneath. I carefully fold the hoodie across the chair and get to my feet, surprised when Hayden pulls me into a hug.

"Remember, you won't see me in your corner, but I'll be in the front of the crowd, all right? If you need anything, or if you want to stop, just tell us."

"I know," I say, pulling back. "Thank you."

He looks like he's going to say something important, but the man comes back and tells me it's almost time. I throw a panicked look at Hayden, who grabs my hand and squeezes it hard. I slip in my mouth guard, and Hayden picks up my helmet before sliding it over my head.

"You'll be fine," he says, his voice low, and he roughly kisses my forehead.

"We need to get your gloves on," Hayden says. He slips the gloves on my hands and I turn to the door. It's suddenly thrown open, and I'm ushered into a dimly lit venue.

What looks like a catwalk leads up to the boxing ring, where my opponent is already waiting. Around the outskirts are crowded dining tables, where people are eating their meals.

My heart pounds in time with my footsteps. I'm acutely aware of all the patrons watching me from their tables, sizing me up. I have never felt more on display. I slip through the ropes and join her, trying to still my heart. She's around my size, with bright blond hair scraped back into a bun, and small, narrowed eyes. A smile makes its way through my mouthpiece, but her eyes remain stony.

The referee is saying something, but I can't work out what. The overhead lights feel hot and blinding. The sound of my heartbeat is thumping through my ears. I pretend I'm back in Hayden's gym, that it's him opposite me now, and it works a little to ease my nerves. Not much, but enough.

The crowd gets louder, and after a simple introduction, the match begins. I circle her the way Hayden would do and try to focus on what he taught me: feet apart, hands up, and with each movement I perfect, I feel the anxiety dissipate.

She suddenly jabs, but I swerve, and her fist goes flying through the air. I hit back quickly, more quickly than she can recover, and land a heavy blow to her cheek. She stumbles back and into the ropes, dizzy. Behind her, I spot Hayden front and center in the crowd, next to the referee. He flashes a grin that makes my heart soar, and I realize it's no longer just fear I feel—it's adrenaline.

The first two minutes feel easy. Maybe I'm quick, or cocky, or maybe she's slow, but I dodge her hits without taking much damage, allowing me to go on the offense. She doesn't dodge—or can't—which means I land multiple blows while remaining unscathed.

It hits me that I have a good chance of winning. I'm still terrified and tired and feel like a fraud, but inside, I have hope. I'm dancing circles around this girl, and she's looking a mess: bloody lip, hair unraveled from her bun. For all my worrying and fear, I am going to win.

And then I see him, sitting at one of the tables. It's hard to make out any faces from here, but I'd recognize him anywhere. Tall and stocky, with dark hair and a wide, grinning mouth.

My father has found me.

I don't see the hit, but I certainly feel it. My face explodes with pain, and I stumble back and grab the ropes, using them to keep me balanced. I gasp and pant as the crowd cheers out, excited by this turn of events.

This can't be happening. It can't be real. I lift myself up and look to where he stands, but I can't seem to find him. There's a man still standing there, watching the fight. He's the same height and build, with light brown skin and jet black hair, but he isn't my father. I search the crowd, over and over, wondering if I'm going insane. Wondering if this is what it feels like to slowly lose your mind. But I don't have time to wonder for long, because another hit comes, this time to my jaw.

The impact throws me back and I land on the floor, watching the room spin. It all feels the same in the end. A punch from her or a punch from my father—it all feels the same.

Crawling to my knees, I stare past the crowd to the back. I keep looking at this man, expecting him to morph back into my father, but he doesn't. When I look at my opponent, I see his face, not hers.

My body is gripped by panic. I get to my feet, and it's him who knocks me back into the ropes. I step forward again, determined to beat him for good this time, but he lands another blow.

Three minutes feels like an eternity when you're suffering. The pain is like nothing I've ever felt before, a shock wave that travels through my face and nose, rattling my teeth. He wants me to stay down—I can tell by his face—but I refuse to be powerless.

Shakily, I get to my feet. Someone is yelling behind me, but I can't work out who. The crowd is too loud, the pain too unbearable, and both of my ears are vibrating.

"Get away from the ropes!"

The voice belongs to Jenson. I move from the ropes, sluggishly aiming for my attacker. My dad's fist makes contact, this time on my cheek. I'm thrown back again, but I don't lose my balance.

I'm vaguely aware of someone pulling me into the corner, where Jenson pours water on my face. "What the hell are you doing out there?" he shouts. "You're not even fighting back. I'm calling the match."

It's like I'm suddenly jerked awake. "Don't." I look to the man, who has now disappeared, and then back at my opponent. It's not my father's face I see anymore, it's hers. "I can do this," I say. "I just froze. I'm fine now."

I look past Jenson, into the crowd, and find Hayden staring up at me. His eyes are wild, and I see something in his expression I've never seen before: fear.

Jenson nods briefly. I walk into the middle of the ring and turn to face my opponent again, ready for round three. I don't know if it was the splash of cold water or the fear in Hayden's eyes, but I can see her so clearly now.

The next three-minute round is like the second round never happened. I fight through the pain, through the fear, and I duck and jab, duck and jab, landing punch after punch. I'm hurting in places I never thought possible; if this match doesn't end soon, I'll collapse. But then, somehow, it does. Above the ringing in my ears, I hear cheering and clapping and the referee shouting, and I realize this is it—I've done it.

I've won.

CHAPTER FOURTEEN

The walk back to the room is silent. I feel like a zombie, sleepwalking my way to the elevator doors without taking much in. I'd been hoping to watch some of the other fighters tonight, but the second I stepped out of the ring, Jenson told Hayden to get me out of there.

He vibrates with anger beside me. We step into the elevator, where he stares straight ahead, but I know it's not me he's angry at, it's himself. He only looks at me once we make it to my room. His eyes trace my face, starting at my pounding eye and nose before ending at my lips. "Shit."

"I won," I say, my voice sounding raspy. My throat feels like sandpaper. "Aren't you going to congratulate me?"

"Congratulations," he says. "You look like something out of a horror movie."

"You said getting hit was a part of fighting."

"You didn't need to get hit. You were better than her, Maddie. A thousand times better. What was that?"

"I don't know."

"At least it's done now," he says. "It's over."

Deep down, I know he's not just talking about the boot camp; he's talking about us.

I'm close to tears, and I have to look away from him in order to blink them back. Hayden turns and runs a hand down his face before moving toward his bag. He'd stopped off at the pharmacy on the way home from the fight, dashing in to get some supplies while I waited in the car. When he turns back around, he's holding some painkillers.

"Here," he says, handing them to me, and I take them and sit down on the bed. "They should kick in soon. Hopefully lessen some of the pain." His Adam's apple bobs when he says the word *pain*, and his eyes cloud over. I feel terrible.

"It doesn't hurt that bad," I say.

"That's because your adrenaline hasn't worn off." He grabs some cotton pads and the disinfectant he bought and then kneels in front of me.

I'm quiet as he opens the lid, dabbing some of the liquid on the pad before he sweeps it across my cheek. I wince in pain, and he stops for a second to let me recover before doing the same to my lip.

I look at my hands, unable to take that look in his eyes. I can't take that my father continues to haunt me, even when he's not really here. "How bad is it?" I ask. I haven't had a chance to look in the mirror yet, and I don't think I want to.

"Bad," Hayden says. He finishes tending to the rest of my cuts and then throws all the pads in the trash. When he turns back around, he pauses as if he's waiting for an answer, some kind of explanation about what happened tonight, but all I can do is stare back. "It's late," he says finally, and I notice just how exhausted he looks. "I know you want your own room, but it's not safe for you to sleep alone tonight. I need to keep an eye on you in case you're concussed. I'll sit in the armchair."

"You can't sleep on the armchair. It's tiny."

"I won't be getting much sleep anyway," he says, and he turns off the light.

Slowly, I climb into bed. I try my best to sleep, but it's almost impossible. I'm in too much pain, and the slightest movement makes me feel like I'm dying. I turn on my side, looking to where Hayden sits on the armchair, only his shadow visible. He rubs at his neck like it's starting to ache, and my guilt returns. "Hayden?"

"Yeah?"

I let out a breath. "I don't want you to sleep on that armchair. You can sleep in the bed, I don't mind."

He doesn't move for a good few minutes before he finally lifts himself up. A black outline moves closer until his face comes into view, and he peels back the covers and climbs into bed.

There's a moment of silence. I can just about make out some of his features through the dark, along with those hazy green eyes. "I'm sorry," I whisper. It's something I've been wanting to say all evening, but I've been too afraid. "There's a reason I froze in that ring."

His eyes soften, and he moves a tendril of hair from my face. "If you don't want to tell me, you don't have to."

"I do want to," I say. I close my eyes and rest my head against his chest, allowing my tears to seep into his T-shirt. "I thought I saw my dad in the crowd. It wasn't him; it was just someone who looked like him, but it's like it all just came flooding back. Like I was going crazy, or something. I just kept seeing his face. Maybe I *am* crazy."

Hayden gently strokes my hair, his other arm around me like a protective cocoon. "You're not crazy," he says, "and you don't have to be scared of him, okay? I won't let anyone hurt you."

I don't know if what he is saying is true, but I want to believe it, anyway. He strokes my back with his hand. I start to feel fuzzy as the pain starts to lessen, which means the pills are kicking in. Hayden leans forward and kisses my forehead; it's the last thing I remember.

When I wake up the next morning, the room is empty—no sign of Hayden—but I can hear the faint pattering of water in the bathroom, so I know he hasn't abandoned me. Beside me, on the pillow where he'd slept, is a small take-out box filled with an assortment of donuts.

My eyes light up and I pick up a glazed one, trying to take a bite. I manage to nibble at the outer edge, but anything else is too painful. Still, it's sweet that he dashed out to get some breakfast for me, even if it's not exactly the healthiest.

A string of texts come through on my group chat with the girls.

How was it?? June asks.

Are you alive? Kavi follows.

I text back: *I won.*

They send a string of congratulatory emojis, followed by June asking if I hooked up with Hayden.

No.

I tuck my phone away and try to get down some donuts. I'm contemplating what to tell my mother when the bathroom door swings open. Hayden stands in the doorway, shirtless, his eyes regarding me carefully. "I forgot how bad you looked."

"Thanks, you're so kind." He smirks a little before reaching for his T-shirt. "Most of them are plain," he says, nodding to the box. "I know how unimaginative you are."

I nod and say thank you before attempting another bite. Hayden just watches me with his arms folded, his eyes shrouded with guilt. I feel awkward all of a sudden, like I don't know where to look. Hayden now knows my deepest, darkest secret. While I'm relieved, I'm also terrified.

"We should get going soon," he says.

"No, thanks," I say. "I think I'll just stay here forever."

I hear Hayden laugh as he crosses the room, and then he slowly pulls the cover down. "And have everyone accuse me of kidnapping?" he asks. "I don't think so."

His eyes shine brightly as they study my face. I don't know what he's thinking; it's always hard to tell, but his hand reaches out and he brushes back my hair. "No more fights," he says. "You can still train, but not like this."

I nod in agreement, because it's the perfect compromise. While I'm jumping at the chance to be in the ring again, boxing is like a part of me now, and I can't imagine not coming to the gym and training with Hayden; it's too ingrained into my routine.

"Get ready and eat your donut," he says, getting to his feet. "It's nearly time to check out."

I sigh and take my time in the shower, working out the knots in my hair. When I finally get a good look in the mirror.

My cheek is slightly swollen, and bruises are starting to form beneath my left eye, but it's not as bad as I'd imagined.

I sleep for the whole drive home. I hardly got much sleep last night, despite the painkillers. I kept leaning on my face by accident, and the pain would wake me up. When we pull up to my house, Hayden shakes me awake and says, "Don't take this the wrong way, Maddie, but you look like a clown."

I frown. Clearly, piling on the makeup hadn't been a good idea. "Yeah, well, I'll look like a dead clown as soon as I get in that house. I'll see you on Monday."

Hayden nods and I get out of the car, slowly walking up to the house. As soon as I open the door, my mom is there ready to pounce. "Funny thing," she says, arms folded. "I bumped into June at the mall today, and—" she stops talking to squint at me. "What's wrong with your face?" She grabs my hand and pulls me inside, into the light. "Oh my God."

I'm about to tell her it's not as bad as it looks, even though it is, but I know saying anything will only make it worse, so all I can do is stare back. "My baby," she whispers, pulling me into her arms. I can hear that she's crying as she holds me close, which scares me to death. She's never been much of a crier.

"It's okay," I say, to comfort her. "I'm okay."

"No," she says, pulling back, and her cheeks are stained with mascara. "Who did this to you? Was it that boy that just dropped you off?"

"No," I say, horrified. "Of course not." She reaches out and puts a hand to my face, her bottom lip quivering. "What is going on, Maddie? Tell me."

Lilly chooses that moment to walk out of the kitchen, and she freezes. "Holy hell."

Dylan comes up behind her in the doorway, horrified. Despite knowing I'd be entering the White Collar fight, his face tells me he hadn't imagined I'd end up like this.

Olly comes up behind *him*, takes one look at my face, and says, "Shit."

Tim arrives and steals his eyes from me to narrow them at Olly. "We don't swear in this house."

Olly looks at me and says, "Maybe we should start."

My mom glares at all of them before turning to face me. "I need to talk to my daughter alone."

The others pour out, single file until it's just me and my mom in the hallway. "Start explaining," she says, folding her arms. "Now." I have never seen her this certain and fiery, and despite the fact I'm about to be in trouble, I like seeing her this way. I like that she's not the meek, quiet woman who is always somewhere else.

I take a deep breath. "I've started boxing." It's hard to look at her, so I focus on looking at my shoes, instead. "That guy you saw in the car—his name is Hayden. He's been training me at the gym. I had my first fight last night." I look up now, unable to keep the smile off my face. "I won."

She looks at me, horrified. "Boxing? Why on earth would you voluntarily do this to yourself, Maddie? I cannot believe you'd be so irresponsible as to go off with a boy without telling anyone, not to mention entering a fight."

"It was just—" I stop, too tired to explain. "It kept me busy."

Her hand goes to her mouth, and she lets out a sob. The look in her eyes is heartbreaking. "This is my fault," she says, pressing her back against the wall. "This is all my fault."

I've been able to keep the tears in until now, but hearing

this sends one down my cheek. "It's not," I say, pulling her into a hug. "Mom, it's not."

Her tears seep into the material of my T-shirt, and soon, we're both sobbing. "You're never doing this again," she says. "You're not training anymore, and you're forbidden from seeing that boy. He's obviously a bad influence if he was willing to put you in danger like this."

"It was my idea," I say, and the desperation is thick in my voice. "He was the one who told me not to. Mom, these sessions are helping me."

"Getting yourself half beaten to death isn't helping you, Maddie. This isn't a healthy way to deal with your feelings. My decision is final. Now I suggest you head up to your room to recover."

There's a part of me that wants to argue until I'm blue in the face, but I know it won't do any good. She doesn't understand why I would put myself through this, and no amount of explaining will make her. Instead, I drag myself upstairs and close the door behind me, falling sideways onto my bed. With one last look at the pictures on my nightstand, I fall into a dreamless sleep.

The whole of Sunday is spent in bed. Not out of choice, but because I'm intent on avoiding the wrath of my mother, and my face hurts too much to do anything else. Hayden texts me at one point to see how I'm feeling, but when I text back to tell him what happened, I don't get a reply.

June and Kavi come over at one point to marvel at my face. June is horrified, like I'd predicted, but Kavi studies the bruises as if she's trying to solve one of her murder documentaries. I tell her to stop, she's weirding me out, and she laughs.

"I'm so proud of you," June says, throwing her arms around me. "I knew you'd win."

Kavi rolls her eyes. "You always say that. *I knew this, I knew that.* Funny how you only ever know after it's happened."

June ignores her and, after several questions about Hayden—namely whether or not we had sex—she tells me things are steaming up with Olly. I pull a face, because it feels like hearing about my brother having sexy time, which only makes June go into detail.

As though he can feel his ears burning, Olly bursts in and joins us on the bed, resting his chin on his hand. "What's the gossip?" he asks. "Any cute boys?"

"We're talking about the steamy night you and June had," Kavi offers.

Olly grins as he looks over at June. "Did you tell them about that thing I did that you like?" He looks all proud of himself, like he's a regular Romeo.

"No," June says. "I don't want to traumatize them. Now can you go away?"

He rolls his eyes, lifts himself off the bed, and takes himself out of my room.

"Better you than me," Kavi says to June, and we all laugh.

The girls go home in the early evening and I snuggle up in bed, trying to ignore the pain in my face. Then, just as I'm starting to drift off to sleep, the doorbell rings. I'm jerked into action by the sound of Hayden's voice. I run to the stairs, watching through the railing as he stands before my mother.

"She's in her room and will no longer be going to your gym," Mom says.

Hayden doesn't move. "I just want to talk to her."

"Absolutely not," Mom says. "You've done enough, young man. How could you let something like that happen to a young girl? What kind of person are you?"

I know she doesn't have anything against Hayden, but right now she'll be thinking of Dad. She used to tell me how handsome he was when they were younger, how enthralled she was by his charm. Looking at Hayden, I know she is just seeing *him*.

Hayden goes to answer, but she shakes her head. "I don't know who you are or what your intentions are with my daughter, but you need to stay away from her." And then she slams the door in his face.

CHAPTER FIFTEEN

With only a few weeks left of school, Mom decides it's time for me to go in again. Most of the bruises have faded by now, and the ones that haven't are easily covered by makeup, so I take a little extra time in the morning to apply my concealer.

As soon as I walk into the kitchen, everyone turns to look at me. Tim asks if I want some pancakes in a bid to lighten the mood, but I tell him I'm not hungry.

"Your face looks better," Olly says at breakfast. "Less killer clown and more Mr. Potato Head."

Lilly watches me from over her coffee cup. She's been doing that a lot these last few weeks, watching us both like she's trying to piece together parts of a puzzle, only half the pieces are missing and she doesn't have the box, so she has no idea what the puzzle even looks like.

"Your mother and I have been talking," she says, "and she would like to talk to you about something."

I glance at my mother, who is sitting by Lilly with her hands in her lap, looking uncomfortable. "Lilly has decided she is going to pay for us to go to some therapy," she says. "To help us to move past your father and I splitting up."

I raise an eyebrow. "I don't need therapy."

"Maybe not," Mom says, "but can you just try? I'm going to go to therapy too. I think it will be good for both of us."

The old Mom would never have agreed to therapy, which is why, despite not wanting to go myself, I say yes.

At school, senior week is all June and Kavi can talk about. Everyone is planning to stay at the beach, which I'll admit, sounds fun, but there's the tiniest part of me that is also sad this is all coming to an end.

I spot Hayden talking to his friends in the courtyard at lunch, but as soon as he sees me coming he darts in the opposite direction. He's been avoiding me ever since my mother told him to leave me alone, which surprises me. Hayden doesn't seem like the type to be scared away by someone's parent.

As soon as I get home, I have dinner with the others and work on some homework before deciding to go to the gym. I've had enough of waiting around for Hayden to grow up, and the lack of training is driving me crazy. I'd almost thought that once the fight was over, I wouldn't want to train, but it's the opposite. The gym is like my safe space, the one place I can go and *leave the bullshit at the door*, just like Hayden had once said. I grab my bag and slip out my bedroom window, crawling across the porch roof before sliding down one of the pillars.

The gym lights are still on when I get there. I find Hayden using one of the punching bags. His jabs come hard, and he's so consumed with pounding the bag that he doesn't hear me approach. I clear my throat and he suddenly whips around, nearly taking my eye out.

"Jesus," he says. "You don't just sneak up on people like that."

I put my hands up. "Sorry, I was trying to get your attention."

He doesn't respond. He's too busy studying my face, searching for bruises behind the makeup, but I've covered them well. "Aren't you supposed to be staying away from me?"

I give him an innocent look. "Technically."

He shakes his head and takes off his gloves, letting them drop to the floor. "Are you all right?"

"I'm fine," I say. "I mean, not skipping through the park, everything's rosy kind of fine, but the pain definitely hurts less."

He reaches out now, lightly brushing the side of my cheek. My heart does this little flip, the way it always does when he touches me. "You shouldn't be here." He drops his hand like he never meant to touch me, and the feeling dissipates.

"I needed to get out of the house. Everyone keeps treating me like I'm an injured puppy."

"You are an injured puppy."

"I know, but still." My expression grows serious, and I force myself to look at him. "I feel lost without the routine. So, what's wrong?"

"How do you know something's wrong?"

I shrug and step closer until there is no more space between us. "Your poker face is worse than mine."

I expect him to smirk or say something sarcastic, but instead, he looks away. "You shouldn't be here."

I knew it. "Wow," I say, looking up. "The great Hayden Walker, scared of my mom."

He glares at me now, those green eyes on fire. "She was right," he says. "I shouldn't have let you go to that fight. I'm not a good influence on you."

"It wasn't your choice," I remind him. "It was mine, but if you want to let your fear, and your past destroy our . . . friendship, then I can't stop you."

For a moment, he is silent. He steps forward and studies me as though he's deliberating something. I can practically see the cogs in his mind as they turn and grind together.

"I don't want to be your friend, Maddie." My heart sinks again. Suddenly, I feel like that clingy person who doesn't get the message. Hayden doesn't want to date me or be my friend—he wants me to leave him alone. "Okay," I say, and I turn on my heel, but he gently takes my hand and spins me into him. He leans in closer, like any second now, he is going to kiss me. My adrenaline pumps as I try to read his expression.

"I haven't changed my mind," I warn.

"I don't care," he says. "I have."

And then he kisses me. His lips feel gentle on mine. I don't know whether it's down to him wanting to protect my injured face, or whether it's for some other reason entirely, but either way, it feels incredible. Slowly, he rests his hand on the small of my back, pulling me into him.

He doesn't break our kiss as his hand brushes mine, entwining my fingers with his. His other hand holds the back of my head, deepening our kiss. It feels different from last time, much softer and more tender, as if he's savoring the moment.

I'm standing on my tiptoes, both of my arms wrapped

comfortably around his neck. It feels like it's been so long since we've done this, but the wait has made it all the sweeter. His mouth leaves my lips to focus on my jaw, leaving kisses down my chin and neck. I tilt back my head and hold on to him tighter, my skin beneath his mouth feeling hot. Being around Hayden is like being slightly drunk—I can hardly think straight.

My breathing comes hard, and so does his. His eyes are hooded, and I can tell he's trying hard to keep this gentle. He takes me by the hand and leads me into the office, lowering me onto the bed.

He lightly kisses my cheek, shooting me a wicked grin. "Look, I'm not used to this kind of thing, but I'm willing to try to be better."

I lean up and kiss him, catching him on the chin. His mouth lands on mine, brushing my lip while his hands roam my body. What feels like electricity pulses through my veins. His body feels heavy and warm against mine, shielding me from the world. It's like whenever I'm with Hayden, I forget everything else. I don't think about my parents or my bruises or worries, I think about how good this feels.

Hayden keeps his hands above my waist, his touches innocent. After a few minutes of kissing, he rolls on his side and scoops me into his arms. I turn to look at him, wondering why he stopped.

"As much as I want to ravage you," he says, "I've decided to be a gentleman. For now."

I laugh a little and reach up to touch him, brushing my thumb across his lip. "Your lips are all red."

He stares at my own lips, looking as though he wants to kiss them again. "So are yours."

I trace patterns on his chest. "Tell me something I don't know about you."

He raises an eyebrow as his hand trails my thigh, making patterns of his own. "How about you ask me a question and I'll answer it?"

"Fine. I know you like boxing, but is there anything else you like doing? I mean, have you got any other hobbies?" When he shoots me a wicked look, I add, "Not that."

He laughs and quickly kisses my cheek. "I'll tell you, but if you laugh, I swear to God, Maddie."

"Why would I laugh? Tell me."

He lowers his gaze, focusing on my neck, instead. "My mom has this home business thing. She makes candles from soy wax. On the weekends, I help her."

I'm truly surprised. I can't for the life of me imagine Hayden making candles. "Really," I say.

"She roped me into helping one weekend," he says, "and then it somehow turned into something we do every weekend when she's not on call." I look at him like this is the cutest thing ever, and he covers my eyes with his hand. "Stop looking at me."

"I love candles. What scents do you use?"

He rolls his eyes at the intrigue in my voice and kisses my neck. "All kinds. The most popular are the ones with vanilla or rose. But some like more earthy scents, like pine." His eyes take on a more mischievous look. "I'm guessing you'd like vanilla."

I can't help it—I just find this so cute and out of character that I laugh. Hayden shoots me a warning look, but I ignore it and kiss his nose.

"I have a question for you," he says. "Do you prefer California or New York?"

“California,” I say. “Now that I’ve had some time to adjust, I think I’m more suited to the beach kind of life.”

“And you look good with a tan.”

I press my lips against his, enjoying the way his hand strokes my back. I’d come to this gym not knowing what to expect, but I’d certainly never expected this.

“As much as I’d love to keep kissing you,” Hayden says, “I don’t want your mom sending a mob after me. We should probably get you home.”

I glance at my watch and realize he’s right. It’s almost nine, and though my mom would have messaged already if she’d noticed I was gone, I can’t push my luck. “What about our training sessions?” I ask. “Can we still do them?”

Hayden thinks for a moment before nodding. With one last seductive glance in my direction, he takes my hand and leads me downstairs. His hand feels warm and solid on my own. It all feels so different from how we were acting last week, like Hayden admitting his feelings has changed us.

We spend the car ride home just talking. At some point, he reaches over and holds my hand without taking his eyes off the road. I find myself smiling for the millionth time; things are finally looking up.

That following night, Hayden texts me to meet him at the gym, so after dinner, I tell Mom I’m going to the movies with June. She watches me as I slip on my jacket, looking like she wants to say more. Deep down, she sees through the lies, the deceit, just like she always did with Dad. But just like with Dad, she’d rather keep up the illusion of happiness than face the reality.

That way, you don't have to end up disappointed in the people you love.

"Have a good time," she says.

"Thanks."

When I get to the gym, Hayden is setting up the mats and equipment, but he stops when he sees me. His eyes light up, and I close the remaining distance between us before standing on my tiptoes to kiss him. He kisses me back, and then we start with some stretches before moving into the plank position.

"So," I say. "How do you feel now that school is almost over? Feeling sentimental?"

He grins and says, "I'm not really the sentimental type."

I glance at him, noting how easy and controlled his plank looks, while my own body shakes from the pressure. "Surely there's something about school that you're going to miss," I say, but really what I mean is, you'll miss me. I don't know what's going to happen once I go off to college, if he'll want to stay together, and the uncertainty of the future is what's scaring me the most.

When he doesn't say anything, I sigh and change the subject. "What did you do after school?"

"Worked on my bike for a bit," he says. "Saw some friends. Helped my mom make a candle." He glances at me, daring me to laugh, but I don't.

"What scent?" I ask.

"Vanilla."

"You seem to make a lot of vanilla."

"It reminds me of you."

I playfully hit him before we step into the ring for our

sparring session. For a minute or two we just circle each other. He doesn't really hit me, he never does, but this time, he doesn't let me hit him either. He moves like a ninja, diving and ducking so quickly that I can't land a single blow. Then, in one quick sweep, he knocks my foot from under me, catches me midfall, and then lowers me down on the mat.

"I win," he says. My chest rises and falls under the pressure of his weight. When I stare into his eyes, they are playful.

"You're squishing me," I say.

"Good." He takes off my helmet and starts kissing me, moving his hands to either side of my face. I kiss him back, but it's not enough. We've kissed a lot throughout this past week, but it feels like ever since he changed his mind about dating, he's been reluctant to take things further.

I prove this theory by taking his hand and guiding it to the top of my yoga pants. As soon as it's there, he's moving it back to my face again. Rejection churns through me. I try to sit up, and Hayden sits up with me until we're facing each other. "What's wrong?" he asks.

I shrug and say, "Nothing," before deciding to be brave. "I just feel like you haven't really wanted to do other stuff. Not like you did before."

Hayden looks confused before his eyebrows crease slightly. "Maddie, I'm trying not to fuck this up." He pulls me in closer until I'm sitting on his lap. Those green eyes stare up at me, bright and intense. "I didn't want you to think I'd only changed my mind so we could do 'stuff.'"

Relief washes through me, and I kiss him again. This is all the encouragement he needs, it seems, because his arms wrap around me, holding me tight as his hands grip my hair. I groan when he breaks our kiss for a second, and so he brings his mouth back onto mine.

One hand moves from my head to my stomach, and he slips it under my T-shirt. In one quick flash, his fingers unhook my bra and he tosses it aside. His hand starts to caress me. My entire body jolts then tingles with pleasure.

I squeeze my eyes shut, feeling like I might just explode when my phone starts to buzz. We freeze, and Hayden pulls back a little so I can pull it from my pocket. It's a text from Dylan, telling me I need to get home right away.

Confused, I sit up properly and Hayden pulls back to watch me. "Can you drop me home?" I ask. "I think something's wrong."

He gets to his feet and helps pull me up, retrieving my bra. I quickly slip it on and then he's taking my hand and we're heading downstairs to his car. The whole ride home, I stare out of the window, wondering what could be wrong. Dylan never texts me, especially not to tell me that I need to come home—it must be something serious.

Hayden pulls up outside but doesn't kill the engine. He turns to look at me, his eyebrows furrowed in what I'm certain is concern. "Do you want me to stay?"

"No, it's okay. I'll text you later." With a deep breath, I climb out of the car and head toward my house, wondering what awaits me inside.

The moment I step inside, I know something is wrong. The house is quiet—too quiet—and all of the lights are off except for the one in the kitchen. I haven't felt this unsettled since New York.

I walk to the kitchen, freezing when I get to the archway. I am right: there, sat at Lilly's breakfast table, is Dad. The effect on my body is instant. My legs go slack, like any moment, I will topple over.

Mom sits opposite him at the table, her hands on her lap. She's nervous, I can tell. Her eyes are looking anywhere but directly into his. A part of me wants to run, but I didn't start training with Hayden just to hide.

I step into the kitchen, forcing them both to look up. Dad's eyes soften, and for a second he reminds me of the man he used to be, before all the drinking and stress.

"Maddison," he says softly, getting to his feet. "It's so good to see you." His tone is different. Lighter. I glance to Mom, looking for that light in her eyes, but it's gone. "Please," he says, his eyes pleading. "Sit. I want to talk to both of you."

I'm frozen, rendered powerless by his voice. I wish I never came home tonight. I wish I never left Hayden. And while I'm at it, I wish he'd never found us.

"Please," Dad repeats.

I cross the room and take a seat at the table. I'm trying to be brave, to look strong and intimidating, because I don't want him knowing how afraid I really am, but my trembling gives it away.

For a minute or so, the three of us just sit in silence. "Where is everyone?" I finally ask, but what I'm really asking is, where are the witnesses? Mom looks up, able to read the expression on my face. Her eyes soften, and she says, "They're all upstairs. They wanted to give us some privacy to talk."

This is all so strange that I don't know what to say, so I don't say anything. After three months of not seeing him, it feels like I'm looking at a stranger. I kept picturing this day, kept picturing what I would do if I ever saw him again. It turns out, I do nothing.

Dad clears his throat before looking at his hands. "I was telling your mother how sorry I am. I was going through a very difficult time, and I took it out on the people I love the most." Finally, he looks at me. There's the green and the brown and the little flecks of yellow, just like there used to be. "I'm so sorry, Maddison. I just want us to be a family again."

Mom stays quiet, but a single tear trails her cheek before splattering on the table. My chest lifts then falls, lifts then falls. Maybe my lungs have forgotten how to work, because I don't think I'm taking in air. Watching her cry is like watching the world end. Parents are the strong ones, the ones who are there to protect and comfort children. To see them cry is like an awful reminder that they aren't just parents—they're human.

"Please," Dad says. "Someone say something." He slowly gets up, walking around the table until he's kneeling right in front of her. Gently, he takes both her hands and holds them in his. "Please," he begs, and his voice cracks.

She is frozen in place as he clings to her legs, tears streaming down her face. This is what she used to pray for, him changing back into the man she fell in love with. This is her dream, but it's also her nightmare: a hardened, abusive man is far easier to walk away from.

"I love you," he whispers with tears in his eyes. "I love you so much, Lorraine. I know what it's like to lose you both now, and I promise I will never do anything to hurt you again. Come back home and we'll go to therapy. We can make it work."

I close my eyes, no longer able to stand it. Sometimes, it feels like there are three of us in this relationship, and I am forever stuck in the middle.

"Lorraine." His voice keeps cracking, and every time he speaks, Mom just cries harder. I can't imagine what this must feel like for her. It's tearing me apart just watching them both, which is how I know: she doesn't have the strength to walk away.

I let this go on for a few more minutes, too scared to speak, but I'm tired and I'm broken, and I want to go to bed, and I don't dare risk leaving her with him. "I think it's time for you to leave," I say, getting to my feet. "We can all talk another time."

It's almost a test. The old him wouldn't like being told what to do. The old him would lash out. But this new him, he just nods and tells us that he's staying in a hotel not far from Lilly's. That if we need him, Mom has his number. Then, with one last look, he leaves.

Mom lets out a sob, as though she can't hold it any longer. I cross the room and kneel in front of her, pulling her into a hug. "We don't need him," I say, and I can hear the panic in my voice. "We were doing so well, Mom. You were doing so well. Let's just pretend like he never came here, okay?" But she doesn't nod. She doesn't say anything. She just sobs.

I don't know how long we stay like this, but eventually I take her up to bed.

Back in my room, I try to get some sleep, but the room is too hot. I kick the covers off, hoping it will cool me down, but I might as well not have bothered. For a while I just lie here, wondering what Dad could be doing right now, and what's going to happen after this.

My phone pings with an alert, and I freeze. I reach under

my pillow and click on the home screen, finding a text from Hayden.

Everything okay?

That's it, just two words, but they offer me the tiniest relief. I think about telling him, but it's a lot to explain over text, and right now, I'm such a wreck that I don't know where to start.

I'm not sure. Talk tomorrow.

A second later, a text comes back.

Night, Maddie.

Night, Hayden.

I turn on my side, my legs tucked to my chest in a fetal position. So, that's that, then. My worst nightmare has come true.

CHAPTER SIXTEEN

He visits me in my nightmares, making me toss and turn until I finally jerk awake. When I do, my face is covered with sweat and tears, and my heart is still pounding in my chest. It's only seven thirty, but I sit up in bed. Sunlight peeks through the windows, casting a haze on the pale yellow walls, but it doesn't cheer me up the way it might have before.

Everyone's going to the beach today for a lazy Saturday in the sun, but I'm too wound up about Dad to be much fun. I pace around my room for a while, trying to kill this anxiety. But it grows and grows, filling my chest and then the rest of my body until it feels like I can't breathe. The first tear slips out, but I flick it away. Crying is useless—it won't change a thing—and I hate that he has this effect on me.

Dylan and Olly are buzzing at breakfast, because school is nearly over. Everyone seems to be on some kind of high, anticipating a future filled with promise and warmth, but across the table, my mother is just as quiet, just as withdrawn as I feel.

It's funny how quickly things can change. The progress she's made these past few months has been stripped away, and in front of me is the same woman whom I've been looking at for years: quiet, vacant, a shell of the girl from that photograph.

"How was seeing Henry yesterday?" Lilly asks. She's sitting across the table from us, watching Mom over the rounded head of Baby Yoda. "It must have felt strange after all this time."

Mom nods but doesn't say anything. I grab her hand beneath the table and give it a squeeze, hoping the action might squeeze some life into her, but she barely reacts.

"Maybe the time apart did you both good," Tim says. "Sometimes you need a break to realize how much you love each other."

Mom looks up now, suddenly uncertain. I want to lurch across the table and slap my hand across Tim's mouth before he does any more damage. "Sometimes distance makes you realize how incompatible you are," I say, and briefly, my mind wanders to Jamie. It feels so long ago that we broke up, and back then I'd thought that I'd never be able to move on again, but I haven't thought about him once in weeks. "We're fine without him. Right, Mom?"

I'm looking at her with pleading eyes, begging her to come back to me, and finally, in a quiet voice, she says, "Right."

Lilly frowns as an awkward silence stretches between us. "Maddie, June's coming to the beach with us today," she says, "and since my car is the only one big enough to fit us all in, we're going to have to take it. Can you catch an Uber to the gym today?"

"Yeah, that's fine," I say, getting to my feet. "Have fun."

I head upstairs and change into my gym stuff. By the time I come back down, the others have already left for the beach, so I grab my phone, call an Uber, and head to the gym. I feel pathetic turning up like this, but I don't know what else to do. At times like this, the only thing that stops me spiraling is our training sessions.

Hayden is doing some press-ups when I walk in. It's almost lunchtime, but other than a burly man going to town on one of the heavy bags, we're the only ones in here. Hayden takes one look at me standing pathetically in the doorway and gets to his feet, pulling out the boxing gloves. Relief washes through me. He doesn't ask questions, doesn't force me to talk; he just knows what I need and he gives it to me.

I cross the gym until I'm standing in front of him. He stills for a moment, his green eyes alert as they study my face. I must look an absolute mess right now: puffy red eyes, dark circles—I didn't think to look in a mirror.

He grabs the tape from the box and wraps up my hands before sliding on the gloves. His hands are warm, gentle as they brush my skin. When I look up, he is watching me.

After a second, I turn to the bag and start punching. Hayden blurs away now, along with the rest of the gym. The only thing I see is his face: eyes flecked with brown and yellow and green. A mouth that used to curl into a snarl. I punch and punch until it feels like I'm dying, but even then, I don't stop.

This is worse than my nightmares. If Dad had come and screamed and shoved us around, it would have been easy. But he didn't. He came with redemption, with tears in his eyes and regret in his voice. I don't know if it's real, and I don't know if it matters, but I know it changes everything.

My punches come faster until my arms start to burn. The harder I punch, the easier it is to forget all the fear; the physical pain takes over.

"That's enough," Hayden says. He moves behind me, reaching around me to hold my arms before pulling them away from the bag. I'm about to tell him no, but my voice feels heavy and thick with emotion, so the word won't come out. "Maddie." His voice is almost pleading. He drops his hands but doesn't move away.

I pull off my gloves before tossing them aside, too afraid to turn and look at him. He must think I'm a basket case, a train wreck. All I ever do is let my anger get the best of me: Why is he still here?

I'm breathing heavily, in and out, in and out. It used to come easy, the ability to breathe; now it feels like I'm running out of air. Without speaking, Hayden takes my hand and leads me into the office, locking the door behind us. His arms wrap around me before I can turn, hugging me from behind. His chin rests on the groove of my shoulder so that his face is near mine. I close my eyes and lean into him, praying I don't cry.

Hayden won't let go. His body feels heavy and solid around me, keeping me secure. Gently, he lowers us down onto the bed, and we just lie with me wrapped in his arms like a baby, soaking his T-shirt with my tears. I should memorize this, the way his skin feels on mine. I should memorize the green in his eyes and the warmth in his skin and the feeling he invokes in my chest. If I don't and we move to New York, I'll forget. And I don't want to.

When I've finally gathered the courage to speak, I lift my head to look at him. It hurts to remember, to even say his name, but Hayden deserves an explanation. "My dad is here. He found us."

Hayden is still. Too still. I wonder if he's stopped breathing. "Did he hurt you?"

I shake my head, and his breathing resumes. "No, it wasn't like that." I stop for a moment to gather my words. "He was emotional. He sat in the kitchen and told us how sorry he was. How much he missed us."

Hayden shakes his head, his grip around me tightening. "And you believe him?"

I falter. Do I believe him? I've seen this side of him before, but never quite like this; it's hard to know what's real. "I don't know. I don't know what to believe."

"I don't like this." Hayden stands and lifts me to my feet, towering over me. "You're not staying in that house with him." He reaches out, brushing away a leftover tear before cupping my face.

"He's not staying with us," I say. "He's in a hotel around the corner. I'll be okay, Hayden. I just can't believe he's actually here." For the longest time, I have managed to separate my life here from my life in New York, now it's like the two worlds are colliding.

"Good." His eyes darken, and he grabs my waist. "I still don't like this. Make sure you're never alone with him, and if anything happens, you tell me straight away, okay?"

I nod, and another tear escapes. Around Jamie, it was easy to pretend everything was fine. I don't know why, but around Hayden, it's much harder to fake it.

The thought is terrifying. I'm trusting him with my secrets, trusting him with things that I haven't even trusted June with. As nice as it feels not to keep this all in, I can't help but worry he might make me regret it. It's like standing in a kitchen with the gas turned up, and I'm just waiting for the whole thing to blow.

"I'm scared." It's the first time I've admitted it, both to him and to myself. I am scared, because I know nothing about this new version of my dad. I don't know his temperament; I don't know his intentions. The old him was predictable, I knew how he worked, but this new him? It scares me to death.

Faster than I thought was possible, Hayden pulls me to his chest. My body syncs with his, molding to his shape like we were always meant to fit. "Distract me," I say, closing my eyes, and his mouth catches mine. It feels different, somehow. *He's* different, as if this isn't just a kiss: it's a declaration. I lose myself to the taste of his lips, which are warm and sweet and will be ingrained into my memory for many years to come.

"Maddie?" His breathing is ragged, his voice deep and warm. All I can do is look at him. "I think I might like you."

His words leave me breathless. For someone like Hayden, this is practically a proposal. I reach for his shirt, pulling him closer until there's no more space left.

I'm touching him everywhere, running my hands along the ridges of his chest while his own hands thread through my hair. But then he pulls back, his eyes uncertain, and I realize he's waiting.

"I think I might like you too."

My words make him grin. His eyes light up in a way I've never seen, and his mouth comes crashing onto mine. There's so much force, so much passion, that I nearly forget to breathe.

Maybe my mother was wrong, after all—this is how it should be.

I take his hand, moving it from out of my hair to my stomach. His hand slips under the T-shirt I'm wearing and brushes my skin. I shiver against him, surprised at the warmth of his fingers.

He pulls away slightly, just enough to look at my face. His hand moves down farther, pausing at the band of my yoga pants. He's still watching me as he does it, watching my reaction as his hand slips underneath.

He lowers his mouth, kissing the sensitive skin on my neck. When he starts to suck, I gasp. "Hayden!" My hands fly to his chest, but I don't apply pressure. Hayden ignores me and continues to kiss me, which sends shivers through my body. But then he sucks harder and harder, until I'm forced to let out a moan. He pulls back slightly to look at me.

"I should get you home," he says, his voice low, and his meaning is clear: otherwise, things will escalate.

I straighten out my T-shirt and follow him to his car, where he opens my door like a gentleman. He slips into the driver's seat and closes his eyes, needing a moment to compose himself. Then, after glancing over and looking at my mouth, he drives me back home.

When we pull up at the house, there's a car I don't recognize sitting in the driveway. My breath catches as I turn to Hayden. "I think he's here," I say. "My dad's here."

Hayden's eyes darken as he quickly kills the engine. "Then I'm coming in with you."

My eyes widen. I can only imagine how much worse that will make things. "My mom will throw a fit if you turn up."

His eyes flash defiantly. "Then I'll hide in your bedroom. If anything happens, I'll just be upstairs."

After a moment or two, I relent. He parks around the corner and I head inside the house, finding Dylan and Olly on the sofa.

"Hey," Dylan says softly. "Are you okay?"

I know Hayden is waiting, but for a moment, I sit down. "I'm okay, I just needed to go and clear my head for a little bit. What did my mom tell you?"

Dylan shrugs. "Not a lot, but she seems really on edge. So do you."

I stare at my hands. "Things got a bit toxic between my mom and dad. My mom just wanted a break."

Olly and Dylan share a nervous look. "Dinner should be interesting, then," Olly says, and I get to my feet. He's not wrong.

I can hear Mom and Dad talking with Lilly in the kitchen. I bypass them completely and head up to my bedroom, signaling for Hayden to come up. He climbs up the veranda and onto the balcony, stepping inside. He brings his hands up to either side of my face, roughly kissing my forehead. "I'll be right here," he says.

I nod and get all the way to the door before saying, "Don't even think about snooping through my stuff."

Downstairs, Lilly has cooked her famous pot roast. Everyone is seated, including Dad, and I take a seat next to Dylan. Dad is on his best behavior—his most charming self. He tells Lilly this is the best pot roast he's ever eaten, and she's lapping it up. Clearly, he's already won her over.

Sometimes, when I sit and watch this side of him, I wonder if maybe I'm crazy. If maybe I only imagined the bad parts. I just can't see how it's possible for two halves of someone to be so out of sync.

At one point, when he's finished telling one of his elaborate stories, Dad turns to me. "How's school here, Maddison? Have you settled in okay?"

If I'm rude to him right now, then I'll look like the bad one, because this is what he does. He works you up until you're ready to snap, and then he comes out smelling like roses. "It's really good," I say, staring at him. "I've met some really nice people. I'm happy here." I put an emphasis on *happy*, a warning that I won't be moving.

"Good," he says, stabbing at a vegetable. "That's good to hear. You look different."

"She's been going to the gym," Tim chirps up. "It's inspiring, really." He taps the pudge on his belly. "She's putting us all to shame."

Any minute, I can see one of them spilling the beans on my fight, so I quickly change the subject. "How's New York been?"

Dad's eyes soften, regarding me in a way I used to crave. "Awful without you two. I'm just glad we're all here together again."

I glance at Mom, wondering if she buys this redemption, but it's hard to tell. Her face looks conflicted, her eyes searching his like she's looking for the truth—like she needs it. I understand that feeling, because I feel it too.

After dinner, everyone heads into the living room to talk. I volunteer to help Dylan with the dishes, so we're washing up at the sink. I bend down to scrub a particularly stained dish, and he suddenly looks at me.

His eyebrows furrow and he pulls my hair away from my neck, his frown deepening. "Who gave you that?"

I turn to look at him, confused. "Gave me what?"

"That hickey." He moves his finger from my hair to my neck, resting it on my skin. "Right there."

"Oh God. Is it noticeable?"

"Your hair was covering it until now." His eyes darken. "Was it Hayden?"

I'm so embarrassed that I don't say anything. I'm going to kill Hayden.

"It was," Dylan says, shaking his head. "If he's marking his territory, I take it he's more than your trainer now?"

I wipe my hands with a cloth and then force myself to look at him. "What do you mean marking his territory?"

Dylan looks at me like I'm being naïve. He falters, unsure of whether or not to tell me the truth. "He's a possessive guy, Maddie. I've seen this before, with Caitlyn. He's doing it to be territorial."

The mention of Caitlyn does something strange to my insides. "No one even knows we're together," I say. "What would be the point in him doing it? How would anyone know it was from him?"

Dylan turns away from me to carry on with the dishes. "Just be careful, all right?"

I suddenly feel sick, like I've been caught doing something wrong. "Are you mad at me?"

"Of course I'm not mad at you. I'm just—I don't know. Worried, I guess."

We finish off the dishes in silence. I feel so unsettled now. It's bad enough that my dad is here messing with us, but now my concerns about Hayden are resurfacing too.

I skip the living-room reunion and head to my room, where Hayden is seated on my bed, playing with his phone. He looks up when I come in, his eyebrows creasing. "Was it okay? Did he try anything?"

I shake my head and sit opposite him, crossing my legs. "He was on his best behavior. It's hard to tell if he's being genuine or not." I close my eyes. "God, I feel like I'm going crazy."

Hayden puts down his phone and pulls me toward him, sitting me down on his lap. Gently, he places his hands on my lower back, keeping me still while he nuzzles my neck. I wish I could close my eyes and lose myself in him, but I can't.

I pull away slightly, needing to look at him. "Hayden, why did you give me a hickey?"

His green eyes twinkle. He grins. "I couldn't resist." His fingers move from my waist to my neck, gently stroking the skin. "You taste too good."

"Are you sure that's all it was?"

He frowns, dropping his hand. "What's that supposed to mean?"

"Are you sure you didn't do it to mark your territory?"

"Mark my territory? What am I, a dog?"

"You know what I mean."

"Is that what Dylan told you?"

My heart beats faster. I shouldn't have told him. "He's just looking out for me."

He gets to his feet, looking at the wall before turning to face me. "What about me?" Hayden asks, looking hurt. "Aren't I looking out for you?"

I get to my own feet, closing the distance between us. "You

are," I say, feeling bad. "I'm sorry, I wasn't trying to accuse you of anything. It's just hard when you're both telling me different things. He thinks you're the untrustworthy one and you think he is. Who am I supposed to believe, Hayden?"

He stiffens before flashing a wicked grin. "Fine, let's make it even." He pulls off his T-shirt until his taut chest is exposed. The longing in his eyes tells me this isn't just about making things even between us.

"Hayden."

"C'mon," he says, staring at me. "You obviously think I'm some dick who goes around marking my territory, so let's make it even." He pulls me toward him, spinning me until I'm trapped between his chest and the wall. His face is so close, I can feel his warm breath on my cheek.

My heart is pounding. Slowly, I move my hands to either side of his neck, pulling him toward me. His eyes come alive, scanning my face and my lips in anticipation. He grabs my thighs and lifts me up, using the wall to hold me. I wrap my legs around his waist and bring my lips to his neck. He inhales sharply, grabbing me harder. I use my tongue to wet the skin. Then lightly, I start to suck. His whole body stiffens, then sinks into me. I do it harder, overcome with the urge to taste him.

A few minutes later, he pulls back to look at me. His eyes are dark, his breathing heavy and shallow, but the longing on his face is unmistakable. He sets me down, and the sound of the front door closing catches our attention.

Outside, my dad's car is pulling out of the driveway, disappearing down the street. Hayden looks back at me. "I guess that's my cue."

He turns to leave, but I grab his arm. There's no way I'm

leaving it like this. "Don't go yet," I say, pulling him back. "Please."

He towers over me. I can tell by the way he frowns a little that he's still pissed off. Finally, he caves. He takes my hand and pulls me down onto the bed. After a second, he throws an arm around me, pulling me into his chest.

He's still angry, I can feel it coming off him like a force field, but he's holding me like he's not. I don't know how long we stay like this, but I end up falling asleep in his arms.

CHAPTER SEVENTEEN

At breakfast, Tim can't stop gushing over Dad. He's only ever met him through brief FaceTime calls, but he's even more charming in person. Mom remains quiet but clutches her coffee, mulling this over. She doesn't look as anxious as when Dad first showed up, which means his "redemption" is working.

"When are we starting therapy?" I ask. "I think you were right; it will be good for us."

Mom looks surprised, and I don't blame her. Therapy is the last thing I want to have to do right now, but if it means stopping her from making a huge mistake, I'll go. She thinks for a moment, clearly conflicted. "I don't know, Maddie. Things are so hectic right now that I completely forgot about it. Soon, I guess."

The rest of the morning seems to drag. I try to concentrate on my schoolwork, but there's just too much going on. If I don't start dealing with some of these problems, I think I'll explode. The first thing I need to do is talk to Mom. I've been scared to ask her what's going to happen because I'm afraid of her answer. But the sooner I find out, the sooner I can come to terms with it.

Kavi catches me at my locker at lunch and asks me what's wrong, but as much as I trust her, this is one secret I don't feel like sharing. "Nothing," I say, linking my arm through hers, "I'm just worried about finals."

"Me too," she says, squeezing my arm, "but you'll be fine, all right? And just think, the sooner it's over, the sooner we can look forward to graduating. Try not to stress, okay?"

"I'm trying," I say. "Believe me."

She gives my arm another squeeze. "I'm going to the bathroom. I'll be back in a sec, and we can head to the library to cram in some studying, okay?"

"Okay." Just as she's leaving, Hayden sneaks up behind me, wrapping his arms around my waist. Shocked, I slowly turn to face him. He's never been this public with me at school before.

"What are you doing?" I ask.

He flashes his typical, boyish grin. "Saying hi."

"Hi."

He continues to look at me, and I get lost in those eyes. There's no Caitlyn or Dylan or Mom or Dad—there's just him, looking at me like he's missed me. He's about to kiss me, right here in the hallway when Dylan comes striding toward us.

We both turn at the same time. I expect Dylan to acknowledge me, but he doesn't. He's looking at Hayden.

Hayden's eyes cool. "Can we help you?"

Dylan looks away for a second. Then quick as a cat, he turns back around and punches Hayden square in the face. I gasp, and Hayden stumbles back a little, completely caught off guard. He recovers quickly and flies at Dylan, shoving him back into the lockers. When he raises his fist, I grab it midair, panicked.

Hayden looks down at me, uncertain. I can see it in his eyes how badly he wants to retaliate, and for a second, I think he is going to. But then he lowers his fist and looks back at Dylan, "That's the only free shot you get." His other hand releases Dylan's T-shirt and he steps back an inch.

Around us, people have stopped to stare and whisper. I turn back to Dylan and in a hushed voice say, "What the hell are you doing?"

For a split second, Dylan looks guilty, but then he turns back to Hayden, those dark eyes wild. "Tell her," he demands. "Tell her what you said to me in the locker room just now."

I look between the two of them before focusing on Hayden. *Oh no.* "What did you say?"

Slowly, Hayden looks at me. For the first time, his eyes are clouded not with anger, but panic. He rubs at his jaw like he's deliberating something. Or biding for time.

"Fine," Dylan says. "I will." He turns to me, some of that anger in his eyes dispersing. "He confronted me after gym about what I said to you. Told me to mind my own business. I told him I was just looking out for you—"

"You called me a psycho," Hayden interjects, but Dylan ignores him.

I look right at Hayden, into those green eyes as they stare at me in desperation. "I want to hear it from you," I say, my voice calm. "What did you say?"

Hayden's jaw clenches, then contracts. "He called me a

psycho, and I told him—" He closes his eyes like he can't bring himself to repeat it.

Dylan steps in. "He said I was following you around like a puppy with a crush. Then he said, and I quote, 'If Maddie was interested in you, she'd be fucking you, not me.'"

I turn back to Hayden, horrified. From the look on his face as he stares at his feet, Dylan is telling the truth. My heart pounds in the silence that follows. I'm so shocked that I don't know what to say. "We're not even, we haven't—" I can't say it. I'm too embarrassed.

Hayden's eyes soften, but before he can speak, I'm pushing past the pair of them and running down the hallway. I need air: I need air and space and quiet. I head to the football field and sit out on the bleachers, staring at the empty pitch.

I used to wonder how my mother could fall for someone like my father, but maybe this is how it starts. Maybe they started off passionate and happy before she let too many things slide. She could have ignored the warning signs. What if Dylan's warnings are right and I'm just being blind?

After a minute or two, Hayden crosses the field and sits on the bench in front, facing me. We are quiet as we regard each other. There is guilt all over his face. Bragging about sleeping with someone is one thing, but to Dylan, whom I live in a house with and have to see every day. Why is Hayden so determined to make my life more complicated?

The silence must get to him. He quickly takes my hand, holding it tightly in his palm. When I look at his face, he is nervous. "I shouldn't have said it. I'm sorry."

"Then why did you? Why would you ever talk about me like that to someone? Don't you have any respect for me?"

"No one else was around to hear it," Hayden says like this makes it all better, "and Dylan was telling me all this shit about how I'm a psycho and how he won't let me hurt you."

"So you decided to prove him wrong by proceeding to hurt me?" I ask.

"No," Hayden says. "I wasn't trying to hurt you. I said it because I knew it would hurt him. The kid's obviously in love with you."

"Of course he's not in love with me, and even if he were, I'm not Caitlyn, Hayden. I wouldn't do that to you." I get to my feet, my chest tight with anger. "I can't believe you would talk about me like that."

Hayden stands up, too, towering over me like the giant that he is. He's just as confused about how to feel as I am. His breathing is heavy, the look in his eyes switching from regret to anger, and back to regret. He leans in closer, his mouth inches from mine. "I'm sorry."

"The thing is," I say, looking up at him, "how am I supposed to know if I can trust you or not?"

He runs a hand down his face. "I'm trying here, Maddie. What do you want from me?"

"I want you to not make me question your intentions, Hayden." I turn to leave, but his fingers catch mine.

"Is this what's going to happen every time you find out some shit you don't like?" he asks. "You're going to run away from me?"

"You know what? Yes, I run away, Hayden. I hate conflict. I hate arguing. I've had more than my fair share of it. I'm done with all the drama."

"Life is drama," he says, his voice low. "You can't predict

and plan for everything. You don't get to just opt out because it gets hard."

He's wrong. I can opt out if I want to. "My life with Jamie wasn't drama. It was quiet and peaceful and safe. Maybe that means boring to you, but is this any better?"

It's the mention of Jamie that does it. His eyes flash with hurt before flitting to anger. "Yeah, that relationship seemed really great. You know what you are, Maddie? You're a sheep."

"Excuse me?"

His eyes gleam back. He's not backing down. "Yeah, you're a sheep. You keep letting yourself be led and controlled. I saw the way Jamie had you wrapped around his finger. Now you're blindly believing everything Dylan tells you when you know the kid hates me, instead of looking at how I've changed. Because I have, Maddie. I wanted to change because of you."

I try to swallow, but there's a lump in my throat. I want to believe him, I want to believe this will be a one-off, but I've seen what happens when you trust too blindly and when you forgive the mistakes: they just get bigger and worse. "I don't want you to change for me; I want you to change for yourself."

Slowly, the anger fades. He lets out a sigh, then brings his arms around me. This thing between us is coming to an end—I think he must realize this.

"I messed up," he says, and when he speaks, his voice is rough. Emotional. "I know that, Maddie. But I'm trying to be better. I'm sorry."

I can't take the look in his eyes anymore, so I close my own, sinking into his chest. "I know what Dylan did to you. I get it, but that kind of betrayal eats away at you if you let it. And I don't need this extra drama. I have enough to worry about." Between this and the thing with my parents, it feels like I'm balancing on a tightrope. One wrong step and I'll tumble to my death.

"I know," Hayden says, hugging me tightly. "That kid just brings out the worse in me. From now on, I'll be the model boyfriend." He freezes like he's realized what he's said, and I pull away to look at him.

"Is that what you are now?" I ask.

I see panic in his eyes—vulnerability. He's terrified of committing after what happened with Caitlyn. But then he grins, and it's the warmest, boyish grin I have ever seen. "What else would I be?" he says, and he kisses me here on the bleachers.

CHAPTER EIGHTEEN

Dad's had dinner with us almost every day this week. Slowly, Mom starts to open up again, and begins to contribute to discussions. He's telling her things like how beautiful she is, and she's lapping it up. A part of me is too. I keep staring at him, keep trying to find traces of the old him in his eyes, but there's no impatience behind his eyes, no silent treatments or criticizing Mom for wearing makeup—it's like the old him is gone.

At dinner one night, when we are talking about sports, Lilly mentions my fight. I freeze and glance at Dad, who slowly looks up from his salmon. "Really?" he asks. "You won the event?"

I nod, still watching him. There's no malice in his eyes, no anger—he looks like a father who's happy for his kid. His green eyes crinkle at the corners. "That's amazing, Maddison. I'm so proud of you. What was it like?"

"It was amazing," I say. "Everyone was cheering for me. It just felt, I don't know. Like nothing I've ever experienced before."

"You've always been good at sports," Dad says, "even when you were little. Remember when I used to take you to your swimming meets? You'd win a medal every time, and you'd search the stands for my face and wave it at me. You always looked so proud."

I try to recall, but I can't. Most of my childhood feels like a blur, like parts of it are missing. The good days were always so close to the bad, that I had to block most of it out.

"Are you still practicing?" Dad asks. "Any fights we can come to?"

I glance at Mom, who is waiting for an answer. "No, I stopped training. Mom didn't think it was healthy."

Dad's eyebrows furrow, and he looks over at Mom. "Boxing is a great sport, same as any other. You should start up again."

My eyebrows fly up. "Really?"

Mom looks at me, then at Dad. Her expression falters. "She was badly hurt. I don't want her fighting."

"It's boxing," Tim chimes in. "Of course she'll get hurt. Doesn't mean she shouldn't do it if she wants to."

Mom avoids Tim's gaze and looks at her hands, instead. If I didn't know better, I'd think she looks betrayed. "Fine," she says. "Train, then."

Things are quiet for the next few minutes until Dad changes the subject. I finish off my vegetables, looking between him and my mom as they look like a normal couple.

After dinner, I tell them I'm going to the gym to train, and Dad tells me to have fun. Mom sighs then says the same. At least I can be honest now.

I get to the gym at ten past eight and hope Hayden won't be mad that I'm late. Inside, the lights are dimmed, and in the middle of the ring is a table and two chairs. It's one of those round tables with a cloth that drapes over the sides and reaches the floor. Hayden is seated in one of the chairs, wearing a black tee and jeans. I walk over and take a seat in the other, realizing he's had a pizza delivered.

"What is this?" I ask.

He doesn't look at me as he dishes up my food. "Our second date."

The smell of pizza tingles my nostrils. "I didn't know what you like," Hayden says, looking up, "so I kept it simple."

I can't help but smile. I'm not used to seeing this side of him. He's so shy and cute, like he isn't sure what to do with himself. I'm still annoyed by what he said, still annoyed that he's the reason Dylan is currently ignoring me, but at least he is trying.

We talk for a little while about different things, and I realize how easy it is with him. There are no awkward silences like when I was talking to Jamie. There's no running out of things to say. Being here with Hayden, it's like my escape; I never want to leave.

"Oh, I got you something," Hayden says, and his eyes cloud over, "but don't laugh."

I suddenly grow nervous. "I'm not going to laugh."

He hesitates, then reaches under the table and pulls out a candle shaped like a small flower. Surprised, I take it from his hands and lift it to my nose. The vanilla hits me, paired with something lighter.

"Honeysuckle," he says.

I laugh. "I love it," I say, breathing it in. "I can't believe you made this. How do you get it to look like a flower?"

He shifts uncomfortably. "You pour the wax into a mold shaped like a flower. It's pretty easy."

I'm still smiling, and it draws a reluctant one from him. "Okay, okay. Stop looking at me like that." He gets up and clears away the pizza box, throwing it in the trash. When he comes back, I'm already waiting for him.

As soon as he gets to me, I throw my arms around his neck, pressing my lips to his. Maybe I'm making a huge mistake being with him, maybe I'm foolish for giving him chances, but I can't help how I feel. I have to trust that this feels right because it does. Around Hayden, I'm stronger. Braver. I laugh more and care less. I haven't thought about rules or my schedule or any of the things I used to focus on: all I can think about is him.

"I meant what I said," Hayden says, breaking the kiss. His eyes burn down at me, bright and intense. "I won't fuck up again."

"You better not."

Our lips touch again, and my body ignites. His hand travels to my hips, his thumb trailing the waistband of my yoga pants. My pulse begins to quicken and I hold on to him tighter, allowing him to lower me onto the mat. He spends a second just looking at me, his eyes slowly searching my face.

"What?" I whisper.

"Nothing. Just thinking how lucky I am."

Before I can get embarrassed, his mouth finds mine again, parting my lips with his tongue; I think I could kiss him forever. Hayden's breathing is rough and heavy. I slip my hands beneath his T-shirt, trailing my nails down his back. He closes his eyes, and I watch as his eyelashes flutter against his cheek. Quick as a cat, he flips us so that I'm now underneath him, my back on the mat. His body feels hard and lithe on mine, keeping me pinned beneath him. My breath comes out ragged and in short, shallow breaths. Hayden looks down at me, his eyes on my lips as his hand slips into my pants.

As always, I shiver. His fingers are warm and gentle as they move. I continue to look at him, lost in the green of his eyes. My heart feels ready to explode. His fingers keep moving and I clutch at him harder, bunching my fists in his T-shirt.

"Hayden," I whisper, and he shivers against me. His finger moves farther until I feel me around him. His breathing is sharp as he slowly starts to move, his eyes dark and hooded. I squeeze shut my own eyes and lose myself to the moment, my skin on fire from his touch.

I have never had this feeling before. Not just physically, but emotionally. Being with Hayden is like being on a roller coaster: it's scary and exciting and not always fun, but you still never want to get off.

Briefly, I wonder if it's the same for him, or if he's felt this before. Maybe he has—maybe he's been with lots of other girls who have made him feel like this—I'm just one on a long list of many. I don't dwell on it for long, because all thoughts are lost. My hands continue to roam his back, his waist, the band of his sweatpants. I'm just touching and touching, needing to feel him the way he's feeling me, but it never seems enough.

He moves deeper, and the feeling inside me gets stronger and stronger, growing and shifting. My muscles contract, and with an arch of my back, I feel the most wonderful relief.

Hayden kisses me gently on the lips, pulling his hand back. I'm breathing too hard, barely able to kiss him back. He sits up properly, no doubt to give me some room to breathe, but I pull him back down and climb on top.

He stares up, surprised. I lean forward slightly, teasing him with a kiss as my hand moves to the front of his sweatpants. He stiffens beneath me, like he hadn't been expecting this, and I like that I've managed to surprise him.

He inhales sharply and rests back his head, closing his eyes. I don't know what I'm doing, but from the look on his face, it's the right thing. His jaw is clenched, angled at the ceiling as I move. After a second or two, I lift up slightly and then align myself over him. His eyes shoot open. My yoga pants are thin, and so are his sweatpants: we can both feel everything.

"Shit." His eyes are electric, like sparks of lightning in a storm. His hands shoot out and grab at my hips, rocking me back and forth. We keep moving like this in a slow and steady rhythm, like waves in an ocean. He's looking right at me, trailing his gaze over my nose, my lips, my neck. I'm doing the same, memorizing every crevice and feature so I can burn it into my memory.

He grabs my hips harder, over and over, his fingers digging into my skin. After a second or two, his body tenses, stiffens, then sinks. He pulls me toward him until I'm flat on his chest, then shudders against me. We stay like this for what feels like forever, me lying on top of him. His arms are around me, holding me tight like he's reluctant to let me go.

At some point, we roll over so that we're both on our side, and he pulls me into his chest. He strokes my hair, and it feels so good that I want to fall asleep, but I also don't want to waste this.

I start to interrogate him with all of the questions I've been dying to ask, and for once, he humors me. I learn that he's lived in California his whole life, but he'd love to live somewhere else when he's older, maybe Hawaii. When I ask about boxing, he tells me what it felt like the first time he won a fight, and what it felt like the first time he lost. His father is a sore subject, but he tells me about the hours they'd spend together training for fights.

We cover everything and anything, except for his relationship with his ex. After a little while, once he's found out all there is to know about me, I gather up the courage to ask. "I know this is probably the last thing you want to talk about," I say, "but I would kind of like to hear your side of things."

He shifts to look at me. "Are you going to ask me about Caitlyn?"

I nod, and he sighs before looking at the ceiling. "She was my first serious girlfriend," he says, still stroking my hair. "I didn't treat her very well."

I tense a little. "How so?"

Hayden sighs and says, "I didn't do any of the things a boyfriend is supposed to. I didn't take her on dates, didn't make her feel special. My dad's death really messed me up, and I just couldn't give her the things she wanted from me. Things got worse when I started focusing on the gym a lot more. She thought I wasn't showing her enough attention." He looks at me now, his expression conflicted. "She was right, but I had to be here. It made me feel closer to him, or something."

I nod, because I get it. "That must have been hard."

"She started trying to make me jealous whenever we'd go out, and it would work. I'd get mad, we'd argue a lot—it kind of got toxic. One night, we had this really big argument, and I guess she went over to Dylan's and kissed him."

He closes his eyes like he's shutting out the memory before he opens them again. But when he looks down at me this time, he doesn't look sad or annoyed like I thought that he would: he looks relieved.

"I used to think about her all the time," he admits. "I thought if I slept with enough girls, I'd forget about her eventually, but it never worked." His hand slowly moves from my hair to my arm, trailing his fingers on my skin. "It was after one of our training sessions when I realized." I'm about to say *realized what*, but he's not finished. "You were spread out like a starfish as if we'd just run a marathon or something instead of a few stretches, and it suddenly hit me: I hadn't thought about her in days. I was too busy thinking about you."

My heart does a flip, then a somersault. He stares at me, his eyes sincere as they quickly scan my face. I've never heard him speak like this. He kisses my forehead, his lips soft and warm, and I feel a quick flutter in my chest. I think I am falling in love.

It's something I hadn't expected when it comes to Hayden Walker. Maybe I'm being stupid or crazy or ridiculously immature, but it's true, I can feel it; I just don't know if he feels the same.

When it starts to get late, Hayden drops me back home and then kisses me good night. I run into my house and get ready for bed, pulling the covers to my chin. My heart is still racing, a constant pitter-patter deep in my chest; I am definitely falling for him.

The next morning, I'm both happy and terrified. Even though things around me are worse than ever, it feels like Hayden and I exist in a bubble. Him and me, me and him, away from my family drama; I wish it could last.

At lunch in the cafeteria with June, she asks me why I look like the Cheshire cat from *Alice in Wonderland*, so I tell her about the flower candle Hayden made, and she looks like she might keel over.

"Like, an actual candle," she says slowly. "Made from wax."

"Yes."

"That he made with his hands."

"Yes."

"Are you sure he didn't buy it from the store and pretend to make it?"

I laugh and steal some of her fries. "His mom makes candles, so he helps out."

"Wow." She shakes her head. "I never would have thought in a million years that Hayden makes candles in his spare time. Was it a good one?"

"Yeah, it smells nice. Vanilla and honeysuckle."

She shakes her head again, laughing. "Bizarre," she says, and for a moment, just like when I'm with Hayden, it's like I forget all the bad stuff and focus on the good, like how Dad can't touch me when I'm surrounded by the people I love.

"What are you doing tonight, anyway?" she asks. "Want to come over and watch a movie? Nothing below a rating of eight on IMDB, though."

I sigh. "I wish I could, but I have to go for dinner with my mom and dad."

She furrows her eyebrows, confused. "Your dad?"

It suddenly hits me that in all the drama, I haven't said a word to June about any of this. Armed with a few more fries, I tell her that my dad has found us, and was hoping to reconcile.

"Wow, are you okay?" she asks.

I think about this for a moment. I suppose I am, to some extent. I've accepted that I can't change the situation I've found myself in, so I just have to see how it goes.

I don't see Hayden for most of the day, but in English, he writes something on a piece of paper then hands it to another student, who passes it to me.

You look pretty today. What are you doing tonight?

I scribble back: *Going for dinner with my parents. :(*

Then I spend the rest of the class thinking about how awkward it is going to be sitting opposite the two of them. At least with my aunt and uncle present, my father is on his best behavior. I have no idea how he'll react once he's got us alone.

Hayden passes the note again, and Johnny narrows his eyes before throwing it over.

Need me as a bodyguard?

I'm about to say no, but the thought of Hayden being there tonight makes me feel a lot better, so instead, I write: *Yes.*

My heart thumps. I shouldn't be so nervous about having dinner with my dad, but I am—I am terrified. At some point, there's a knock at my door and I call for whoever's outside to come in. The door creaks open, and Dylan hovers cautiously in the doorway.

"Hey," I say, surprised.

"Hey. Can we talk?"

I clear away the clothes on my bed so he can take a seat opposite. For a second, things are silent as we look at our hands, at the floor, at anywhere but each other. Then, finally, he says, "I shouldn't have hit Hayden in front of you like that. It was a dick move, and I'm sorry. He just gets under my skin."

I sigh and say, "I don't want to be involved in this, okay? If you guys aren't mature enough to be civil, then at least be mature enough not to put me in the middle."

He nods and gets to his feet again, holding out his pinkie. "Friends?"

I hook my pinkie through his. "Friends."

At six thirty, I head downstairs and find my mom and dad are already seated on the couch, waiting for me. I haven't told them Hayden is coming, and I don't plan to. I'm going to wait until the last possible second.

Dad gets to his feet, smiling when he sees me. "You look nice, Maddison."

I straighten out the dress I'm wearing. "Thanks."

Once Lilly has gushed about how nice we all look, we climb into Dad's car and head to dinner.

My foot taps the whole ride there. I try to control it, try to keep still, but my nerves won't allow it. Finally, Dad pulls up outside and I spot Hayden already waiting, leaning against the wall.

My heart skips a beat, then another. He looks so handsome standing there, like a boy from a different time. He's wearing a pale blue shirt that makes him look more tanned, and dark blue jeans.

When I step out of the car, he looks over, straightens

up, and walks toward me while my parents climb out. Mom glances at him, recognition crossing her features.

"I invited Hayden to dinner with us," I say. "Is that okay?"

Mom's lips purse and Dad looks over, then back at Mom. "Sure," he says, taking Mom's hand. "The more the merrier."

Inside, the restaurant is dark. We're led over to a booth in the corner, away from everyone else. Mom and Dad slide into the booth seats while Hayden and I take the chairs. As I go to sit down, Hayden pulls my chair out for me, then tucks me in.

Mom picks up the menu, refusing to look at me. She hates change, hates anything that could upset my dad, but this is what we need. The more we challenge him, the easier it will be to tell if he's faking.

Things are awkward for the first few minutes. Dad makes a few jokes about the menu and Mom laughs like a schoolgirl. For once, she looks happy. "So," Dad says, smiling at Hayden. "Hayden, was it?"

Hayden nods and says, "Yes, sir."

I tense. This isn't exactly how I'd imagined Hayden meeting my parents—I'd never imagined this at all, in fact—but if he's uncomfortable, it doesn't show. "Hayden is the one who's been training me," I explain, picking up my own menu.

Dad looks at him, surprised. "You're a trainer? You look so young."

Hayden moves his hand to my thigh, resting it above my knee. "I inherited the gym from my dad," he says. "I've been running it ever since he passed away."

Dad's eyes soften. He looks genuinely concerned. "That's terrible. I'm sorry for your loss."

"I appreciate it."

"What do you think?" Dad asks. "You think Maddison could ever go pro?"

Hayden laughs and squeezes my knee. "Sure, she's a natural."

Dad nods like Hayden's being serious, but I can tell from the playful glint in his eyes that Hayden is just being silly. I squeeze his hand harder as punishment, and he moves his hand farther up my thigh.

When the waiter comes over, we order our drinks. Dad orders a bottle of red wine, and when it arrives, goes to pour Mom a glass. She puts a hand out to stop him. "Oh, no thank you," she says. "I'm not a fan of red."

Dad looks surprised. "You used to love it."

Her expression falters, and I can see the cogs in her mind turning as she tries to recall. "Did I? I don't remember."

He nods and says, "It was the drink you would order whenever we'd go to a restaurant. Remember our first date and we nearly polished off three bottles?" He laughs at the memory.

Mom lets out a nervous laugh too. "My memory is getting awful these days. Go on, then. I'll have a little."

For the next fifteen minutes, things feel normal. I could almost forget everything that's happened until now, everything he put us through. The man in front of me is nothing like the man we left in New York—I don't know what to think.

Hayden's fingers continue to trail patterns on my thigh. He's in the middle of telling my dad about boxing, but his hand doesn't stop. It almost feels soothing, having him touch me. I try not to close my eyes.

At the end of the meal, when we're waiting for the check, Mom and Dad look at each other. My stomach drops. I lean forward slightly, staring at my mom in particular. "Everything okay?"

She nods and looks to Dad again. "Should we bring it up now?"

Dad puts his wine down. "Maddison, I know we've all been through a lot these past few months, but your mother and I have been talking and we'd like to give things another try. I want us to be a family again."

I'd think time had stopped if it weren't for the beats of my heart. One, two. One, two, like pattering rain in a storm. "What does that mean?"

"It means he wants me to move back to New York," Mom says. "Permanently."

It feels like the air has been sucked from my lungs. Hayden's hand moves from my leg to my waist, like he thinks I'll slip away. "My life is here now," I manage. "I'll be graduating in a few weeks and going to UCLA. I can't just move."

Mom's eyes soften. "I know, that's why we don't expect you to move, Maddie. It would just be me."

I shake my head over and over. I want to throw something at her, to tell her she's being ridiculous, but I can't with him here; I want us to be alone.

The check comes, and when the waiter asks if everything was okay, Dad nods and gets to his feet. I turn to the waiter, like a deer caught in headlights. *No*, I want to scream, my heart still pounding. *Everything is not okay.*

As soon as we get home and Hayden and Dad have said good-bye, Mom hurries upstairs to her bedroom. Lilly steps out of the living room and asks me how dinner was, but I don't say a word. Hands shaking, I head upstairs and into Mom's room, where she's already curled up on the bed. Just as before, I curl up next to her and wrap an arm around her waist, her body feeling warm against mine. It feels like so long since I've touched her, felt her warmth on my skin, and she must think it, too, because she turns in my arms.

"Everything is a mess," she says.

"I don't want you to go," I say. My voice makes me sound like I'm a little girl again, when I'd beg her not to go to the store. Even though she was only ever gone a few hours, I hated when she left me. "Please." My voice cracks now. I'm on the verge of tears.

The first tear rolls down the curve of my cheek, and she gently wipes it away. "It's not that simple, Maddie."

"It is that simple." I hate that my voice rises, that I'm so angry at her, but sometimes I just want to shake her out of this dream world she's in.

"How do you think you're getting to UCLA?" she asks. "Your father is paying for it. If we sever ties completely, he might change his mind."

Her words stop me dead in my tracks. "Is that why you're doing this? Because he's blackmailing us?"

"No." But she says it too quick, like the word feels foreign on her lips. "I mean, he mentioned it, but I do think he's changed, Maddie, and it's not like I'm making much money right now, I can't live off Lilly and Tim forever, and your father loves us."

I believe her on the last part. I'm not stupid, I know enough about psychology to know that my father is a deeply flawed man, and I believe that he loves us, but sometimes people don't love you in a way that is right, or is healthy. Sometimes, people who are broken end up breaking you too.

My mother closes her eyes and lets me hold her for a while, her fingers entwined with mine. There's no sense in arguing or making her see reason, because in her mind, she is saving me. I'm going to live the life she had always wanted for herself, a life of freedom and college, things that were stripped from her the moment she became pregnant and had to drop out of college to raise me. But as I watch her fall asleep, her face free from lines as she slips away to dreamland, I'm not willing to let her be my sacrifice. I won't let him break her anymore.

CHAPTER NINETEEN

At breakfast, Lilly and Tim are in the kitchen, drinking coffee at the table. When I hear their hushed whispers, I linger behind the archway to eavesdrop.

"I'm telling you," Lilly says, shaking her head. "I'm not happy, Tim. Something is going on under this roof—I can feel it."

I'm about to step away, but the floorboard creaks, and they both jerk their heads toward me. Guilt lines Lilly's expression. She gets to her feet, indicating to the table. "Come and sit down, Maddie. Do you want anything to eat?"

"No, thank you, I'm not hungry. Where's Mom?"

"She's upstairs. Is everything okay? And be honest."

Slowly, I look at her. As much as I hate this question, I know that she means well. Which is why, when I look at her face, which looks so much like Mom's, I start to cry. Lilly's face softens. Her arms fly around me, cocooning me in her embrace.

"Tim," she says, without looking at him, "Maddie and I need a minute alone, please."

He grabs his paper and coffee and heads into the living room, leaving us alone. After a few minutes of her quietly stroking my hair, she pulls back to look at me. "What's going on?"

I want to tell her so badly—I do, but telling Lilly the truth is too risky. If Mom gets defensive, it could drive her away from us and closer to Dad. Turning to Lilly, the dread in my stomach starts to shift and grow.

"I'm fine," I say, wiping my eyes. "It's just my mom is thinking of moving back to New York with my dad. I'm going to miss her."

Lilly reaches out, pushing back a lock of my hair. "I know," she says softly. "She told me a few days ago. I don't want her to leave either. I've loved having you both here, but you'll still be able to FaceTime and visit each other during holidays. Everything will work out."

I nod, but I can't shake this feeling that something terrible is about to happen, it's only a matter of time.

At school, yearbooks are all anyone can talk about. My yearbook quote is "*To accomplish great things, we must not only act, but dream; not only plan, but also believe.*" —*Anatole France.* I think it's fitting, in a way, because for all the planning and preparation I've done, I never really believed in myself. Training with Hayden for the White Collar boot camp gave me confidence I never knew I was lacking—a chance to be brave.

They say senior year is all about figuring out who you want

to be, and how you want to be remembered. The previous three years of high school went by in the blink of an eye, and senior year has been no different. Navigating the final year of high school feels eerily similar to the first, with a lot of nerves and high expectations for the best year ever, but in some ways, it's been the worst.

The old me would have seen this year as a failure. But I've realized the pressure to have everything perfect and wrapped up with a pretty little bow isn't realistic. This year may not have been perfect, but I've learned things about myself I never would have back home, and I'm even more determined not to let Dad come into the new life we've built and tear it to pieces, which is why I need to get him away from Mom.

Later at training, Hayden has me working on the punching bag while he sorts out the equipment box after the busy day at the gym. It feels good to let all of this anger out, to feel in control for once. My situation is spiraling, my future on the line, but at least in this gym, I feel safe: home. Afterward, Hayden and I sit on the mat for a while, lost in our thoughts. His hand is in mine, large and solid. I squeeze it tighter, loving the feel of his skin.

"If he wants to be a family so bad," Hayden says when I've told him what happened, "then why can't *he* move here?" He's got a point, and of course, this would be the logical solution, but I know my dad. He wants things his way, on his terms—the way it's always been.

"I don't think I can just let her move," I say. "I can't leave her alone with him. I might have to defer a year and move back to New York."

Hayden's eyes darken. "You're not going anywhere with him."

"I can't leave her."

"Then go to the police," he says, sounding desperate. "Get a restraining order. Just don't leave, Maddie."

He makes it sound so easy, and maybe it is, but there is something that has always stopped us from taking that step. Some misguided loyalty that makes the thought of turning him in break our hearts. And for the longest time, letting anybody know the truth about Dad, even the police, felt like the scariest thing in the world. It still does.

Hayden gets to his feet now, pulling me to mine. "Do you want me to just take him out? 'Cause I'll do it." The way he looks down at me, so serious, makes me laugh.

"Yeah, you ending up in jail is the perfect ending to this story."

He raises an eyebrow. "What ending did you have in mind?"

"A happy one."

"Easy," Hayden says. He picks me up by my thighs, wrapping them around his waist, and I throw my arms around his neck. For the briefest moment, I just stare at him through my hair, which hangs in tendrils around his face. Those green eyes stare up at me, eager and warm and intense, just like my own. He spins me around, kissing me as he does it, and my heart bursts at the seams.

It is moments like these that I'll remember.

When I finally get home, it is late. The lights are off except for the one in the living room, where Mom and Dad are cuddled on the sofa. I freeze at the sight of them, taking in the bottle of wine on the table. Mom looks up, her expression like a kid who's just been caught doing something they shouldn't.

They've always looked good together, like a couple you might see in a furniture commercial, or on the front of a cereal box—how misleading appearances can be.

Dad rises to his feet. "Now that you're back, we've got some good news." I can't take this—I've never felt worse. "I've bought you both some plane tickets. I'd like you to come back to New York with me. I know you'll just be back for the summer, Maddie, but it will be nice to be a family again."

Half of me expected as much, so I don't react. My mother is staring at the coffee table like it is the most interesting thing in the world. "Can I talk to you alone?"

She nods, and when Dad gets up and disappears into the kitchen, I take his seat next to her. She takes a deep breath as though whatever she's about to say will pain her.

"Before you get mad," she says, "listen to what I have to say. I don't want to keep uprooting you, especially when you seem to have settled in so well. If you wanted to stay here and spend the summer with your aunt, I'd understand. I spoke to Lilly earlier. She'd be happy to let you stay."

"Even if he's changed, so what?" I say, leaning forward. "He hurt us, Mom. That's not something you just forgive."

She nods like she understands, but I don't think she does. "I know, but I've been seeing him a lot recently, Maddie. He's a lot better now. I can't just walk away. That's not what marriage is about."

"It's also not about being abused by your husband."

My eyes fill up, and I wipe away a tear that falls. There's a part of me that wants nothing more than for us to be a family, a real family, but none of this is real. Even if he's redeemed himself, it doesn't erase what he did in the past: I can't just forgive.

"I don't want you to move," I say. "You're happy here, Mom. You can't just give that up for him."

Her eyes tear up, and she looks at her wine glass. When Dad comes back, she flicks away a tear that falls. "You don't have to decide right now, Lori," Dad says softly. "I know it will take some time to come to terms with. The flights are booked for next week, so you have until then to decide."

I don't respond. I just get to my feet and then hurry to bed, pulling the covers to my face. Hayden is wrong, I realize. Happy endings aren't easy at all.

The next few days are a nightmare. Mom's rarely home anymore, which leads me to believe that she's staying with Dad, so we never get the chance to talk. Occasionally, Lilly will ask me if everything is all right, if I've made a decision, if there's anything I want to talk about, and every time, I say no. I know that she's worried, but there's nothing she can do. If I'm right and my dad hasn't changed, then he'll get his own way in the end; he always does.

But a part of me thinks, what if he has? Isn't this what I've always wanted, to see my mom and dad happy? I used to lie awake during the worst of their arguments, a pillow over my ears, and pray to God that he'd change. What if this is our only chance?

On Friday, when Mom is out for dinner with Lilly, I head to Dad's hotel. I don't know why I do it, but I think I just want to get him alone, to sit face to face. There are so many doubts and thoughts and feelings I have, and if I want any chance at that happy ending, I can't wait around for it to fall into my lap; I need to take control.

The whole drive there, my foot taps. My body is vibrating, that fight-or-flight instinct kicking in. I shouldn't be so terrified to see the man I call my father, but I am. Still, the tiniest part of me is hopeful. Maybe I'll get there and I'll look in his eyes, and I'll know. His redemption is real, he loves us the way a father is supposed to love his family; he's changed.

I pull up to the hotel just as my phone starts to buzz, and I pull it from my pocket, finding a text from Hayden.

My mom's in Santa Barbara for the weekend. Do you want to come over?

I tense in my seat. Hayden has never invited me over before. It shouldn't be a big deal when we've shared a hotel room together, but this feels different. Scarier. I think for a moment before writing back.

I might be able to come later. Send your address.

Hayden texts back straight away with his address, and I tuck my phone back into my pocket. The hotel is one of those small, boutique-type places with palm trees outside. I take a deep breath, and, when I've gathered up the courage, step into the lobby.

Dad is expecting me. I'd messaged him before I left to ask if we could talk, and he'd jumped at the opportunity. I wait in the lobby and mess with my sleeve, with my top, my hair, with anything that distracts me.

Finally, he shows. He walks toward me, wearing his typical handsome grin as he pulls me into a hug. "Thank you for coming to see me, Maddison," he says. "It really means a lot to me."

I pull back to look at him, searching his eyes like the answers might be written there, but they're not. "It's fine."

"There's a beautiful courtyard restaurant outside. Are you hungry?"

I hesitate. While I'd feel safer talking to him out in public, it means that if this is an act, he'll be on his best behavior. "Actually," I say, "I kind of just wanted us to talk alone."

His eyes soften, and we head over to the elevator and shoot up to the fourth floor. When the doors open, Dad leads me over to Room 414 and opens the door. The room is beautiful, with traditional Spanish designs and a four-poster bed. In the corner, there's a small leather armchair that I quickly slip into, while Dad sits down on the bed.

For the first few minutes, things are silent. Finally, Dad says, "I know you must be worried about your mom moving, but we'll come visit you all the time."

I rub my hands on my jeans because they're starting to sweat. "I think it's a lot for you to expect her to move back to New York so suddenly. It's not fair."

"I know, I know," Dad says, sighing, "but I can't take any more time off work to be here, and I don't want us to be apart anymore, Maddison."

My stomach unclenches. I understand now why Mom is so quick to believe him. His voice, his expression, everything about him is quietly desperate, like a puppy you want to protect.

"I need some time, okay?"

Dad nods and gets to his feet. "Come and visit whenever

you want, okay? I've missed you." He pulls me into another hug. I tense, not used to such displays of affection, but soon I'm hugging him back.

Afterward, I head straight to Hayden's, pulling up to a small but cozy-looking house. It's painted a pale orange and is surrounded by shrubs, like a mini Spanish courtyard. As soon as Hayden opens the door, he grins and hugs me. I allow myself to sink into him, resting my head on his chest.

"How did it go?"

I take a deep breath. "It's hard. I want to believe him so badly."

His eyes soften. He pulls me into his arms again, roughly kissing my forehead. "I know," he says, his voice low, and I reach up to kiss him. He's the only one who can do that, the only one who can make me feel happy when I'm supposed to feel sad; I love that about him.

The next few hours, he acts like the perfect gentleman. We sit in the living room wrapped up in a blanket like a human burrito, watching movie after movie. I learn that despite wanting to punch people in the face for a living, he's a sucker for quirky romances. We end up watching *Barefoot*, *Excess Baggage*, and *The Back-up Plan*, one after the other.

At some point during the last movie, I look over at Hayden to see he's fast asleep. He looks so innocent and vulnerable right now, like a little kid. His eyelids flutter, and his lashes gently brush on his cheekbones. I lean over and kiss him right there on the cheek, and he smiles. I find myself smiling too.

It's late when I get home, so I end up sneaking in. The lights are all off except for the living room, where Dylan is alone watching TV. I hover in the doorway, surprised to see him—he usually just watches in his room.

"Hey," I say. "Isn't it past your bedtime?"

"Hey," he says, nodding at the TV. "Wanna watch something?"

I nod and sink onto the sofa next to him. He goes to grab the remote from the table, but I swipe it first, holding it just out of reach. "I'm deciding."

"No way," he says. "I'm not watching *Buffy the Vampire Slayer* again."

He reaches for the remote, but I hold it away, laughing when he misses. He grabs my hand now, trying to pin it down on his lap, and I laugh as I struggle against him. Just as he's about to go for the remote, I shove my other hand under his armpit, and he clamps down so hard that my fingers get stuck. Dylan lets out a laugh that mixes with mine, then stops to look down at me, his dark eyes unreadable.

Eventually, we call a truce and stop to catch our breath, but he doesn't let go of my hand. "Uh, Dylan?"

He looks down at our hands like he hadn't even realized. "Oh, sorry."

We shift apart, and Dylan picks up the remote, flicking through channels while I look at him.

"What?" he asks, not looking away from the TV.

I'm silent for a moment, trying to find the right words. "Dylan, do you have a—" I stop to close my eyes, because this is just so embarrassing. "Do you have a crush on me?"

When I open my eyes, he is looking right at me. "Is this about what Hayden said?"

I bite my lip, because the truth is, since Hayden

mentioned it, it's been stuck in the back of my mind. Dylan shakes his head, annoyed. "You've let him get in your head, haven't you?"

I frown. "He's not in my head. I just want to make sure that there's nothing, you know, that we need to talk about."

"Let me ask you this," Dylan says, turning to face me properly. "Would you have asked that question if Hayden hadn't said something?"

"No, I wouldn't have, because I didn't notice anything then."

He furrows an eyebrow. "What do you notice now?

I think for a moment then say, "I don't know. Nothing, I guess. I just wanted to check."

For the next few minutes, Dylan looks ahead, his jaw clenched into a hard, narrow line. I sigh and say, "Look, I'm sorry if I've upset you. I wasn't accusing you of anything."

He turns back to face me, his eyes softer now. "It's not about that, it's about the fact that he's doing it again."

"Doing what?" I ask.

"He makes up stuff in his head and then he goes around trying to convince everyone his way is the truth, and it's not. He did it with Caitlyn, and now he's doing the same thing to you. He's gaslighting you."

I have no idea what he's talking about, but I hate that he mentions Caitlyn. Being compared to Hayden's one true love all the time doesn't do much for my ego. "Gaslighting?"

Dylan arches an eyebrow. "You've never heard of the term *gaslighting*?"

I scowl. "Yeah, I'm just asking for fun."

He rolls his eyes and gets out his phone, typing something

into Google. After a minute or two of scrolling, he silently passes me his phone. I click on the description, which reads:

> Gaslighting is used to describe abusive behavior, specifically when an abuser manipulates information in such a way as to make a victim question his or her sanity. Gaslighting intentionally makes someone doubt their memories or perception of reality.

I look up now, confused. "This doesn't sound like Hayden."

Dylan's eyes darken. "It's still early days. He's already trying to convince you of stuff that isn't true. Soon he'll have you doubting what's real and what's not."

What's real and what's not. Those words play on repeat in my head, over and over. I think back to Dad's comments about swimming and wine, memories he's certain happened, but no one else could remember. What's real and what's not—the phrase doesn't sound like Hayden at all, but it certainly sounds like someone.

"What else does it say?" I ask. "What are the other signs?"

Dylan looks concerned at my frantic tone, then takes back his phone. After a second or two, he hands it back, allowing me to scroll through the list. It seems this gaslighting thing works because it's done gradually, over time. A lie here, a lie there, a snide comment, and then it starts getting worse. According to this article, even the brightest, most self-aware people can be sucked into gaslighting, which explains how he's won over Mom. She's been through this so long that I doubt she knows what to think anymore.

I flick through the other signs, like how their actions don't match their words, and how they throw in positive reinforcement to confuse their victim. Briefly, I remember the way Dad compliments us, the way he acts like our biggest fan. The doing things and then denying he'd ever done them, like hiding Mom's things and my Disney doll.

Suddenly, I feel sick. I don't need to read the rest, because I already know. Despite what Dylan says, Hayden isn't the one gaslighting me—my dad is.

CHAPTER TWENTY

I can barely concentrate during the week of finals. I've crammed in as much studying as possible with Kavi, so it's not that I'm worried about not doing well; it's more that my mind is too focused on Dad and whether or not he's really changed.

On the day of my last exam, instead of heading to the beach with Kavi and June to celebrate our freedom, I drive over to Dad's hotel to surprise him. Maybe I'm wrong and he really has changed, or maybe I'm crazy, but I just can't ignore this feeling in my gut, telling me something is wrong.

I step into the elevator, studying my reflection in the mirror opposite. I look scared, uncertain, like the girl I used to be back in New York, not the fighter I thought I'd become.

On the fourth floor, I knock on Dad's door. He takes a minute or two to answer, and when he does, he's surprised.

"Maddison," he says. "You didn't tell me you were coming. Now isn't really a good time, I'm in the middle of a video meeting."

Behind him, I see the shadow of someone else on the wall. Bile rises up the back of my throat, and I slip through the gap between his arm and the door, into his room.

Scrambling to get dressed is a woman a few years younger than Dad. Her eyes widen when she sees me, and she hurries to do the last few buttons on her shirt before she slips right out of the door.

"It's not what you think," Dad says. "Maddie." His voice sounds soft, pleading, and it rips at my heartstrings.

Slowly, I turn. My heart is beating a mile a minute. "How could you?"

His eyes soften. He extends a hand toward me. "You can't tell your mother, Maddie. It would crush her. Here, sit down."

I step away from his hand. I don't want to sit down. Sitting down leaves me vulnerable. Powerless. In an even voice, I say, "Mom won't be moving to New York."

He pauses for a second to study my face. His eyebrows furrow and I can almost see the cogs in his mind, turning and turning. "That isn't your choice to make, Maddie. Your mom has already agreed."

I step forward until I am inches away. "Can you believe that for a moment I actually thought you'd changed?"

The muscle in his jaw twitches, so I know he's getting angry. "I have changed, Maddie. When you and your mom left me, it forced me to take a good, hard look at myself."

I shake my head, trying to hold on to this resolve. "Yeah, I could see that. I'm going to tell her exactly what I saw, and she's not going to want to go anywhere with you."

"Would you really want to hurt her like that?' he asks, and I falter. Suddenly I feel like the one who is doing something awful, like I'm purposely out to destroy her.

"She deserves to know," I say, my voice shaking, but now there is doubt behind my words.

Dad shakes his head as he takes a step closer, gently pushing the hair from my face. "I made a mistake, Maddie, I admit that, but your mom is finally feeling happy again. She's chosen to be with me despite all my faults. Are you sure you want to take that happiness away?"

Once, when I was twelve, my parents argued so loud that the neighbors called the cops. It had been over something so small, so insignificant, that I can no longer remember what it was. But I remember when the cops showed up, my dad put on this confused, innocent face, and it made me wonder if I'd imagined it all. This is the expression he is wearing now. It is his *I don't know what's happening face*. His *this is all your fault, not mine* face; I want to slap the expression straight off.

"Maybe she has chosen," I say, "but even if that's true, it was a choice made out of fear. Is that what you want? You want her to stay with you out of fear? There's a word for people like you: *pathetic*."

My dad steps forward. He stands so close that the tip of his shoe touches mine. It takes all of my strength not to step back. "What, you took a few boxing lessons and now you think you're somebody? You're not somebody, you're nobody."

My heart breaks a little, even though it shouldn't. A part of me had still held on to hope, still believed in his redemption, but now it's been shattered before my eyes. My dad hasn't changed—he's the same man he always was, and now he has proved it.

"We're done," I say, looking up. My voice sounds steady and even for once, masking the fear behind it. "*You're* done, Dad." I go to shove past him, but he grabs my wrist, yanking me back.

"You think you can talk to me like that?" he asks.

In one quick movement he shoves me again, and I back into the edge of the table. Pain radiates down my lower back, and I'm transported back to being that helpless girl in New York. Despite everything I've learned, despite how strong I thought I'd gotten, this man has the power to render me helpless.

Something wet starts to trickle down my nose. It trails down my lips, dripping down my chin and onto the front of my shirt, and only when I look down do I realize I'm having a nosebleed. I raise my hand to wipe away the blood, and Dad, disgusted, takes a step back. I scramble for the door handle, yanking it open before running to the elevator.

When the doors slide open, I get a good look at my reflection. My eyes are red, my nose smeared with blood. I use the bottom of my T-shirt to clean my face, then zip up my jacket. I click on the ground floor button then lift up my sweater, turning to see the damage. There's a red line across my lower back from the impact of the table, and when I roll up my sleeve, I see imprints of his fingers on my skin.

I try to breathe the way Hayden taught me: in, out, in, out, but it doesn't seem to work. The pressure in my chest is growing and twisting; it is shifting into something dark. I'm so mad at myself for not fighting back that a part of me wonders if maybe I deserve this.

I'm frantic as I drive to Hayden's, barely able to see through the tears. As soon as I pull up, I spend the next few minutes trying to calm myself down and make myself presentable. The last thing I want is for Hayden to find out and for things to potentially get worse. With a glance at my jacket to make sure no blood is visible, I cross the lawn to his house.

Hayden opens the door on the third knock, practically half asleep. It's only around six, but I know he likes to nap after getting back from the gym, which explains why he looks so groggy.

For a moment, we just look at each other. I must look desperate or pathetic or both, because, without a word, he pulls me in closer and wraps me up in his arms, where I bury my face in his chest.

"You're shivering," he says, closing the door behind me. I don't say anything, because it's taking all of my strength not to burst into tears. He raises a hand, pushing back some of the hair from my face before he studies me, concerned.

He's about to ask what's wrong, and I don't want to talk, so I kiss him instead. He hesitates for a moment before kissing me back, moving his hand to my waist. His lips are soft as they part my own, his tongue warm and urgent. With everything that's happened, I should be unraveling, but Hayden keeps me together.

"I missed you," he whispers.

"You only saw me yesterday."

"I know. Do you see my predicament?"

He kisses the tender spot below my ear, and I shiver. Kissing Hayden isn't just a distraction, it's what I need. It's a reminder that despite all the bad I've had to deal with right now, there's still something good—I need to hold on to this.

He pulls back a little to study my face. "Are you all right?"

"No," I admit, because lying to him feels impossible, "but I don't really want to talk about it right now."

He frowns a little, looking uncertain. "You sure?"

Throat thick, I kiss his cheek. "I'd rather take a tour of where the elusive Hayden Walker lives."

There's a brief hesitation before he takes my hand and gives me a tour—the small but cozy living room, the open-plan kitchen, and then to what he calls the "magic" room.

When he opens the door, I see why. The room is long but narrow, with big bay windows that fill it with natural light. All four walls are covered in shelves, holding candle after candle in various sizes and shades.

It feels like I've been transported into a magic shop in the Harry Potter magic world. Different scents tickle my nostrils, like vanilla and pinewood, but others are so subtle that I can't quite place them.

On the far side is a long wooden counter with a device on top, and two patchwork stools. I walk toward it, imagining Hayden and his mom sitting there as they craft and mold candles.

"I love it," I say, turning to Hayden. "Can you show me how to make one?"

He looks into the distance like he's deliberating something, and I wonder if maybe this is something he wants to keep just for him and his mom. Finally, he nods, and for a moment I'm able to forget about Dad and just enjoy the moment. I turn to face the counter, and he slips behind me so that my back is against his chest. His arms come around me, trapping me between them as he reaches for the cupboard above the counter.

He pulls out a bag of soy wax and then opens the smaller cabinet next to it, revealing hundreds of fragrance oils. Gently, he gathers up my hair and pulls it over my shoulder, exposing my neck. "What scent do you want?"

I close my eyes, enjoying the warmth of his breath on my skin. "Mmm, what scents go well together?"

He lowers his head so that his mouth is near my ear. "Most candles have what we call top notes, middle notes, and base notes." His voice is low and husky—how does he make talking about candles sound so dirty?

"And what does that mean?" I manage.

"The way the fragrance notes combine is what gives every scent its own unique profile." His hands lightly brush my arms as he says it, sending goose bumps along my skin. "Top notes are what you can smell first and are usually floral or citrusy. They fade the quickest. The middle note provides balance. The base notes give depth and are what tend to linger, like vanilla and spices."

It sounds so strange hearing Hayden talk about scents and notes that I have to stop myself from grinning. "What's your favorite?"

He stiffens behind me. "I'm not telling you."

"What, why not?"

"Because I'd have to kill you."

I frown, about to turn around, but he keeps me pinned to the counter. "Tell me."

His hands move from my arms to my waist, wrapping around me. "Fine, but don't you dare laugh, Maddison."

I smile. I'd started to hate being called Maddison, but coming from Hayden, it doesn't sound like a slur; it sounds like a confession. "It's called 'Baby,'" he says. "It's a mix of the scents baby powder, lavender, and lilac. It sounds stupid, but the scent is so clean, like smelling fresh sheets."

"Okay, let's make that one."

He pulls out three vials and rests them on the counter. Then he reaches for the wax flakes, pouring some into a measuring jug. The whole time, I watch his arms reaching around me, taking in his bronzed, taut muscles as they work. Despite the fact we've been intimate, having him this close still gives me butterflies.

He flicks a switch on the device, then pours in the wax. He presses himself against me as he does it—either by accident or on purpose—and it sends little pulses of heat to my thighs.

While we wait for the wax to heat up, his hand starts to trail over my inner thigh. He says something about the wax needing to be the perfect temperature before adding the fragrance, but I'm barely even listening. The machine next to me pings, and I jump, causing Hayden to laugh. He slowly removes his hand and reaches over. "It's time for the fragrance."

I sulk and say, "Seriously?"

"It's an exact science," he says, kissing my neck. "If I don't add it now, it will mess up the whole candle." He reaches for the fragrances, adding a little bit of each to the melted wax. Then he stirs it for two minutes before leaving it to cool. "Once it cools to a certain heat, we can start to pour it."

"Hayden?"

"What?" he asks.

I shake my head, but it doesn't get rid of the grin. "You're kind of a nerd, you know that?"

He frowns and reaches down, taking my face in his hands. "Oh really?"

"Yes, really."

He gently tilts my head back, his eyes falling to my lips. "Such a smart mouth," he says. His thumb brushes across my lower lip, making me tremble. "Maybe I need to put it to better use."

My whole body freezes, then burns. His eyes dart to mine, the color of pure, unfiltered energy. His hands move up to the back of my head, gathering a fistful of hair. He brings his mouth closer, stopping just short of my lips. When I think I'm about to burst with excitement, the timer goes off.

Hayden sighs like he's regretting this candle, then hands me the jug of hot wax. "What shape do you want?"

I think for a moment. "A heart."

He pulls two molds from the cupboard, putting them on the counter. "Pour it slowly," he says, "or else the wax won't set properly."

Together, we slowly pour the wax into each of the molds, then leave them on the counter to set. He kisses me again, slowly unzipping my jacket, before he pauses.

"What?" I glance down at myself, remembering my T-shirt is spotted with blood. "Oh, I had a nosebleed." His eyes widen, and I notice the look on his face. "My dad didn't do it, it just happened."

He frowns and takes me by the hand again, leading me up into his bedroom. I stand in the doorway like I'm afraid to go in. The walls are dark blue, the floor a polished walnut that matches the rest of the furniture. In the middle is his double bed, which he leads me to.

I take a seat as he reaches for his drawer, pulling out an

oversize black tee. "Here," he says, handing it over. "Change into this."

My hands shake when I take it from him—I don't know if it's down to being cold or being nervous. I get to my feet and Hayden turns his back. The T-shirt is long enough to reach my upper thighs, so I take off my jeans, leaving them in a heap on the floor. "Ready."

When Hayden turns around, his eyes briefly fall to my legs. I stiffen as he peels off his T-shirt, revealing his tanned, taut chest. "It's getting pretty late. You should stay here tonight."

My heart does this quick, pulsing flip. It's not exactly the first time Hayden and I have shared a room, but tonight I feel decidedly more vulnerable. I nod anyway and get out my phone, letting Mom know I'll be staying at June's, and then I turn to face Hayden.

Carefully, he tucks a strand of hair behind my ear. "Can we talk about what happened yet?"

My eyes stay glued to my hands as I give him a brief update. Hayden listens intently, keeping his fingers wrapped around mine. "You know, a part of me really started to believe that he'd changed," I say, "even after everything I know about him. Isn't that stupid?"

"You wanted to believe that there's good in your dad," he says. "That doesn't make you stupid."

I turn to face him properly, taking a minute to study his handsome face. I can't imagine the boy before me sleeping with countless other girls and then ignoring them. It's like the Hayden I know is different from the one everyone else sees; I don't know if they're the ones who are blind, or me.

Then I think, how do people do this? How do people go

through cheating and misery and betrayal and still want to trust another human? Still know how to? Because I look at Hayden, and I want to believe that he's everything I think he is, but a part will always wonder: Am I wrong? Is he lying? Is this real? If growing up with my father has taught me anything, it's that my guard must stay up, always.

"What are you thinking?" Hayden asks. His eyes are dark as they study me back, his finger trailing patterns on my knee.

With a deep breath, I ask, "Do you trust me?"

It's something I've wondered for a long time now—whether his issues with Dylan and Caitlyn have affected us, somehow. Does he really trust me, or does he expect me to do to him what Caitlyn did to him? His finger stops moving, and he lifts his hand to my face instead, forcing me to look at him.

"What?" I ask.

He looks back at me, surprised. "I was about to say I don't trust anyone." I feel my face fall, and he adds, "But then I realized . . ."

"Realized what?"

He shrugs and says, "I tell you things I've never told anyone. So, I guess I do." He grins again, like learning this is a revelation for him—a nice one. "Do you trust me?"

"I want to," I admit. "I think I do." I look at him through my lashes, feeling entirely exposed. With another deep breath, I think of my father cheating on my mother and say, "Just don't do anything to ruin it, okay?"

He nods, and when he looks at me, I know he is serious. "I'll try." He shifts closer to me until our noses are practically touching. His hand reaches up again, cupping the side of my cheek.

Then, gently, he kisses me. It's like every nerve in my body wakes up, just for him. I kiss him back, slowly at first, but then this primal need takes over; I just need to feel him and taste him and touch him, so I do.

My hands stroke his back, running along his spine. His skin is so soft, so supple, that it glides against my fingers like silk. He touches me back, lightly trailing his hands up my arm, before stopping when he gets near my shoulder.

"Take this off," he whispers, pulling at my T-shirt, and I nod. He lifts it right off me, throwing it to the floor before pulling back to look at me. I sit naked from the waist up, cold and exposed, and entirely too vulnerable. But then his arms wrap around me, solid and strong, and I am suddenly warm again.

He pulls me toward him so that I am sitting in the space between his legs. Up close like this, I can see the flecks of yellow in his eyes from the light of the bedside lamp. His mouth moves near mine, but he doesn't kiss me; he's savoring this. His fingers are gentle as they brush along my arms. It is terrifying being this exposed, but the feel of his chest on mine more than makes up for it.

His fingers move upward, reaching the red marks on my arms, and I watch the muscle in his jaw contract. He shifts me, lifts me up so that I'm on his lap, my hair falling over him.

His eyes slowly drop from my lips to my chest, taking me in. I want to cover myself, but my arms are locked around his neck. His eyes turn hooded. He rests his hand on the back of my head, wrapping his fingers in my hair.

Gently, he brings his other hand up, sliding it across my stomach until he's cupping me in his hands. I gasp as he runs his thumb across my breast. His touch sends a quick electric pulse to my stomach; I shudder. This feels different from any other time we've touched. It's not the urgent, desperate passion we are used to, it's more than that: it's intimate and scary and vulnerable. I feel like I'm naked in the middle of a crowd, my secrets laid bare.

My heart pounds with every touch, every brush of his thumb. He's rubbing so softly that I can barely even feel him, but it's enough to send jolts through my skin. I close my eyes, losing myself to the rhythm of his strokes.

He rubs softly, then pinches, his large hand the perfect fit for my body. He moves his hand to wrap it around my back, lifting me up higher. I'm about to demand that he moves it back, but his fingers are replaced with his mouth.

My chin rests on top of his head, my arms locked around him, tight. Unraveled, but in a good way. He doesn't stop touching, stop sucking, and any minute now, I feel like I might come undone. I could stay like this forever—I want to—but Hayden flips us and lies me down on the bed.

For a second he leans over me, green eyes bright, trailing over my body like he's memorizing it. I think of the time he'd scrutinized my body during a training session, almost clinically, assessing my fitness levels. The way he studies me now, it is the complete opposite.

His mouth is so close that I want to reach up and kiss him, but I don't. It's almost nicer this way, having to wait; it just makes me want him more. When he looks down at me, I can tell he wants me more than anything too. I tug at his sweatpants, which are getting in the way, and he laughs and pulls them off.

He leans over me again, still wearing that sweet, boyish grin, like a kid at the candy store. His hand snakes up the front of my thigh, stopping at my panties. They are black and old, because never in a million years did I ever foresee this happening. I suddenly feel embarrassed, but Hayden just grins. He hooks his fingers around them, pulling them down my legs. Tossing them aside, he places both of his hands on my legs and kisses me.

Every so often, in between kisses, he takes a second to look at me. Really look at me, like he can't believe this is happening. It is the kind of look I have always longed for—the kind that tells me I'm desired by someone. He moves his hand from my waist to my chest, resting it just above my cleavage. His eyes search mine now, looking for an answer to a question he's yet to ask; I know what my answer will be.

"I want to . . ." my sentence trails off, but it doesn't matter. From the look on his face, he knows exactly what I want.

"Are you sure?" he asks.

I hesitate. I don't know if I am sure; I don't know if I'm 100 percent ready, but then I don't know if I ever will be. All I know is that right now, with him, this feels right. "I'm sure."

His eyes light up like he's just won the lottery, and it fills me with warmth. He grins and leans closer, burying his face in my neck. "I've wanted you for so long, Maddie."

He kisses me again, and with his other hand, reaches into his bedside drawer and pulls out a condom. His movements are smooth as he reaches down to put it on without breaking our kiss. He moves a little to position himself, then his mouth brushes mine again.

Nerves settle in, but when Hayden looks down at me, any

fear melts away. He presses himself against me, and when I rest both my hands on his chest, I feel his heart drumming through his skin. "Are you nervous, Hayden?"

"Yeah." This answer surprises me—Hayden has done this a million times, with a million girls. Why would he feel nervous? "Why?"

He doesn't answer for a second. I can feel him down there, hard and ready. Now that the fear has subsided a little, I wait in anticipation, searching his eyes for a sign that he's ready. "Because," he whispers, looking down at me, "I'm in love with you."

Then, slowly, he's pushing himself into me, and all the words and thoughts that consume me suddenly slip away. If they hadn't, though, if I'd been able to speak, this is what I would have said: *I think I'm in love with you too.*

CHAPTER TWENTY-ONE

I've been lying in Hayden's arms for hours. He's fast asleep, his chest gently rising, then falling, in rhythm with my own. I'm too scared to move. He looks so peaceful when he's sleeping that I don't want to accidentally wake him. I lie as still as possible, tracing his features with my eyes.

It's dark outside, but fragments of the moon fall in through the window, dusting his nose and cheeks. It's the same way he'd looked when I'd straddled him at the party—soft and boyish and vulnerable: beautiful. His lips look so soft that I can't help it, I lean in slightly and close my eyes, pressing my lips on his.

Carefully, so as not to wake him, I prop myself on one elbow, watching him sleep. I feel different all of a sudden, like I'm finally at peace. I'm not—my life right now is anything but peaceful—but Hayden has this way of convincing me otherwise, of making me believe everything will turn out all right.

My lips still taste like his kisses. Everything about last night had been warm and gentle. I always thought my first time would be with Jamie, one day, eventually, but I'm glad it wasn't. Even if Hayden and I don't last, even if everything falls apart, I will never regret this night.

Slowly, I ease my head onto his chest, listening to his heartbeat. It's light and fluttery, the kind of hum I'd imagine the wings of a bird to make. It calms me, this sound, and I lose myself to the rhythm.

Hayden *loves* me. He'd actually said it, all three words and eight letters. But what if it was just in the heat of the moment? What if all guys say it during sex? I sigh and stroke his chest, trailing the body of his serpent tattoo with my finger.

It's a scary tattoo, and a part of me wants to wake him just so I can ask him what it means. Finally, when I can no longer lie still, I gently flick his face. He jerks awake, and I pretend to be asleep. He shifts a little to prop himself up, so I open my eyes, blinking a few times like I'm just waking up.

He watches me carefully, pushing back a curl from my face. "Did I wake you?"

"It's fine," I say.

He nuzzles my neck, pulling me toward him until there's no more space left between us. Slowly, his fingers stroke my naked back, drawing patterns across my skin. He thinks I haven't noticed, but it's love hearts he's drawing.

I stroke him back, trailing the serpent again. "What does this tattoo mean?"

His green eyes find mine, soft and steady. "I knew I needed to change, so I did. I threw all of that anger and pain into running the gym. Then, as a reminder, Wiley took me to get this tattoo." He looks at me now, brushing his thumb across my chin. "The snake is a symbol of rebirth or transformation. I wanted a reminder that change is always possible, even if it doesn't feel like it at the time."

"I like it," I say, and then I kiss the tattoo, right over his heart. I feel him inhale, a sharp, rough breath that sends my pulse racing. His lips fall on mine again, teasing my bottom lip. His hands move up my body, light as feathers. I shudder when they cup me.

The room has turned colder, but his hands are like fire, warming me up. I run my own along his back, trailing my nails on his skin. He tenses, then flips me so that I'm lying underneath him.

"I meant what I said," he says, pinning my wrists to the bed. When his eyes search mine, they are vulnerable. "Before, I mean. I wasn't just saying it." He inhales slightly. "I love you, Maddie."

My heart soars, the same way it did the first time he said it. He's waiting for my reaction, searching my face for some kind of gesture; now is my chance. I say, "I love you too."

He grins, and for a second, he looks so happy that his whole face lights up. His mouth comes crashing onto mine, hot and sweet. I wrap my legs around him, pulling him closer, and he instantly hardens.

He's got me trapped underneath him, hands pinned to the bed, but I trust him—not just with this, but with everything. I don't know when it happened, or even how, but I know that I do. And maybe it's not a bad thing. Trusting Hayden makes me feel like I'm weightless or like I'm free-falling, but I'm not afraid; I know that he is waiting to catch me at the bottom.

He moves a hand, resting it over my heart. When he smiles, I am certain he feels it racing under my skin. I reach up and kiss his neck, nibbling on his skin the way he always nibbles mine; the thought of going home to more chaos and drama makes me wish I could stay here forever.

Hayden slowly shifts until I feel him down there, ready. His eyes flit to mine, asking for permission; the second I nod, he slips on a condom then slowly moves into me. It's even better than the first time.

For once, my dreams are peaceful. They aren't about Dad cheating or being dragged back to New York; they are about Hayden and me, sitting on a beach, looking out at the ocean, his fingers entwined with mine.

In the middle of the night, when I wake up again, I close my eyes and try to hold on to it, but it doesn't work; the dream slips away. I must fall asleep again, because at some point, creaking footsteps sound in the hallway, jerking me awake. I expect the noise to be coming from Hayden, but when I sit up, he's fast asleep next to me.

Panic grips my throat, and I shake him awake. He stirs slightly, letting out a grumble before turning back on his side. I flick him again, and he jerks awake, twisting his body to look at me.

"Did you just flick me?" He must notice the look on my face, because he doesn't wait for an answer. "What's wrong?"

I pull the covers up and nod toward the door. "I just heard a sound out there, like someone walking."

In my head, even though it's likely impossible, I'm

imagining my father out there, ready to get rid of me. I'm the only thing in his way now, the one person who sees through his facade; there's no way he'll just accept that.

Hayden's eyebrows furrow, and he looks toward the door. "Are you sure?"

"Yes, I'm sure." I hate the fear that twists in my chest, but I can't help it. I've spent so long being afraid of that man, it's hard to just stop.

Quietly, Hayden gets out of bed and stands up, naked. He looks glorious in the sunlight, like one of those Greek god statues. The light hits his skin in long, feathered strips, revealing every scar and ripple; it is wonderful.

I avert my gaze, suddenly feeling shy, and Hayden grins. He slips on some boxers, then his sweatpants, and rustles for something under the bed. When he straightens up, there is a bat in his hands. He notices the alarm on my face. "In case of an emergency," he says. Then he holds up his knuckles and adds, "These babies aren't always enough."

He inches toward the door, and I reach for the pile of clothes on the floor, grabbing his black T-shirt before slipping it on. When I look up again, Hayden already has the door open and is creeping down the stairs. He disappears, and I hover on the steps. Then I think, why am I cowering on the stairs when Hayden could be in danger? So I turn and search the hallway, spotting a large, empty vase on top of the cabinet.

I grab it and turn around, able to hear raised voices coming from the kitchen. My heart rate quickens, and I tighten my grasp on the vase. With a deep breath, I charge down the stairs and into the kitchen, the vase raised high like a weapon.

Then I pause. Hayden is leaning on the counter, his

baseball bat on the table as his mom stands near the counter, holding shopping bags. Slowly, she turns. She glances at my legs first, which are on full display. Her eyes make their way up the rest of my body and land on my face. I've seen that look she's wearing before: disapproval.

She turns to Hayden, who's grinning, and says, "I sure do love coming home to half-naked girls in my house." She says it like this isn't the first time, and my heart sinks. "You better wipe that grin off your face, Hay." Without looking at me, she adds, "Are you planning on bashing my brains out with that vase? Because it was expensive."

Embarrassed, I lower the vase and rest it on the table. This is not how I'd expected to meet Hayden's mother properly. I am horrified.

"I've told you about this kind of thing before," she says to Hayden, and she doesn't look happy. She starts to unpack the shopping away, but Hayden swoops down and does it for her. "You can't be left alone for a second, can you?"

Hayden glances at me, then steps forward and says, "Mom, this is Maddie." He grins before adding, "My girlfriend."

To say his mom is surprised is an understatement. She opens her mouth, but words seem to fail her, because she closes it again. She turns to face me, and that look of disapproval morphs into relief.

"Holy hell, I never thought I'd see the day again," she says, pulling me into a hug. It is warm and motherly; the kind of hug I have sorely missed. "Nice to meet you, Maddie. You're completely forgiven for trying to kill me with my own vase."

"That's a relief," I say. "It's nice to meet you, too, Dr. Walker."

"Please," she says, pulling away, "call me Sam."

Hayden and I help with the rest of the shopping, and then his mom cooks us a breakfast of bacon and waffles while we sit at the breakfast table. She's in the middle of telling us how her trip to Santa Barbara went, when, under the table, I feel Hayden's fingers thread through mine.

At one point, I head to the bathroom to freshen up, and when I come back, Hayden and his mom are talking about me. I hover behind the doorway, watching as Hayden wolfs down his waffles.

"I like her," his mom says, leaning against the counter. "She seems like a good person."

Hayden stops eating and says, "She is."

She walks around the table to give him a kiss on the forehead. "It's so nice to see you happy again, Hay." When she pulls back, she says, "Don't mess it up."

Hayden drops me home around four, and for a few minutes, I sit quietly in the passenger seat, watching the house. The engine hums quietly beneath us. Hayden fiddles with the key in the ignition, holding it in his palm before releasing it again. It knocks against the steering wheel, letting out a slow, soothing jingle. I wish he could do something; I wish he could slam on the gas until we're hurtling down the road—anything to get me out of here.

"Okay, I'm going in," I say, turning to the house, but I don't move. I realize this isn't about being afraid of my dad anymore; this is about her, my mother—maybe it always has been. If I go in there, everything changes. I could tell her the truth about Dad, and even after everything, she could still choose *him*; that is what scares me the most.

Hayden brings his hand to my face, brushing my cheek with his thumb. I turn to find those green eyes already on mine. They are dark and concerned, the kind of look I'd never have imagined him to give me; I love him.

"She needs to know," Hayden says. "At least you've got evidence now. Tell her about the cheating—show her the mark. You can go to the police together and get him out of your lives once and for all."

Gently, his fingers brush the marks on my shoulder, his eyes darkening. I shake my head because he doesn't get how this works. Evidence is not the deciding factor here—not even close. There could be a mountain of it, stacked and presented with a neat little bow, but it won't make the slightest bit of difference.

To an outsider looking in, the thought of my mother staying with her abuser must seem unfathomable, but I have had a taste of both sides, both viewpoints, and I see what they don't. Being controlled and hurt and beaten is traumatizing. It leads to confusion, doubt, and guilt: Did I provoke him somehow? Upset him? Did I do something to deserve this? The abuser crawls their way in, burying into your skin and settling in your veins, whispering, *You're the one to blame. This is your fault.* My father was good at twisting the tables, and everything became my mother's fault. In this way, he broke her, then built her back up into a shell of herself—one that was easy to control.

Looking back, I realize now that she'd shielded me from the worst of it, kept it to herself; I never even thanked her. Hayden might look at someone like my mother and think, *How can she stay?* But he doesn't see the times she'd tried leaving, only to be punished for it. He doesn't see the tears or the pain or the mental abuse, which stays long after the last bruise has faded. He looks at her, at what she's become, and thinks, *How can she stay?* But I know the question she asks herself: *How can I leave?*

"It's not enough," I say, gnawing on my nail. I'd known it the moment Dad's fingers left a mark, the moment he pushed me. It isn't enough—maybe it never will be. "There could be a mountain of signs and evidence to prove he hasn't changed, and she'll miss every single one."

"We don't exactly have a lot of options here," Hayden says. "Just tell her the truth. Maybe she'll surprise you."

"Maybe," I say but I don't believe this for a second. For my mother, giving in to my father's harassment is easier than walking away.

Hayden leans into me, taking my face in his hands. "Do you want me to wait out here for you?"

"No, it's okay. This is something that I need to deal with alone."

"Go. You need to talk to your mom."

"Okay, okay, I'm going."

He kisses the tip of my nose. "Call me if you need me. I'll come straight away, and if she tries to stop me, I'll kidnap you."

I laugh a little, into his neck. "I'll be sure to pass the message along." I give him a quick peck, then turn to leave, but he grabs my arm and pulls me into him, kissing me properly. I sink into his lips, not realizing how much I need this right now.

"I love you," he says against my mouth.

"I love you," I say back.

Inside, the house is dark, except for a lamp in the kitchen. I'm about to head on up to my room, but the sound of footsteps stops me. A little click follows, like somebody quickly shutting a door. I inch toward the kitchen. It's empty, but the blind on the patio door is gently rocking back and forth.

The doorbell rings and I jerk into action, racing to open it. Dad stands on the other side, holding a bottle of red wine and a bouquet of red roses—Mom's least favorite flower.

"Maddie," he says, and his eyes soften. "I didn't expect to see you here. Your mother made it seem like everyone would be out. Are you joining us for dinner?"

My fingers clench around the door frame. I glance back to the kitchen, expecting to see someone peering from the shadows, but there's nobody there. "What are you doing here?"

"Your mom and I are going for dinner. Okay if I wait inside?" He steps past me, into the hallway, putting the flowers on the table. When he turns around, those eyes of his are soft again, regarding me with warmth. "Look, I'm sorry about what happened," he says, extending a hand, but I don't take it. "I love you so much, you know that? Everything I've ever done, I've done so that we can be a family."

Whenever he talks like this, his voice goes straight through my heart like an arrow, stabbing me where it hurts most. Time and time again I find myself wanting to believe the sincerity in his voice. It doesn't matter how many times he turns around and hurts me—it's like the moment he apologizes, I forget. I forget what came before it.

"I should put these in water," I say. I pick up the flowers, and a few of the petals break off and flutter like feathers to the floor. I scoop them up and hurry into the kitchen, where I fill up a vase with water and put the flowers inside. My fingers are shaking as I turn off the faucet. The blinds have stopped rocking, and I wonder if I've imagined those footsteps I heard.

Dad follows me in and stands in the doorway, folding his arms. He's getting more and more impatient but is trying to hide it. "Do you know when your mom is supposed to be getting back? You know what they say: arriving late is a way of saying your own time—"

"—is more valuable than the time of the person who waited for you," I finish. I have heard him say this a hundred times. More.

He beams like I've made him proud. "It's not your mother's fault, it's spending all this time in California. Everyone moves so damn slow here. She'll be back to normal once she gets to New York."

"The thing is, Dad," I insist, "Mom isn't moving to New York."

My heart pounds, threatening to break through the wall of my chest, but I don't look away. Dad doesn't, either, he just stands in the doorway, arms folded, watching me.

"We've talked about this, Maddie," he says. "We're family. Family sticks together through thick and thin."

In my head, I am thinking about all of the times we weren't a family, like when he'd scream at us for disagreeing with him, or for looking at him the wrong way. I think about how he would react to my mother saying thank you to the cab driver, because he thought this was flirting. Or how my mom would stand up for herself, only to be called irrational.

I resented her for a long time for staying. For not protecting us. But the truth is, she defended and protected me until she no longer could. Until she had no more fight left. This fight burns in me now, deep in the pit of my stomach. It sparks and ignites, consuming my body until all that is left is chaos and fire.

"Family?" I say, stepping forward. "We're not a family."

He frowns as if I've hurt his feelings. For a brief moment, I wonder what he was like by himself in New York, whether he's the same soft, collected man when there's no one around. It's like the old proverb goes: If a tree falls in the forest, and there's no one to hear it, does it still make a sound? I don't know.

He swallows hard. "Maddie, I'm trying here. I really am. I know I haven't always been the best dad or husband, but I want to make things better. Please." His voice breaks on *please*, which feels like an arrow to the heart.

"Stop, Dad."

"I will not," he says, "because you're asking me to stop loving you, and that's never going to happen. Maybe I sometimes lose my temper a little, but that doesn't mean I don't love you or your mother. It means I love you too much. I'm in the process of getting help, Maddie, but it takes time. I need my family to support me."

His eyes have started to water, and it throws me. I'm looking into them, into the green with flecks of yellow, into eyes that are just like mine, and I'm searching for the truth. For an answer. Is he just a sick man who needs help to get better? Do Mom and I have some moral obligation to help him, or is this just another tactic?

"You cheated on Mom," I say. "How can you say you've changed?"

He steps forward, confused. "I would never cheat on your mother."

"I *saw* you."

"I love her," he says. "Why would I cheat on someone I love?"

"Stop *lying*." I can feel the anger I've worked so hard to control start to make its way up my throat. "Just stop!"

He turns slowly, and the surprise in his expression only lasts a moment.

"Maddison," he says, grabbing my hand, "you're acting crazy. You need to just calm down."

My name sounds like a curse word as it rolls off his lips. He's still fighting for composure, but spit has started to froth at his mouth, and a droplet lands on my cheek. I'm stuck in a time loop, imagining all of the times that he made Mom feel worthless—all of the times he made me feel that way. His fingers clench my wrist, squeezing harder.

"You're angry at me," he says, still squeezing, "and you're trying to punish me by turning your mother against me." He's squeezing, squeezing, his fingertips digging into my skin.

I yank back my hand, but the force in which he lets it go sends me stumbling to the ground. Staring up at him, I realize I have never, in all of my eighteen years, seen him like this, and it slowly starts to dawn on me why. In New York we were always under his control. The threat of his hand as he raised it in the air, the tone in his voice as he yelled, was often enough to get us to comply.

He doesn't have that power here. He's losing his hold, and the more he realizes I'm not bending to his will, the more Mr. Hyde is coming out.

Slowly, I straighten up. "You need to get out of my house."

In one quick movement, his hand comes out, shoving me back. I stumble to the ground, and for a second, I am still. Fear tells me to stay down here, to not get back up. It tells me to appease him, to apologize until that anger inside of him has subsided enough, the way we used to back home, but I can't anymore. I *won't*.

"I'm sorry," he says, extending his hand, "I'm just—I don't understand why you're doing this to us."

I sit up slowly, heart pounding, then rise to my feet. Dad looks surprised. He'd wanted to be the one to pull me back up, to be the savior again. He thought the times he'd raised his hand in anger would keep me afraid of being hit. But I've been hit before; I've fought in a ring, and if I could see myself now, I think I'd see someone who looks fierce and strong; I think I'd see a fighter.

"You need to leave," I say calmly. My bravery coaxes the rage in him. He steps forward again, grabbing my arm before yanking me closer.

For a moment, it looks like he's about to play the *sorry* game again, but then something closes down in his expression. His hand feels like fire as it connects with my cheek. All of that anger that burns in his veins, that quiet frustration—he channels in this one slap. I squeeze my eyes shut as my skin starts to prickle. The fire inside of me bursts into flames, burning and scorching my skin.

I try to look up, but he's a faceless blur through the tears. "Get away from me."

"Just apologize," he says, but what he really means to say is, *Submit*.

When I don't react, he holds out his hand like I'm a little girl waiting to take it. I shift into my fighting stance, hands held high the way Hayden once showed me. "I mean it," I say. "Get away from me."

"You need to—" he begins, but the second he grabs me, my fist is connecting with his face. The sound of skin against skin is loud, and he stumbles back, colliding with the wall behind him.

The front door clicks open. A chorus of voices travels through the corridor before stopping dead. The whole of my family is standing in the kitchen doorway, taking in my hunched-over father. Mom rushes over without saying a word, holding my face in her hands.

"Oh God, Maddie," she whispers, her fingers brushing my tender cheek. "Are you okay? What happened?"

"She attacked me," Dad says, getting to his feet. "I came inside to wait for you, and she just lost it."

He sounds so convincing that I almost believe him.

"I didn't," I say, voice shaking. "He slapped me. He wouldn't let me leave."

Dad steps toward me, but Mom steps in front of me, blocking my body with hers.

"Don't take another step," she says, and when she reaches behind her to squeeze my hand, I squeeze hers back. "Tell the truth, Henry. What happened?"

Lilly and the others are silent in the doorway. I don't blame them for being so shocked. "I *am* telling the truth," Dad says. "She kept saying she won't let me take you back to New York, and how she's learned all these boxing techniques, and then she hit me."

Mom turns to look at me. I prepare myself for what she will say, for how much it will hurt to hear. She'll believe his lies, I can feel it in my gut, because his story makes perfect sense.

"Lilly," Mom says, still looking at Dad, "I need you to call the police."

In the brief silence that follows, Lilly pulls her phone out and heads into the hallway. Dad looks from Mom to me, and back to Mom again. His eyes soften in that way they do when he's trying to win someone over. It's a look he has perfected over the years, so well executed that I think he must practice it in front of the mirror.

"You're doing the right thing," he says to Mom.

"Just wait," Tim says, stepping into the kitchen, "I don't know what's going on here, but—"

"That's right," Dad says, spinning to face him, "you don't." His face is lumpy and swollen from the hit, like something out of a horror movie. "She assaulted me. She needs to be charged for this."

Panic grips my throat, and I glance at Mom. "I was defending myself," I say, my voice thick with emotion. "Mom, you have to believe me."

Mom steps away from me, no longer my shield. I take in a breath, then shrivel and fold like I can no longer stand. This is the moment I've been dreading: the moment my mother breaks my heart. She doesn't look at me when she speaks. "I'm sorry, Maddie, but actions need to have consequences."

The relief that floods Dad's face is unmistakable. "Thank you, Lorraine. I know it's hard right now, but we'll get through this. Together."

It feels like I can't breathe. My chest rises and falls, rises and falls, but my body is no longer under my control; I am once again powerless. Tim crosses the room, ignoring Dad and Mom and hooking an arm around my waist. "All of this . . . madness . . . can wait. We need to get some ice on your face."

"*Her*? Look at me." Dad takes a step toward me—to do what, I don't know—but Dylan steps in front of me, blocking Dad's line of fire.

"You take one more step and you'll be eating through a straw," he says.

I turn to look at Mom, who hasn't spoken a word. This is the hardest part. Not the bruises or cuts or having a monster for a father. It is the realization that my mother might not believe me. Here I stand, bruised and battered and barely holding on, and it might as well all be for nothing.

Dad takes another step. Olly moves now, taking a position next to Dylan. "I thought you were told to stay still, old man."

My heart swells. I'd convinced myself I was alone in all of this, but I was wrong. I have a family, and it might not be in a conventional way, and I might not have a doting father, but I have Lilly, and Tim, and Olly and Dylan; I have people who love me.

The knock at the door jerks me to my feet. Lilly's eyes widen, and we rush into the hallway at the same time as my parents. We all look at the door, able to see blurred shadows behind the frosted glass. Dad tries to get there first, but Lilly knocks him to the side with her hip and pulls on the handle. Behind it are two police officers, who glance behind Lilly and look straight at me.

"Thank God you're here," Dad says. "My daughter assaulted me."

In the seconds that follow, it feels like my head is underwater. My ears are blocked, my breath is held, and all I can hear is the pounding of my heart as it thumps like drums in my ears.

Then, as the police step forward, Mom does too. "He's lying," she says, pointing to my dad. "He broke into our house and assaulted my daughter. You need to arrest him."

CHAPTER TWENTY-TWO

My dad ends up getting arrested. He shouts and curses, telling my mother that he'll come back and kill her, that he'll kill *himself*, but if she's scared, she doesn't show it. She just squeezes my hand, looks straight ahead, and watches as he's carted away.

As soon as the police leave, Lilly sets me and Mom up in the living room with a fort of blankets and two hot chocolates, and after asking if there's anything else we need, she and the others disappear upstairs to give us some space.

Now that the adrenaline has worn off, I feel exhausted, but when I look at my mother, who is curled next to me in a ball, I know it was worth it.

It is silent until she bursts into sobs, and then there's no stopping her. I pull her toward me, allowing her head to rest on my lap as I gently stroke her hair. "I'm so sorry," she cries. "I'm so sorry, Maddie."

"Shh," I say, trying to soothe her. "It's okay, Mom."

She lifts her head, eyes wet with tears. "I had to say those things. If he caught on that I didn't believe him, he'd have tried to leave."

I nod, and we spend what feels like forever just sitting there, crying. Eventually, when the tears run dry, she tells me she's heading to bed. "I think I'm going to just stay here for a while," I say. "Could you turn off the light?"

She gets to her feet, switching off the living-room light before giving me one last look. "I love you."

"I love you too."

I sit quietly for a while, the blanket pulled to my neck. The dark used to scare me when I was little—I was convinced there were monsters under my bed. Now I know that the monsters are out there, in the real world, disguising themselves as people.

"Hey." My head snaps up. Dylan stands in the doorway, looking hesitant. "Can I sit for a moment?" I nod, and he takes a seat next to me on the sofa, looking at me through the dark. "How are you feeling?"

The hot chocolate Lilly made still sits on the table, so I reach out and clutch it in my hands. I haven't taken a single sip, but I like how it warms my fingers. Dylan watches me from the sofa, waiting for me to move, or speak, or do something other than stare at my mug. "I'm okay," I say at last. "I think I feel more relieved than anything." I look at him now. "You all must think this is insane."

"Kind of, but we've pretty much put the pieces together after seeing the way your dad reacted when he was arrested. That man is a psychopath."

Somehow, against all odds, I laugh. "You can say that again."

"That man is a psychopath."

I lightly push him with my hand. "Can you believe we're graduating soon? It feels like everything is passing in a blur."

"No, I can't," he admits. "I'm kind of a little scared about going off to college."

"Me too," I say, and it feels good to admit to my fears out loud, like I don't have to hide them anymore.

"Listen," he says, "with everything going on with your dad, I just wanted to say that I'm sorry for being on your case about Hayden. It's none of my business who you want to hang out with, and I shouldn't have put my Caitlyn issues on you. I'm sorry."

His apology surprises me, but I'm grateful for it. "Thank you."

When I start to get sleepy, I head upstairs and crawl into bed, pulling my pillow toward me. I still can't wrap my head around everything that's happened this evening. It feels like everything until now has been a horrible nightmare, and it's one I can't seem to forget. I spend the whole night sobbing, needing to get it all out. As relieved as I am that my father's been arrested, I'm still a jumble of different emotions. Eventually, when the tears run dry, I fall into a dreamless sleep.

When I finally wake up, I find several texts from Hayden, asking me how it went with my mom. I don't want to explain what happened over text, so I ask him if he can come over that night. He replies immediately with an okay, and I pull my pillow over my face and fall asleep again.

The next time I wake up, it's to the smell of bacon. I head

into the kitchen, where Lilly, Tim, and my mom are at the table, in the middle of a serious discussion. I'm about to back away, but Lilly looks over and tells me to take a seat. I do as I'm told, pulling out the chair opposite Mom.

After a few seconds of silence, Lilly reaches over and squeezes my hand. "We've been talking all morning," she says, shooting me a motherly look. "Your mother has told us everything, Maddie. You don't have to keep anything a secret anymore."

The relief that floods through me is unmistakable. I glance at my mother, whose eyes are red and heavy with bags like she's been fretting all night.

"We've discussed where we go from here," Lilly continues, "and we've come to the decision that you and your mother will stay with us. Your mother's going to keep her job at the bookstore, you'll go to UCLA in the fall, and you'll both attend therapy twice a week."

"What happens to Dad?" I ask.

Tim steps in now, his expression businesslike. "You don't need to worry about any of that right now, Maddie. We're dealing with the charges brought against your father. You'll need to speak to the police further at some point and give a proper statement, but we'll take care of everything else. You have nothing to worry about—you're safe here." He looks at Mom now, smiling. "Both of you."

Mom slumps with relief, and as Lilly and Tim go on about therapy and healing, I reach beneath the table and give her hand a squeeze, like old times.

It's late when Hayden gets here, almost eleven, and I've already changed into my pajamas. Slowly, I cross the room to the balcony doors, where he hovers behind the glass. As soon as I open them, he takes a step forward and then pauses. Outside is dark, but the moon tonight is bright and round, shining a light on my face.

He steps forward, into my room, and pulls me into his arms. "Are you all right? Did something happen with your mom?"

"I'm fine," I say into his hoodie. "I'm fine now, I just didn't want to explain over the phone."

He stiffens. "Explain what?"

"My dad came over after you left." I sink my face into the groove of his neck, but he's entirely too still. "He's in jail now," I say in a bid to relax him, and it works. He takes my hand and leads me to the bed, where he pulls me onto his lap.

"Tell me everything," he says.

I start from the moment he'd left, explaining the noise I'd heard in the kitchen, which I'm certain now must have been my dad lurking around, to the moment the police came and took him away. Hayden listens intently, not saying a word, even after I've finished the story. Then, just when I think I can't take any more silence, he pulls away to look at me.

"I shouldn't have left," he says, his jaw clenched. "I should have—"

"I'm glad you did," I say, stroking his face. "If you were there, you'd have tried to save me, and I needed to be able to save myself."

When I was little, I used to pray that someone would rescue us from Dad, that I'd find a Prince Charming. But I realize now that waiting for a savior isn't the answer; I am my savior.

He looks away, his jaw a hard, narrow line. "I'd have killed him."

"I know," I say, kissing his cheek. "That's why I'm glad you weren't here."

He finally looks at me, his eyes softening. "This mean you're staying in LA? You're not deferring?"

"Yes, I'm staying."

For the first time all night, Hayden grins. "I wouldn't have let you go, anyway."

I lean into him slightly, needing his touch. He shifts me so that I am underneath his chest and then he runs his hand beneath my T-shirt. "I'm proud of you," he whispers, looking me in the eyes. "I mean, I'm mad, but I'm proud of you."

My whole life, I'd been desperate to hear my dad say those words, but in the end, they mean more to me coming from Hayden.

"It was because of you," I say. If it hadn't been for Hayden, I would never have found the strength to defend myself—I would never have known how to.

"No," Hayden says, kissing my neck, "it wasn't. It was you, Maddie."

I close my eyes and sink into the pillow. It feels nice being able to relax for once. I'm not worried about my parents or anything else, I'm just present in the moment, happy and free; it is bliss. I go to kiss his cheek, but he moves his head so that my mouth catches his. I grin against him, and his arms snake around me and pull me on top of him, refusing to let me go.

"Maddie?"

"Mmm?"

"I've never felt this way before," he says, "and I just wanted you to know. I trust you."

I'm so surprised that I roll on my side to face him. He peers down at me, cautious and vulnerable. I touch his face, lightly brushing my fingertips over his cheek.

"I trust you too," I say, and it feels stronger than just *I love you.*

It feels like a promise of forever.

CHAPTER TWENTY-THREE

On the day of our graduation, I lie in bed, staring at the strips of light that fall through the window, grateful to have made it here. The familiar sounds of my family hum through the walls. Dylan and Olly's footsteps stomp around in the corridor, and Lilly's and Mom's voices travel up through the kitchen, where Tim is no doubt cooking up something delicious for breakfast.

It's been a week since my dad was arrested, and life has started to settle down again. I'm going to miss all of this when I start UCLA, but knowing that my home is just around the corner is a relief.

On the car ride to school, I keep smoothing down my flowing white dress and fixating on my hair. I'm just so nervous that the day I've been anticipating for months is finally here, and I don't know what to do with myself.

"Quit fidgeting," Olly says as I smooth down my hair yet again. "You're making me nervous."

"You look fine," Dylan says with a thump to Olly's ribs. "This is a happy day, remember?"

"I remember," I say, but I double-check that my cap is in my bag for the fifth time since we left. It feels like a dream that I'm graduating today, like maybe I've fallen asleep during breakfast or something and none of this is happening. It feels like senior year has been both the quickest and longest year of my life.

Tim pulls into the parking lot, and we all clamber out of the car. I'm excited to see Kavi and June in their gowns and I'm scanning the busy parking lot for signs of her convertible, but they must not be here yet. As always, there's the tiniest part of me that is sad my dad won't be here for this, that he's missing all of these important milestones he'd always promised to be a part of. I don't know if that's a normal feeling or if it will ever go away, but I don't reject the thought instantly like I might have before. I just accept it and move on.

Graduation is all of the normal things, like the valedictorian speech and Mom waving wildly from the crowd when my name is called by the principal to collect my diploma. But it's also things I hadn't expected, like hugs with friends that I'd never thought I'd have, and promises to spend an amazing summer together before going off to college. It's throwing myself into Hayden's arms despite the surprised look from my mom, because even though I'm sure she's probably thinking the worst, this is graduation right now, and I want to be happy.

As soon as we've got our diplomas, it's the typical throwing our caps in the air as our parents take pictures. I throw mine the highest, making sure to take a mental picture to savor this moment and commit it to memory. One day I'll be old and I'll look back on this year, and I'll remember I made it, I survived—I *thrived*.

"We survived," Hayden says as he kisses me on the lips. His mom is standing in the distance, talking to the woman beside her, but she's staring at us fondly. "How does it feel to have graduated?"

"Strange," I say, taking his hand, "but in the best kind of way."

What comes next is a blur of hugs that feel like good-byes from Kavi and June. Everyone's so emotional that I feel my own eyes press with tears, even though I promised myself I wouldn't cry. I've always seen it as a weakness, a sign that I was being irrational or crazy, and even though I know that's not true, some things are still hard to forget.

After we've taken enough photos to last a lifetime, we all go back to the house for a graduation barbecue, and I pray that having Hayden in the same room as Mom, Dylan, and June isn't going to be awkward.

This is my way of dealing with things, now. Not praying, exactly, but believing. Trusting. I am taking the good when it comes, and the bad the same way, knowing each moment is fleeting. I think I've spent so long living in fear, that somewhere along the way, I forgot how to just live, but it's not too late to start—it's never too late.

June and Kavi come upstairs with me while I change out of my graduation dress into something a little more summery. According to June, with my "new outlook on life," I need a new, sexy wardrobe, so she rifles through my closet and throws out half of my clothes before settling on a white, floaty dress.

"Here," she says, handing it over. "This one is perfect. It screams, 'My dad is a psycho but at least I am hot.'"

I laugh and take the dress from her hands, running my fingers over the soft, white material. June has picked a dress I brought with me from New York; another one Jamie didn't like. I'm about to put it back when I pause, realizing Hayden was right. I wasn't a person back in New York, I was a shadow, floating along while trying not to rock the boat. My dad, Jamie, my mom—everything I ever did, I did for them. Now it's time to do something for me.

I slip it on and glance in the mirror, running my hands down the front. It is light and airy, the kind of dress a girl might wear to run across the beach; I love it.

"I like it," I say.

"I told you," June says, smiling at my reflection. "I have an eye for these things."

"No one loves you quite like you love yourself, June," Kavi says.

I laugh before turning to June. "June, are you going to be okay with Hayden being here? I mean, you guys have never really hung out before."

June gets to her feet and walks toward me, letting out a sigh. "Is that what you're worried about? Maddie, we had a brief, drunken kiss a million years ago, and I'm with Olly now. As long as Hayden treats you right, I'll put up with him."

I grin and give her an almighty hug. "Okay."

"Good," she says, pulling away. "Now, let's get down there and grab some food. I'm dying for some chicken."

The three of us hold hands as we head out in the back yard and over to the food.

Lilly's gone all out with the barbecue. She went and bought a white gazebo that sits in the corner, surrounded by chairs and tables. Each table has a huge bouquet of daffodils on it—Mom's favorite—and paper plates.

On the patio is the buffet, a long table filled with every type of meat and vegetable one could possibly imagine. Tim stands at the grill, talking to some of his friends as he tries to flip burgers in the air like some fancy chef. Lilly floats from person to person like the social butterfly she is, and Mom floats with her, not as sociable, or as vibrant, but she's trying.

She's wearing a pale pink dress that cuts at her knee, and her hair is down for once, flowing down her back in long, glossy curls. I have never seen her look so beautiful, so weightless, before. And while Dad's out on bail, free until the trial, he can't come within fifty feet of us. It's not much, but it's enough to give us some semblance of peace.

It's hard to imagine going off to college without her, but knowing she's only a short drive away makes it easier. And maybe me leaving is exactly what she needs to feel independent again. I'm about to turn when a pair of big, warm hands cover my eyes. They smell distinct and familiar, like vanilla mixed with pinewood. I grin and turn around.

Hayden.

For a second, my eyes take him in like it's the first time I'm seeing him. In some ways, I am. Now that I'm freer, I can appreciate everything—everyone—so much more now. I recognize details that I'd barely taken in before, like the light sprinkle of freckles on his nose, or the flecks of yellow in his eyes; it feels like I'm finally awake.

He grabs my hand and spins me into him, grinning at me. "I like this dress," he says, allowing his eyes to drop. My heart flutters, and I lightly swat his arm.

"Behave yourself," I say. "My family is at this barbecue."

When he grins again, my heart melts. "I always behave myself."

"Sure you do," I say, hooking my arm through his. "Come on, let's go and talk to my mom."

Hayden looks alarmed, but he allows me to drag him over to where Mom and Lilly are standing. I know he feels awkward by the way he suddenly tenses, but Mom's still under the impression that he's some kind of thug, and I need to prove her wrong. While compartmentalizing things has served me relatively well, I'm tired of keeping things separate. I want my family to know Hayden and Hayden to know my family; I want everything out in the open.

"Mom," I say, and both her and Lilly stop talking to their friends to turn to face us. Lilly beams and steps forward, pulling Hayden into a hug. He kisses her cheek, and the pair pull back.

"Hayden," she says, craning her neck to look at him. "Nice to see you."

Hayden grins, and if that smile doesn't win them over, I don't know what will. "Nice to see you, too, Mrs. Applegate. You've really outdone yourself with the barbecue."

She smiles and touches his arm before looking at Mom. "Lori?"

Mom nods, her eyes still cautious. She pulls Hayden into

a hug, whispering something in his ear before pulling back. Hayden smiles and takes my hand before nodding at her. "Fair enough, Mrs. Goodwright."

I wait until we're over at the buffet before I turn and ask him what my mother had said. He doesn't respond for a minute, because he's too busy piling his plate high with food.

"She told me if I ever did anything to hurt you, she'd chop me into pieces."

We look at each other now and burst out laughing. "She's still dealing," I say softly. She's put on a brave face, but I know, deep inside, she's still hurting. So am I—maybe we always will be.

"You looking forward to therapy?" Hayden asks once we've found a table. He's wolfing down his food like there's no tomorrow, and I grin. It reminds me of that time at the diner, when he'd ordered us a mountain of food for the *protein*. Really, I just think he's greedy.

"Yeah, I actually am," I say. I didn't think I would. I thought going to therapy and dragging up all those feelings would make me feel worse, but it hasn't. We've only been to two sessions so far, but it's been nice to see Mom open up a little. In time, I think she'll be okay. I like to think that I will be too. It's hard not knowing what happens next, or what my future might hold, but if one thing is certain, it's that whatever comes my way, I'll survive. I have fire inside of me, and that fire came from suffering.

Olly, Dylan, and June come over at one point and take the seat opposite. I can tell June and Dylan are tense around Hayden, but June smiles and tells us about the cabin her mom said she can borrow this summer.

Halfway through June's invitation to join her, Dylan glances at Hayden, and Hayden glances at Dylan. I hold my breath in the seconds that follow, watching as a thousand words are spoken in one look. Then, after a second, Hayden does what I thought was impossible: he grins at Dylan.

My heart bursts. I know he's only doing it for my benefit, but watching him be the bigger person despite everything that's happened just makes me love him more. Dylan returns the grin, and I squeeze Hayden's hand, letting him know how much I appreciate it. When he squeezes mine in return, I know we're all going to be okay.

Olly starts talking about something silly, and the rest of us laugh. It's starting to feel more natural between us, and for a fleeting moment, I get a glimpse of my future and what it could be like.

I can't wait.

ACKNOWLEDGMENTS

It goes without saying that without the continual support from so many, this project would not have been possible.

First, I'd like to thank the Wattpad team for this incredible opportunity and for creating such a wonderful community. It's because of the overwhelming support I've received that I've been able to grow and develop as a writer, and for that I'm so grateful.

To Deanna and Rebecca, my editors, for believing in this story and for always being there to support and advise me. You have truly helped shape this book in so many ways, and it has been a pleasure working with you.

Finally, thank you to my wonderful readers. The kindness you have shown me over the years is what kept me writing, and it's because of all of you that this story has made it this far.

ABOUT THE AUTHOR

Rachael Rose grew up in Solihull, England, and graduated from Brunel University of London with a BA in English. Her passion for literature led to the writing of her debut novel, *Gaslight*, which has amassed over ten million reads. When she's not writing, Rachael can be found teaching, candle making, or watching quirky romance movies with her two cats.